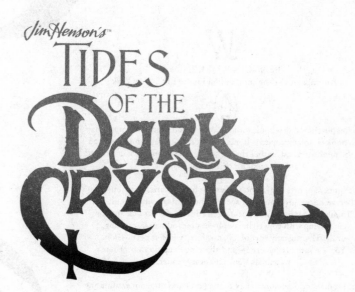

Jim Henson's™

TIDES
OF THE
DARK CRYSTAL

PENGUIN WORKSHOP
An Imprint of Penguin Random House LLC, New York

TM and © 2018 The Jim Henson Company. JIM HENSON's mark and logo, THE DARK CRYSTAL mark and logo, characters, and elements are trademarks of The Jim Henson Company. All rights reserved. First published in hardcover in 2018 by Penguin Workshop. This paperback edition published in 2019 by Penguin Workshop, an imprint of Penguin Random House LLC, New York. PENGUIN and PENGUIN WORKSHOP are trademarks of Penguin Books Ltd, and the W colophon is a registered trademark of Penguin Random House LLC. Printed in the USA.

Visit us online at www.penguinrandomhouse.com.

Library of Congress Control Number: 2018041657

ISBN 9780399539855

10 9 8 7 6 5 4 3 2 1

Jim Henson's

TIDES
OF THE
DARK CRYSTAL

BY J. M. LEE

ILLUSTRATED BY
CORY GODBEY

Penguin Workshop

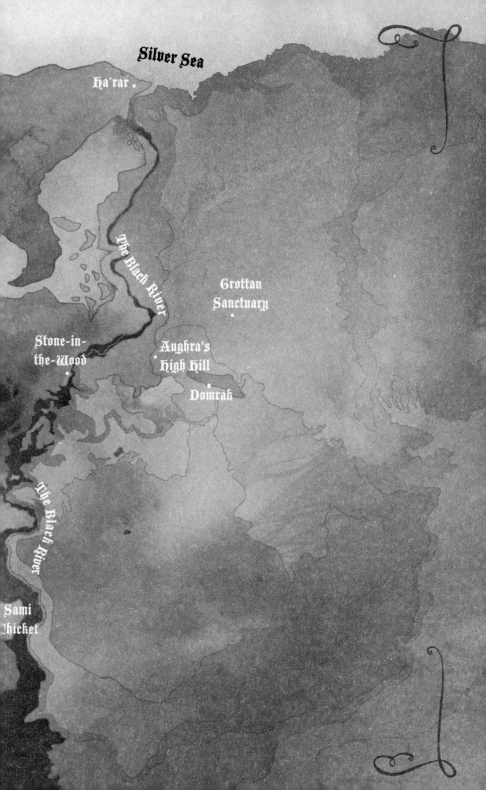

Silver Sea

Ha'rar .

The Black River

Grottan
Sanctuary

Stone-in-
the-Wood

Aughra's
High Hill

Domrak

The Black River

Sami
Thicket

We shared thought, and I taught them to feel the trembling

of the rocks as they sang to the Crystal they could not see.

The World of the Dark Crystal

CHAPTER 1

The daylighter world was unbearably bright.

Even at night, the smiles of the Sisters seemed excessive, especially surrounded by all those stars. And then, during the day, the Three Brothers drowned the sky with light. Amri could only hope that his eyes would adjust over time.

Until that time, the Grottan Gelfling wore his hood, trying to keep his face in shadow even as he followed his companions through the sun-dappled mountain wood. His eyes moved across the moss- and grass-covered earth, like a pelt over the mountain's stone skeleton, whose soggy soil bled into Amri's sandals.

Through the brightness, Amri caught something stirring in the wood. Whatever lurked ahead was distant enough to be seen but not heard. Were they being watched?

He reached out and tugged on Kylan's sleeve. The Spriton boy walked just ahead of him, using a stick to clear brush away from their path. Under his free arm he held a scroll with a map he'd drawn, and hanging at his breast was his *firca*, a Y-shaped musical instrument made out of bone.

"Kylan," Amri whispered. Maybe his new friend's green daylighter eyes could make something out. "Do you see something? To our right. Under those trees!"

"Where?" Kylan lowered his voice instinctively, ears swiveling back and forth, straining for any sign of danger.

"What are you two whispering about?"

Naia appeared behind them. She had been farther up the hill, breaking the trail, when she'd realized that the others had stopped. Amri wasn't surprised she had returned so stealthily. Dagger in hand, camouflaged in tan and brown leathers, locs pulled back in a loose knot, she was every inch a Drenchen warrior.

Somewhere nearby, a twig snapped. Amri drew the sword that hung at his hip, though he had no idea how to use it. Naia ducked to a crouch as six tall white-and-gray animals emerged from the trees, only a stone's throw away. The big-eared creatures' long, slender legs carried their furry bodies high among the branches. The beasts grumbled softly to one another, flicking their proboscises to taste the sweet sap that dripped from the wintry trees.

Kylan fell back in relief, wiping his brow. "Wild Landstriders. And here I thought the Skeksis had found us."

Amri stared at the Landstriders as they passed, trying to absorb every detail of the wondrous creatures. Naia watched him with an amused smile.

"Landstrider rear ends can't be *that* interesting," she teased.

"Maybe not to you. I've never seen a Landstrider front end, so . . ."

"Fair," she chuckled. "Well, come on. We've got to keep moving."

Naia and Kylan left, forging ahead on their trail without a

second glance as the troop of Landstriders disappeared into the wood. Amri wasn't surprised. The others were from this world, after all. Kylan's clan, the Spriton, had named the Landstriders as their sigil creature. Even Naia's clan, the Drenchen of Sog, lived under the sky and had contact with the outside world—when they wanted it. Amri, on the other hand, had been born in a cave deep in the Grottan Mountains, only exploring the daylighter world in tiny, forbidden excursions that had to be taken at night.

Naia moved with an unbreakable pace, eyes always fixed ahead with focus and determination. As they reached the top of a small wooded hill, the green gave way to a brilliant white. A cold wind came down, smelling of salt and crystal; snow and frost felted bark and every leaf. The cold, white stuff reflected the day even more than before, but even so, Amri couldn't deny it was beautiful. He stooped to touch the wet crystals, squeezing the snow into a melting lump in his hand.

A tiny voice sounding of chimes and whispers came from Kylan's shoulder. "The frost line means we're near."

Perched in the folds of his collar sat a shining blue creature with eight needle legs. Tavra had lost her Gelfling body—that of a Vapra soldier, with iridescent wings and trained hands that had wielded the sword that now waved uselessly in Amri's clumsy grip. She now inhabited the form of a crystal spider.

Amri sheathed the sword back at his belt before he cut someone with it by accident.

"To Ha'rar?" he asked. He was curious to see the Gelfling capital and its legendary citadel.

"To our destination," Tavra replied.

"I thought Ha'rar *was* our destination," Kylan said, raising a brow.

Amri couldn't make out Tavra's little spider face, but the impatience was evident enough in her voice: "Eventually, yes. But we cannot simply charge into the citadel."

"Why not?" Amri asked. "Do we need to make an appointment or something?"

Naia looked over her shoulder, nodding in agreement as she marched up the mountain slope. "I'll barge into All-Maudra Mayrin's personal chamber uninvited if I have to," she said. "She needs to know about the Skeksis, and fast. Rian should be here, too. If we find him and get that vial of essence in front of the All-Maudra, there will be no way she can deny the truth."

"It's not about invitation, Naia," Tavra said. "We've been alone in the wilderness since Kylan sent our message from the Grottan Sanctuary Tree. We have no idea if anyone has received it, much less whether they believe."

Amri shivered. What they'd done was monumental, especially if the pink petals dream-stitched with their message had reached each of the seven Gelfling clans. That had been the whole point, after all: to send the warning as far and as fast as possible, so what had happened in the Grottan caves would never happen again.

Naia's pace slowed until she stopped, sighing and putting her hands on her hips. The three of them were quiet so they could hear Tavra's voice over the wind that whistled through the snowy pines.

"Naia, Kylan. Amri. I know you want to reach Ha'rar. What the Skeksis have done—are doing—is a horrible crime and must be stopped. But the Gelfling have lived in the hand of the Skeksis for generations. It is not easy to change the way things are. People are learning our names and faces. But like Rian, we will be known as traitors. Not heroes. For this reason, we must be cautious, even with my mother. We must understand the weather before we inadvertently walk into a blizzard."

"You think your mother might still side with the Skeksis, even if she saw that vial of essence?" Amri asked. The idea was a disheartening one. "Even if she saw what happened in Domrak—saw what happened to you?"

"Belief is only half of the task we face," Tavra replied.

Naia's eagerness deflated, her green ears flattening.

"Fine," she said. "Then what should we do?"

"We could disguise ourselves as Podlings and sneak into the citadel," Amri suggested, trying to lighten the mood. Being so serious all the time was exhausting. "Spy on the All-Maudra from the rafters. Oh, I guess Podlings wouldn't be very good climbers."

Naia laughed, and even Kylan cracked a grin. Tavra, as usual, had no sense of humor about any of it.

"Chase the scent of the sea," she said. "When you see the seafarer's lanterns, follow them down the cliff to the shore."

As they heeded Tavra's directions, the earthy trail gave way to more snow and stone. The cliffs and mountain forms shimmered and glittered, like smoothed crystal reflecting the bright blue of the sky. Amri had never experienced the scent of the sea. He wasn't sure what to expect. But when a draft of salty air gusted across their path, there was no mistaking it.

"Smells like it's coming from that mountainside," he said.

Naia nodded, looking the wall of rock up and down.

"Pretty steep," she remarked. Amri didn't think so, but then again, rocks were his specialty. Maybe his only specialty. It didn't matter, anyway. If his friends couldn't follow, then there was no point to making the climb. That much could have been said of their entire journey.

"There's a passage through," Tavra said. "That way."

They waded through the snow, into the shadow cast by the cliff. For a grand moment, Amri's eyes had a rest from squinting, though it wasn't for long. A spot of light shone through the trees. They followed it, in moments finding a low tunnel through the rock. Amri traced his fingers along the tunnel wall as they walked through it.

"You're so smooth, like you were polished," he said to the stone, falling behind a step or three. Naia and Kylan were more interested in reaching the other side. He pressed his hand against the glossy surface, soaking in the cold of it and closing his eyes. "What made you? Hm?"

"Are you talking to the wall?" Naia called back to him, over her shoulder. She and Kylan stood at the end of the tunnel, their silhouettes the only relief from the blasting of the daylight. "Come on, crawly-foot!"

Amri sighed and gave the wall a goodbye pat. He hurried down the tunnel, grunting when he slipped on the icy path. Normally the tunnel would be no problem for a Grottan like him, used to caves and rock, but the sandals strapped on his feet made him clumsy. *Crawly-foot indeed.*

When he reached the other side of the tunnel and stopped beside Naia and Kylan, all he could see was blue. An endless ocean stretched below, the texture of living granite. The tunnel opened like a mouth, its tongue a steep, rocky trail that wound down to the coast. There was no snow here. Instead, thick silver mist glittered and swirled, broken only by the tops of a few tall trees that grew along the shore. The mist must have frozen into snow as it passed over the top of the ridge, Amri guessed. The mist that had given the Silver Sea its name.

Kylan tilted his head when he caught sight of a peculiar rock sitting just outside the tunnel's opening, nearly touching his left hand. On the rock, a carving in the likeness of a scaled, finned sea creature peered at them. Jewels were set in its head as eyes, reflecting the golden flame in the lantern hanging out of its mouth.

"Seafarer's lantern," Tavra said, as if it explained everything.

"Who keeps the lantern fires lit?" Amri asked. He knelt by it, looking into its old, shining eyes.

"No one knows. Old mauddies tell the song of a water spirit that lights the lanterns to lure childlings into the sea. More likely they're kept lit by travelers. However it happens, their lights have led sailors and travelers for hundreds of trine. Showing the way up the coast to Ha'rar . . . Come, then. Down we go, along the stone's way for the sake of you two boys."

Amri exchanged a glance with Kylan. The Spriton shrugged and, as the spider on his shoulder said, began the long descent.

Amri could see Naia's black-and-indigo wings twitch as she looked over the cliff into the open air above the mist.

"You could glide down and we'll meet you," he suggested.

She smiled. "And I'm sure you could easily climb down the cliff if you kicked off those shoes. That would just leave poor Kylan alone with Tavra . . ." Here she winked and added, "I'm used to the stone's way. We'll go together."

It would have been nice to have wings, though the idea of drifting through the open sky sounded a bit terrifying, too. Amri preferred the ground, even if the path was gravelly and loose under his sandals. When his foot slipped out from under him, Naia grabbed his hand to keep him from tumbling down the side of the ledge. She righted him and he sighed.

"Sorry," he said, ears twisting back in embarrassment. None of the others seemed to be having the same problems, but they were all used to the sandals. It was a daylighter thing. Naia only smiled, the corners of her eyes soft with sympathy.

"Walk heel-first," she said. "And keep your back straight. It'll help with balance."

He tried it, and they followed Kylan together. Heel-first felt unnatural. Dangerous, like he was going to step on something sharp at any moment. Walking toe-first made more sense, barefoot in the caves where any step could turn sharp and painful. But that was what the sandals were for.

"I had the same problem when I first left Sog," Naia added. "You'll get the hang of it. You're already better than when you first started."

Amri tried to imagine Naia getting used to shoes for the first time. "Even so, it'll only take one slip to go tumbling into the sea. And I'll bet this far north that water's cold as a Vapra's kiss," he said with a grin.

Naia chuckled, then realized she was still holding his hand. She let go, leaving a cold spot in his palm. "And you've kissed how many Vapra?"

Amri had never kissed anyone, let alone the one Vapra he'd ever met. Who also happened to be a spider.

"Oh, so many," he said. "So many."

When they finally reached sea level, Amri's knees ached. The forest thinned as the land ended in a rocky shore where the ocean's waves rolled up the land. The stones that washed up from the sea were round and smooth, in shades of black and silver and blue. Amri wanted to stoop down and bury his hands in them, close his eyes and listen to their tales. But his friends were already on the move, Kylan pointing to another lantern monument ahead, a spot of gold in all the silver mist.

Something small and pink flitted by. Amri caught the petal in his hand, and memories sprouted in his mind. A forest full of shadows and whispers and a terrible monster. A huge tree in the Dark Wood called Olyeka-Staba—the Cradle Tree—calling out in agony as its roots touched poison in the ground. The wild red eyes of the Skeksis Hunter as he chased Kylan and Naia—his confession on that terrible night that echoed the screams of the Skeksis back in the castle: that they had found a way to make a life-giving elixir by draining essence from the Gelfling. The

Gelfling, who had served the Skeksis with unquestioning loyalty for hundreds of trine.

Amri opened his hand and let the petal free before the dream could take root and fully blossom. He didn't need to see all the awful memories again.

"They made it to the coast after all," Naia said, watching it fly away. "I wonder if they've gone all the way to Ha'rar."

Amri tried to let the memories fly away, too. Tried to replace them with what was in front of him: Naia, whose smile was undaunted. Who had healed Olyeka-Staba and eased its pain in the Dark Wood. Who had faced the Skeksis without fear, and had seen the darkened Heart of Thra and survived.

"I hope so," Amri said. "Hey, Kylan! Wait up!"

Kylan slowed, staring out into the fog that rolled in off the sea. As Amri and Naia caught up to him, a shadow shivered into view. It was a ship, tied to a big tree that leaned out over the water. Its long, narrow hull and three sails spread along its yards and battens like the fins of a spiny fish, dyed crimson, rich blue, and a deep purple.

"Someone you know?" Naia whispered. "Is that why you brought us here?"

Tavra's response was breathy with uncharacteristic relief.

"Yes. Go, please."

Amri paused, looking out into the water. He thought of the water spirit Tavra had mentioned, that lit the lanterns. It was just a song told to keep childlings away from the dangerous waters, no doubt. But real creatures did lurk in the water, as they lurked

in every part of the world. Amri tried not to think about it and followed his friends.

They climbed out along the branch to which the ship was tied, using the bough like a dock and hopping, one at a time, down onto the rocking deck. Amri nearly lost his balance again. He hated wearing shoes, but he decided quickly that he hated wearing shoes on a boat even more.

"Do you think they'll recognize you?" Naia asked. She didn't seem to have any trouble keeping her balance on the water, probably because she'd grown up in a swamp. "I still have your pearl circlet, and Amri has your sword, if we need it to prove your identity—"

The door to the cabin opened just as Naia raised her hand to knock. A Sifa with thick, windswept red hair stood in the doorway. She was young, about Tavra's age, dressed in a heavy sailing coat embroidered with knotted ropes and sashes, strings of shining jewelry hanging from her belt and woven through her crimson braids.

Her gaze went straight to Kylan's shoulder.

"Onica," Tavra said, voice stumbling. "It's—"

Without hesitation, Onica reached out and gently scooped up the tiny spider in her hands. She held Tavra close, and her ocean-colored eyes filled with tears.

"Tavra," she said. "Thank the suns. You're alive."

CHAPTER 2

The inside of Onica's cabin was barely big enough for the five of them. It was a single room above deck, though Amri could see a hatch that went below. Red and dark blue cushions embroidered with shining thread and beads littered the floor, and bouquets of fragrant herbs dangled from the ceiling, swaying gently in time with the rocking of the boat. Over-melted candles lit the dim chamber, and any chill in the air was warmed away by the round clay stove against the far wall. Rose-colored glass in the porthole windows made the unending mist seem distant, nothing more than a veil of fog.

Onica wove through the hanging herbs and flowers like a fish through kelp. She still held Tavra in one hand. With the other she set a water vessel on the hearth plate.

"Please, sit," she said. "Anywhere will do."

Amri found a cushion that fit his bottom and sat heavily, hoping the uneasy feeling of water below his feet would subside. He didn't like it at all, not feeling the earth sturdy below him. But this was where Tavra had brought them, and if she thought it was safe here, then Amri wouldn't complain. No one else was, after all.

Onica cleared the floor in the center of the small room. Beneath the cushions and blankets was a leather strap-handle, which she grabbed, twisted, and pulled until a square of planks rose. Amri hunkered down, looking under the panel as it came up, assisted by wood gears below. At last the panel clanked into place, transforming the floor into a table. The daylighter world was full of surprises.

While her friend went back to the water vessel, Tavra hopped from Onica's hand onto the table. She looked like glass, with a silver-and-blue body and black legs. On her abdomen was a symbol, etched there by Kylan when he had stitched her soul into the spider's body to save her life.

"Onica has been my friend for a long time," she explained.

"Since we were young and naive," Onica added, bringing two cups of *ta*. "Daughter of the All-Maudra, sneaking out to meet a Sifa by the seafarer's lantern . . . It was quite a scandal."

Onica returned with two more cups and sat with them at the table. Amri sipped the *ta* eagerly. It was spicy and balanced by sweet flowers. Wrapped in the warmth of Onica's cabin, he almost forgot about the sea of perpetually shifting waves.

"So good," he said. "What's the spice?"

"Fire dust, shaved from coral along the Sifan Coast . . . Here, take some. It's bountiful in Cera-Na." Onica found a small sachet in her cache and gave it to Amri, who stuffed it in his belt pouch along with the other packets and bundles he'd picked up along their way. "But be careful not to use too much. It's quite potent."

"How did you know about Tavra?" Naia asked. She got a look from Kylan and backtracked. "I'm Naia. Tavra came to find me when my brother—"

"Gurjin, yes," Onica said. "Heroic friend of Rian of Stone-in-the-Wood. And you must be Kylan the Song Teller, who dream-stitched your message onto the pink petals of the Grottan Sanctuary Tree . . . and you're Amri."

Just Amri, like usual. He was going to have to figure out how to make a name for himself soon.

"How do you know all . . ." Amri stopped and tried to answer his own question. The herbs hanging over their heads bore scents as broad and diverse as their colors and the shapes of their leaves, some spindly and piney from the north and others wide and flat from the swamps of the south. Lovingly arranged bundles of dried incense rested near the clay stove, and hanging against the walls were wood mandalas carved with the shapes of the Three Brother suns, the Three Sister moons, and other figures of the sky.

"You're a Far-Dreamer," Amri said. "A soothsayer."

Onica smiled. "Far-Dreaming and soothsaying are two different things, but I suppose I've done both."

"Onica has always dreamed of things," Tavra said. "Things far from here, both in space and time."

Onica sipped her *ta*, and the smile went away. "Only glimpses. Rarely more than that. But I saw you all at the Sanctuary Tree. In dreams, Kylan, I saw you playing the *firca* that dream-stitched your memories onto the petals. Naia, I saw you heal the Cradle Tree and leap from the top of the Castle of the Crystal, when your wings came. And Amri, the Grottan . . ."

Her face was so sympathetic, Amri wriggled, a blush creeping up his neck.

". . . are strong and resilient!" he finished. "Not to mention good-natured, as a rule."

Onica nodded slowly. She didn't try to finish her thought, or her sympathies. None of them needed to be reminded of what had happened to the Grottan, defeated horribly by the spider race deep in the Caves of Grot. Sympathies would not rebuild Domrak, the Grottan village, nor restore the lives that had been lost.

Tavra, whose spider body was only more evidence of the hardships they'd suffered on their journey north, picked up on Amri's uneasiness and cleared her throat.

"Onica," Tavra said, her tiny voice filling the small room. She rotated to face the Sifa girl, touching one of her fingertips with a gentle tap of a crystalline leg. "We need to know what has happened in Ha'rar. Before we go there and are taken captive as traitors, or worse. Can you look? Into the fires and the smoke, and tell us if there is anything to be told?"

Of course! If Onica was truly a Far-Dreamer, perhaps she could hear the secret whispers of Thra. Perhaps the shadow songs might warn them if there was danger waiting for them in Ha'rar and the court of the All-Maudra. Amri waited for Onica's response, hoping she would say yes. He'd never seen such things and wanted to learn what incense she used. What herbs and incantations.

"Yes, of course," Onica said. "Let us see what we can see."

Onica rose and selected a bundle of herbs from among the hundreds hanging from the rafters, pressed the end of it into one of the coals that glowed white in the little hearth. When the bundle smoldered, she blew it out, letting the smoke weave through the room in a thin silver line. She set the bundle in a stone bowl and put it in the center of the table. She sat across from Naia and rested her hands, palm up, on the table, wiggling her fingers to invite Amri and Kylan to join her. Naia took their hands in turn, so the four of them were linked.

"Close your eyes," Onica said. "Open your mind. As if in dreamfast, but not that of the past. Connected. You and I. By the heart that beats in the breast of the world. By the blue fire that flows through our Gelfling bodies. By the earth. By the wind. By the water. By the fire."

Amri closed his eyes. That part was straightforward. Dreamfasting with a stranger, however, was not so easy. He tried to settle, relax. Remember that although he'd just met Onica, Tavra trusted her. So much, in fact, that she had brought them to Onica instead of her own mother. Amri took in a deep breath and let it out. He didn't realize his palm was sweating against Naia's until she gave him a firm, reassuring squeeze.

When Onica spoke next, her voice was lower, like the eerie still before a storm.

"You may each ask one question," she said, though now he wasn't sure if her voice was through the air or inside his mind. "Thra will answer, as it may."

Then the dreamfast began.

It was like a song without sound. Exchanging a meaningful glance with eyes closed. The feeling of understanding another Gelfling just by *knowing*, that connection when two minds met as one without a single word spoken. This time it was not just two minds, though. It was Amri's and Naia's. Kylan's and Onica's. Even Tavra, in her spider body, had joined. He could feel her—see her, almost—in his mind's eye. With long silky hair, beautiful and regal and Silverling.

The world lurched, as if the boat had capsized, and Amri grabbed tight on Naia's hand. It wasn't the sea under the ship but the swooping thrill he'd felt jumping off ledges in the Caves of Grot. That fleeting uncertainty of danger, wrapped in confidence.

Ask, said Onica. Or perhaps it was not Onica at all.

They were all hesitant. Onica had said they each had one question. To ask Thra, their world that gave them life. Amri had no idea what kind of question to ask, and neither, it seemed, did the others.

Kylan spoke first. *Did our message reach Ha'rar? Did the Gelfling this far from the tree see the dream I stitched upon its petals?*

Suddenly they were flying.

High above the mist on the coast, so it looked like an undulating cloak of silver fur or feathers, ebbing against the shore. Mountains ran the length of it, green on the sea side and snow white on the other. Amri still felt Naia's hand in his, now clinging as tightly to him as he clung to her. He couldn't see her, or Kylan, Onica, or Tavra. He couldn't even see himself, as the wind gusted against them, blowing them northward toward a shining white light that glowed on the horizon like a star. They raced toward the light, carried in the wind's rough embrace. As if they were riding atop one of the thousands of pink petals from the Sanctuary Tree—

No, that's what they *were*. They were the petals, racing

through the sky in clusters and flurries of pink. This was the dream memory of the pink blossoms that had blown from the Sanctuary Tree of Grot. The blossoms upon which Kylan had stitched their message, using his magic *firca*, so that their words of the Skeksis betrayal might be spread far and wide.

The mountains split to the left and right—the west and east, as they entered from the south—swooping like wings of faceted ice and crystal, protecting a snow-laden village of thatch-roofed buildings connected by winding stone paths.

The petals really made it all the way to Ha'rar, Kylan said, disembodied voice just audible over the wind and light. *Our message . . .*

The petals were everywhere. Bright and pink against the pure white snow, frothing on the silver sea waves that crashed against the wharf. Decorating the domed roofs of the Silverling houses, dancing along the stone streets and atop the frigid rivers that wound under bridges and walkways on their way to the northern shore. As the Vapra of Ha'rar touched the enchanted petals, they saw Kylan's dream. Heard the message stitched within.

Kylan had told his song to the petals and sent them on their way. But Amri and his friends had not yet had a chance to find out how the message was being received. Dreamfasts were always truth, but normal dreamfasts were hand to hand. Not carried by petals. Would the Gelfling believe?

Whispers came to Amri's ears:

This can't be. The Skeksis wouldn't do this to us . . .

But isn't this proof? It is a dreamfast, if a strange one . . .

As they flew through Ha'rar, they touched the cheeks and the backs of the Vapra's hands, landing in palms and nestling in locks of silver hair. Some were moved by the dream. Others threw the petals aside or burned them in fear. Some shared the dream with their families, while others brought the rumors to the very steps of the citadel, waiting for the All-Maudra to tell them what to make of it. But through the muddled doubt, the quiet rumors, one powerful thought came over and over. From suspicious hearts, hardening like stone.

It is a trick by the traitor Rian. He's trying to turn us against the Skeksis Lords.

Do not believe his lies.

Amri felt the heavy hand of disappointment when Kylan sighed.

As I feared, the song teller said.

Don't give up just yet, Amri said. *Your effort wasn't lost. Many must believe. There wouldn't be rumors otherwise.*

The vision faded, and Amri became aware of Onica's boat rocking below him again, smelled the smoke of the herb bundle under his nose. They still held hands, and Onica said again, "Ask."

This time Tavra spoke: "What of my mother and sisters?"

Her mother. All-Maudra Mayrin, chosen by the Skeksis to be the ambassador of the seven Gelfling clans to the Castle of the Crystal. And her daughters, of which Tavra was one of three. The question might have been selfish coming from anyone else, but from Princess Katavra, it was crucial.

The winds of the dreamfast stilled until they were floating in space, the world turning without them. Time passing, though whether backward or forward, Amri couldn't tell. Then the currents of the dream shuddered, once again moving, but this time in a different direction. Up and up they went, swirling through Ha'rar and ascending the face of the citadel itself. Through a window and into a chamber made of ice and white stone. It was night, some evening in the past. The petals of their consciousness drifted in and settled on the soft fabric draped across a small table. Other petals clung to the gossamer curtains, lay across the vanity where the All-Maudra kept her jewels and pretties.

Three Gelfling spoke nearby. Two were clearly sisters, Vapra, dressed in white and silver, with long pale hair and silver circlets on their brows. One was Amri's age, ink smudged on her cheek. The second was older, wearing a mantle of flowing gossamers. Amri saw Tavra's likeness in their smooth brows and silver hair. Her sisters, one younger, one older.

The third Silverling was their mother: All-Maudra Mayrin. There was no one else she could be, with that silver crown on her brow. Voice like snow, face wizened and stern.

None of them took note of the petals that had been brought in by the wind. The petals whose memories Amri and his friends were experiencing in this strange dreamfast.

"Seladon. Brea. This endless bickering will not do!" she scolded her daughters. The two of them that had been there, anyway. She couldn't have known her third daughter, who had been missing since she was sent to find Rian and Gurjin, the traitors, would be seeing this moment later.

The younger of the sisters bunched her hands into fists.

"I told you! I saw a sign, in the—"

"I don't have time for this, Brea!" In that moment, she sounded like any other mother frustrated with her wayward daughter. She finally took note of the petals, waving at them in distress. "The Ritual Master and the General will be here soon. I already have to explain the rumors of these pink petals somehow. I can't have you running off to the Sifa and distracting me with their Far-Dreaming witchcraft!"

"But—"

"Brea, give up! No one is going to believe you," Seladon snapped. The cruel words echoed in the chamber, and even Amri winced, though the moment was long eaten by history. Brea looked down, her hands still in fists.

"Tavra would have," she whispered, and the dream faded. As they left the memory, Amri became aware of Tavra's presence, stronger than before.

Brea went to the Sifa for answers instead of to your mother? Kylan asked.

Brea is young, but she is not stupid. If she had reasons to doubt my mother, then so do we. The All-Maudra may not be as ready to leap into war with the Skeksis as we hoped, Tavra finished in her dour, unreadable voice.

Even if All-Maudra Mayrin weren't Brea's mother, she was still her *maudra.* The head of her clan. It seemed strange that Brea wouldn't trust her own mother with her problems . . . but then again, after seeing the All-Maudra's response, Amri wondered if maybe Brea had been right to visit the Sifa instead.

He wasn't completely surprised, but kept his disdain to himself. The Vapra and their All-Maudra had left the Grottan clan to toil away in the caves for trine upon trine. Of course she'd be afraid to get her silver cloaks dirty tangling with the Skeksis.

Ask.

Amri couldn't be sure who Onica was speaking to until she squeezed his hand. His real hand, though her touch wasn't strong enough to break him from the dreamfast. He gulped and tried to calm his heart. It was his turn.

How do we win?

His voice echoed in the dreamfast of their joined minds, his question bold and bare. No answer came, so he tried again, struggling to make his words heard amid all the darkness of the dream:

Please, Thra. How do we defeat the Skeksis?

The wind of the dream shook like a storm rising. Like a monster waking, or a song erupting from the dawn. Amri had asked, and they braced themselves for the answer.

CHAPTER 3

The answer to Amri's question was a wall.

Just a wall, in the middle of an abyssal darkness, illuminated by the light of the dreamfast. There was no fire, no sun. It was almost as if the wall itself were the source of the light, though it looked like any regular wall. A tall slab of tan stone, rough under Amri's fingertips when he touched it, though it still had the surreal flavor of a dream.

Hello? he called, but no one answered. Not like before when Thra had shown them the memories from afar. The Far-Dreams. This time, it seemed, Amri was alone.

Unlike the first two answers, he experienced this vision as himself. A Gelfling, not a pink petal. He hoped perhaps it was because this was a message, not a memory.

He stepped back, trying to see how high the wall rose, or how far it extended on either side. But it was infinitely tall. Infinitely wide, stretching endlessly into the shadows. He touched the wall again, trying to listen to its hidden voice. But there were no trembles, no vibrations. Not in this place, it seemed. In this place, there was nothing but the wall.

Amri sighed. Of course this would happen. The first thing he shouted out to Thra was to ask it how to defeat the Skeksis. If

Thra cared about the Gelfling, and knew what to do, then wouldn't it have told them already? Through the Sifa Far-Dreamers or through the stars. Through the Crystal. Or through Aughra, the Helix-Horned witch who lived on the High Hill. Thra had endless mediums, but when Amri asked it a direct question, this silent wall was its response.

What am I supposed to do with this? he asked of the empty dream.

The wall's surface warmed under his fingers, and Amri jumped back. Fire had blossomed below, seeping out from the foot of the wall as if it were a door closed shut on an inferno. He stumbled away as the fire grew, blazing red and gold, stinging his eyes with its hot light as it lapped at the wall with greedy, hungry tongues. He turned and ran from it as the flames lunged upward, burning heat washing across the dream, casting its orange light upon the darkness.

The gold changed to silver. Amri stopped running when he felt the heat subside from his back, turned to see what had happened.

The fire had engulfed the wall, but where it had been ravenous and red, it was now blue as the midnight sky. The wall itself had crumbled in places from the teeth of the fire, and where the rock had fallen away, Amri saw shining light. Crystal veins, white as starlight, bared as the wall crumbled, bit by bit. And revealed in the light of the crystal were words. Images. Figures . . .

Then he was back on the boat, his hands clammy against Onica's and Naia's.

"What was that?" he asked, nearly breaking the circle. The

dreamfast still bound them, like a blanket, and despite what he had seen, he was loath to believe it.

A wall, Naia said. *You saw it, too?*

I think we all did, Kylan replied softly. *With the blue flame . . . What does it mean?*

None of them, not even Onica, had any answers. Or at least that was what Amri took the silence to mean. He felt Naia hesitate, tensing her fingers around his and almost pulling away. She hadn't asked her question yet, though after what they'd seen and how little it made sense, Amri didn't blame her for being unsure.

Onica took in a breath. Let it out.

Ask, Naia, she said. *Ask your question.*

What remained of Naia's hesitation vanished. She clasped Amri's hand and said,

Please, tell us where we can find Rian.

Amri felt the chill of the mountains before he saw them. A carriage raced through the snowy wood, drawn by two rolling armalig slugs. It was of Skeksis design, with sharp edges and angular, nearly grotesque sculpting along its sides and canopied top.

Amri looked from the carriage to the mountains that surrounded it on either side. The snowy backs of the rocky ridges were familiar, as if he'd seen them very recently. As if he'd tasted the scent of the trees just that day. This dream was not of the distant past, he realized as he caught the angle of the three suns. They were not witnessing the memory of a pink petal, nor was this a strange and puzzling message. This was a vision of now, of something that was happening not far from them.

The dream suddenly died as Naia pulled her hand from his, jumping to her feet and drawing her dagger as if she would stab a Skeksis with it right then and there.

"That's back where we were!" she exclaimed. "That was a Skeksis carriage!"

"Rian must have gotten to Ha'rar and run into the Skeksis," Amri said. "But what are we going to do? If that's a Skeksis carriage, then that means—"

"Then it means we don't have any time! We've got to go rescue him!"

Naia barged out of the cabin door and sprinted across the deck, leaving them all behind as she charged back toward the cliff.

The sword at Amri's hip felt unbearably heavy. Had they left Domrak behind, ruined by skekLi and the spider race, only to find the Skeksis were still a step ahead? Only to find that the All-Maudra in Ha'rar might not be trustworthy, despite how hard they'd worked to reach her?

It didn't matter now. If Rian was in danger, they had to save him. He had the vial, after all. The proof of their message. The proof they weren't the ones who had betrayed the Gelfling.

Tavra caught Amri's sleeve as he stood with Kylan. She crawled up his arm and he resisted the urge to swat her away. Even if she was a Silverling in her mind, her body was still a creeping crystal-singer spider.

"Naia's right," she said in his ear when she reached his shoulder. "Hurry. Onica, please wait here. If something has happened to

Rian, we'll need a place to hide him."

Onica followed Amri and Kylan out onto the deck. Naia was long gone, rushing at her unstoppable pace back up the side of the cliff toward the other side. Kylan struggled out of his heavy traveling pack, leaving it on the deck of the ship. It would only slow him down. Amri's heart pounded in anticipation of the tough race they had ahead of them.

"Be safe," Onica said. "Those trees we saw, near where the carriage was headed. The fluttering pines."

Amri nodded to her. "Thanks."

They sprinted across the beach, trying to retrace their footsteps back to the winding path. The seafarer's lanterns led the way, but even once they reached the cliff, Amri knew it would take them far too long to go up the way they had come down.

"Take your time, I'm going up," Amri told Kylan. Without waiting for a reply, he ran straight for the sheer rock, ignoring the footpath and taking hold of the first lip in the stone. It would have been easier if he hadn't been wearing the sandals. Even so, within moments he had left Kylan behind him. He might even be able to catch up with Naia, he thought, if he kept at it.

His foot slipped, his toes unable to grab through the soles of his shoes, but he clenched his teeth and hoisted himself over the last ledge. The passageway between the misty coast and the snowy wood was up ahead, and he thought he could even see the snow kicked up from Naia's feet as she ran toward the ravine where they'd seen the Skeksis carriage in the dreamfast. He chased after her, Tavra's legs pricking his shoulder when she said, "The fluttering pines. Quickly. Right here, up the incline!"

A small path broke to the right, branching away from the rest of the rocky land that began the steady descent down to the ravine. As they passed under the snowy boughs, Amri realized that it wasn't just snow that coated the trees. Fluttering clusters of unamoths gathered on the emerald needles, flitting between the flakes of snow drifting from the clouds.

The trail transformed gradually into a ridge, overlooking the ravine. Within moments he could see Naia below, running with her dagger in hand. And up ahead, where Naia's path connected to the ravine, he could just make out the snowy commotion of the Skeksis carriage.

"Just a bit more. This trail follows the main way from above. We'll be able to get the drop on them . . ." Tavra trailed off. Taking a high path was good and all for a girl Gelfling with wings, but it wasn't going to do him any good. The Vapra swore.

"Eel-feathers. Stone-weighted boy!"

Amri pointed ahead. "I see the carriage!"

They neared the edge of the ridge for a better view of the bulbous, filigree-encrusted carriage. It wasn't going fast on the ice and snow, but it was steady. If they stopped even for a moment, they'd fall behind.

"There's Naia!"

Naia had mounted the ridge on the other side of the carriage trail. As they caught sight of her, she threw back her cape and launched herself with a surge of speed. Her wings spread, rippling rainbow light against the black and indigo, catching the wind as she dived for the carriage. She landed and plunged her dagger into the canopy and dropped down inside.

"Help her!" Tavra cried.

A Skeksis scream curdled the air, high-pitched and nasal. A moment later, Naia and another Gelfling crashed through one of the carriage windows. The carriage tipped, the armaligs squealing in distress at the disturbance. Amri's lungs burned from effort but he didn't stop running.

"If only I had wings!" he cried.

"The fallen tree up ahead—you can make it, can't you?"

He saw the tree. It had fallen over the ridge cliff, its roots barely holding on to the earth while its top pointed down, its long inverted body like a slide into the ravine below.

"I hope Kylan tells a nice song at my funeral!"

Amri leaped for the tree, landing and sliding down at an impossible speed. As he slipped and nearly fell, he jumped again, aiming for a snowbank below as the carriage swerved wildly and collided with the rocky wall of the ravine. He landed in a pile of soft snow and as soon as he could, got to his feet. He shook off the snow just as Naia and a Stonewood Gelfling with dark brown hair surfaced from another bank nearby. They watched as the armaligs dragged the carriage against the unforgiving rock until the last of the rigging poles broke.

The spooked beasts abandoned their post, rolling away in a spray of snow and ice.

"The vial," the Stonewood Gelfling said. Amri recognized him from the blue streak in the hair above his eye. "He has the vial!"

"Rian, wait!" Naia chased after him, but he broke away from her and ran toward the carriage.

"Who?" Amri panted.

They were about to follow Rian when the ruined door of the carriage flew open. Amri froze as cold as the trees and rocks around them.

Out of the carriage, coughing and swearing and spitting, came a Skeksis. He emerged, reptilian snout first, like a black bird from an egg, almost too big for the door. His feather-lined cloak squeezed out, then billowed as he stepped into the snow, rising to his full height. His eyes smoldered beneath his prominent purple brow, black pupils tiny and livid as he cast his gaze upon them.

"Gelfling," he said as if it were a curse, spittle spraying between his wicked teeth. Next, he saw Naia. ". . . Drenchen. The halfsies one. So you live. Hmmmm."

"Give me the vial, Chamberlain," Rian said. The confidence in his voice was impressive; Amri's stomach felt like it was wrinkling into a tiny ball in front of the Skeksis Lord. The Stonewood soldier stepped forward, holding out his hand. "The vial!"

The Chamberlain glared, then reached back to fluff the black collar around his neck so it framed his face.

"The vial? The *vial*? After ruining our carriage—*MY* carriage? Stupid Gelfling. Stupid Rian. After all we've done for you, you stand there and defy us. Defy *me*."

Rian's hand wavered where he held it out, but he didn't back down. Naia stomped up, flicking her wings so the snow shook free, and took a place beside him.

"Give it," she said. "Or we'll take it by force."

Amri shifted his weight and tightened his grip on Tavra's sword when the Chamberlain jerked his hand, but he was only flipping his sleeve back. He reached into his cloak and slowly, as if teasing, withdrew a tiny glass vial of blue liquid.

"The vial . . . *this* vial?" he asked.

Amri had never seen the vial in person. He had only heard about it from Naia, and seen it in Kylan's dream-stitched petal. The tiny thing and its contents were the proof of what Rian had seen in the Scientist's laboratory. The thing only Gelfling could give, and the thing the Skeksis had betrayed them for. Life essence.

Gelfling essence.

"Give it!" Rian repeated, voice shaking. He started to step forward, but the Chamberlain pulled the stopper out with a sickening, wet *pop*.

"Stop where you are."

The command wasn't the whining, nasal sound it had been a moment ago. Now it was dark and heavy, roiling with deep-seated fury. The Chamberlain looked between the three of them, darkness filling the hoods around his beady eyes. He held the vial as if he would pour it out into the thirsty snow, and Rian stopped short.

"You think you can command me?" the Chamberlain asked, a low growl growing in the back of his throat. "You, puny Gelfling? Giving *me* orders? A Skeksis? One of Twice-Nine? You dare to command *me*?"

"The Skeksis won't rule the Gelfling much longer, not once we prove to them what you've done," Naia said, brandishing her dagger. "To the Crystal, and to our people."

"So hand over the vial before we make an example of you," Rian said.

He leveled his eyes at the Chamberlain. An uneasy silence followed. Hot clouds puffed between the Chamberlain's uneven teeth as he regarded the three, clutching the open vial in his talons. His eyes darted back and forth between them, and Amri tried to still the struggling fear in his heart.

"I've always wondered," the Chamberlain began, "how Vapra tastes."

Then he tilted his head back and emptied the vial down his toothy maw.

"No!" Rian cried. "*Mira!*"

"Rian, don't!"

Naia tackled Rian as he threw himself at the Chamberlain. They rolled to a stop in the snow and watched with Amri in horror.

The Skeksis had gone motionless, hands outstretched as he closed his eyes and sucked in a long, deep breath. He shivered violently from his balding crown to the tips of his claws, dropping the empty vial in the snow.

"*OH YES. SWEET AND BRIGHT AS SPRING SYRUP! Mmm-MMMM!*"

The terrible words echoed off the cold cliffs. The Chamberlain's back straightened, and what feathers and spines remained on his serpentine neck filled with long-lost luster. His head tilted down, and when he looked upon them this time, his ancient yellow eyes had a spark of lightning within them.

"Now," he said. He threw back his cloak and drew a short, sharp blade, smiling at them with a mouth of razor teeth. "What were you saying about making an example of me?"

"Amri, raise your sword."

Tavra's voice was like a snowflake in Amri's ear. He did as she said. He didn't know how to use it, but he couldn't stand by and do nothing while Naia pulled Rian to his feet. The Stonewood could barely stand, shuddering and stiff with rage.

"Rian, we have to go," Naia urged. "We have to go."

"No—the vial—Mira—"

Amri stepped before the Chamberlain. It took every muscle in his body to keep from crumbling under the Skeksis's heavy, terrible gaze.

"Widen your stance," Tavra directed calmly. "Do not look away from his eyes—"

His eyes.

Amri lowered his sword and reached into his belt pouch.

"What do you have there, little Vapra?"

As the Chamberlain drew nearer, Amri threw the sachet of fire dust. The tiny packet struck the Skeksis in the snout and exploded in a cloud of red spice. Snow fell from the trees and the mountaintops above when he screamed.

"MY EYES! AHHH!"

"And I'm not Vapra!" Amri shouted. Then, to Naia and Rian: "*Run!*"

Even revitalized by the Gelfling essence, the Chamberlain dropped to his knees, shoving clawfuls of snow into his burning eyes and nose. Without waiting to see how long the effect would last, Amri and the others ran, leaving the Skeksis Lord's gurgling screams behind them.

"What are we going to do without the vial?" he panted. "That was our proof!"

"We can't worry about that now," Tavra replied. "Keep running!"

In the cold air, Amri's head started to spin. He tried to shake it off, hoping they could escape from the Chamberlain before he recovered from the burning dust.

The wood passed them, white and silver. As if the sky were looking after them, it suddenly began to snow. Amri whispered a quiet thanks, hoping the big, fluffy flakes would cover their footsteps as they escaped. They climbed the foothills until they could no longer hear the Chamberlain's bellows, nearly to where the air smelled of ocean.

The vertigo returned, and Amri stumbled, then leaned against a tree as the world spun. In every swirl of snow, every spot of shadow, he saw Skeksis faces. Phantoms, rising out of his worst fears. His throat felt tight, locking air out of his lungs.

"I don't feel great," he tried to say.

"What's wrong? What's—"

Tavra's voice fell away, and all Amri could hear was . . . humming. An intense droning, a chant, coming from deep in the earth and high in the heavens at the same time.

Rian pressed his hands against his ears. "What is that sound?"

If anyone replied, Amri didn't hear it. Blinded by the dazzling snow, deafened by the cyclic chant pounding inside his head, Amri could barely get one foot in front of the other. What was happening? Was this some sort of spell or hex—some evil Skeksis magic? He wondered where Kylan had gone, if he had ever made it up the cliff. He could only hope the song teller was safe.

The three of them stumbled to a slow walk, though Naia tried to push on.

"He's coming . . . We have to keep going . . ."

The drone vibration sharpened, and Amri heard words. Coming from the earth. From the stars. From the suns and the moons. It drowned out the cold and the bright light. It chanted in time with Amri's heart, in time with the pulse of the world. Of Thra.

Deatea. Deratea. Kidakida. Arugaru.

The voice was familiar. A voice present through the lore and songs of the Gelfling people. His mind awoke with a moment of clarity as he recognized it—

And then the world vanished.

CHAPTER 4

*D*eatea. Deratea. Kidakida. Arugaru.

The chant had been imprinted in Amri's heart long ago. Before he was born, he imagined, as he floated in nothingness. It was the sound the wind made blowing against the mountains. The song of the Black River winding through the Dark Wood. The cosmic sound that fell from the sky in the form of sun and rain and snow, and the earthy rhythm that rose up from the depths of the world as plants and creatures and Gelfling.

Deatea. Deratea. Kidakida. Arugaru . . .

Amri opened his eyes. He was in the dark, in a deep, cold cave. It smelled familiar, like water dripping. He looked up and gasped.

Hanging from the ceiling of the dark-filled cavern was a tree. It grew from the ceiling, down toward the depths, made of stone and rock and glistening with crystal specks. Still, he knew where he was. Knew the blue color of the rock, the scent of the fresh water flowing. He was in the Caves of Grot, far below Domrak.

"Tavra?" he asked, but there was no spider on his shoulder. He was alone.

Deatea. Deratea. Kidakida. Arugaru . . .

The chant was only a whisper now, a mere draft seeping from the world above. Amri remembered thinking just before he'd come to this place—wherever it was—that he had recognized it, and struggled to recall. Through the darkness, in the ancient embrace of the stone tree, something flickered.

DEATEA. DERATEA.

The world of the dream shuddered. The voice boomed like the voice of the heavens itself: *KIDAKIDA. ARUGARU.*

Light glared around him, and he covered his eyes against it. But when he closed his eyes, he saw another dream, this one deeper inside his mind. As if when he'd closed his eyes, he'd actually opened them.

And he saw *it*.

Spinning before him, larger than life, a spire of faceted stone shining a brilliant white. It rang with a deafening song, a cry that might pierce any darkness. A voice that turned the world, that beat with the pulse of the planet. It was the Heart of Thra. The Crystal of Truth: blazing from the depths of the world where it had always been, dwarfing Amri as he gazed upon it.

"Yes! Good! There!"

The voice was of the earth, rough and dirty, ancient and wise. It spoke to him from the Crystal, or from the dream. It was then that he finally recognized it.

"Mother Aughra?" he asked. "Did you do this?"

His question went unanswered, irrelevant and faint and drowned out by the ringing of the Crystal. He heard other voices all around him, but when he looked, he couldn't see other faces. The Crystal was too bright. He could only hear them asking the same questions he'd asked: *Is that you, Mother Aughra? Where are we? Why?*

"Quiet!" Aughra's booming voice silenced the chatter until all Amri heard was the pulsing of the Crystal and Aughra's rough breath. "Quiet, and listen! Not much time. Skeksis might find out. About this dream-space, this source of magic and prophecy."

"Dream-space." Amri recognized Kylan's voice, let out a breath of relief. At least the song teller was all right. "The world within our world . . ."

So they were in a dream, after all. Aughra ignored Kylan, speaking in her strange, impatient way. "Rian, brave Stonewood! Naia, fierce Drenchen! You listening? You here?"

"I'm here."

It was Rian's voice, followed by Naia's: "Me too."

"Good. Yes. Naia, who saw the blighted Crystal itself. Rian, who saw what the Skeksis have done to infect it. Your truths will light the way. You must share them, now! In this dream of menders!"

"Share my dream . . . you mean, dreamfast?" Rian asked.

"Yes!" Aughra bellowed. "Now, and with haste!"

Amri felt the familiar warmth of a dreamfast in his mind, through the dream-space of Aughra's making. Through the projection of the Crystal that blinded him. The dreamfast was Naia's, feeling of her essence—trees and fresh water, the scent of lush flowers and the symphony of the jungle forest.

The dreamfast came more vividly than any other. Clear as if he'd been there himself, Amri saw the Swamp of Sog—Naia's home. A huge, gnarled tree broke the overgrown wetland, protecting the glade the Drenchen clan called home. In the memory, Naia was leaving, with her father, Bellanji, as well as a silver-haired soldier. Tavra of Ha'rar, who had come with news of Naia's twin brother's betrayal . . .

Then the trouble in the swamp. A wild Nebrie. Its monstrous tusks sent Naia, wingless, falling into the deep water. And there, below the layers of silt and mud, she'd seen the crystal vein. Purple, like the eyes of the darkened Nebrie.

The darkening had reached as far as Sog. Naia's voice was in the memory and in Amri's mind.

I saw it, too, said another voice. Was it Onica's? *In a dream of the deep ocean.*

And I, said another. *In the Crystal Sea, there was a terrible storm . . .*

And I saw nurlocs with purple eyes, deep in the Caves of Grot!

How many Gelfling were listening? How many had Aughra summoned to this dream-space—how many *menders* had she named?

Naia's voice was solemn when she went on.

I went to find the Crystal, to be sure it was safe from the sickness . . .

The Dark Wood. The bone-masked Skeksis Hunter. The Skeksis and the Castle of the Crystal. It was all a blur of cloaks and claws and laughter, cruel Emperor skekSo as he ordered Tavra to be taken to the Scientist skekTek's laboratory. All as Naia beheld the horror in the Crystal Chamber. That the Crystal of Truth, once white and pure, was damaged and dying. Bleeding darkness into the world like wildfire.

But it was the source.

Naia's dream rippled, losing detail. Amri felt as if he were breaking the surface of a lake, returning to the sight of the projected Crystal in the dark. It was all in his mind, the dream within a dream. No sooner had it ended than another dream began, this time with Rian's voice guiding it.

The Skeksis are responsible for the state of the Crystal, he said. *Because of what they've done with it.*

Now Amri was in the Castle of the Crystal. Sneaking down a hallway through the eyes of Rian, deep in the catacombs. Catching a sliver of red light, the hushed whispering of Skeksis. Looking in, and seeing . . . a *machine*. A hole in the wall, filled with the fiery light of the Crystal. A Vapra soldier—Mira—forced to gaze on the beam of deadly light that shone from the Crystal that once had protected Thra. Now, instead of giving light, it took. It took and took, until she had nothing left, the whole of her life's essence distilled to a single vial of blue liquid.

It was my only proof, Rian said, his mental voice breaking with anger and remorse. *She was my only proof. And now . . .*

The final memory. One Amri had borne witness to in person. The Chamberlain, leathery tongue flapping against his pointed teeth, swallowing the last drops of the precious essence in the vial.

The dreamfast ended. Rian's voice was rough and broken, near as if he were standing just out of Amri's sight.

"It was our last hope. But now it's gone. She's gone . . ."

"It doesn't matter," said Naia. "Even without the vial. We must reach Ha'rar. We must tell the All-Maudra—"

"You already have."

All-Maudra Mayrin's voice rang through the dream-space like

42

the sea crashing against a cliff of ice. As she spoke, her image came into focus on the face of the dream-Crystal. As they had seen her in Onica's Far-Dream: noble and solemn, her wings like prismatic ice.

Amri wondered if Tavra was in the dream with them. If she was, why hadn't she spoken, if only to tell her mother that she was still alive? Or maybe she hadn't come into the dream-space with them, because of her spider body. Either way, the Silverling soldier's voice did not rise from the quiet.

"I have seen the petals that came on the wind from the south," the All-Maudra continued. "I've heard rumors, rippling through the Vapra of Ha'rar. Of Mira's disappearance. Of Rian and Gurjin, the traitors." Her emotions were hidden on her stolid face when she added, "But now I understand the truth."

Aughra grunted.

"Yes, yes. Now you know. Now you *all* know. Your many dreams are one. Your many truths are one."

"Why have you taken so long to help us?" It was Kylan again, though he hadn't been called on to speak. "If you had the power to do this—the *will* to help us—"

Aughra paused, dropping them into a silence that threatened to dismantle the dream-space altogether. The light of the Crystal dimmed, and Amri felt himself begin to wake. Until Aughra's voice brought him back, this time softer and sadder than before.

"Aughra made this place, this *dream*-place. To ask Thra the same thing! Thra answered," Aughra muttered. Amri wasn't sure if it was an answer to Kylan's question or just a continuation of her thoughts.

"Now, Thra has answered," she continued. "And here is what it has said: Seven fires of resistance must be lit. Seven fires by seven clans, before the Skeksis destroy the Crystal with their greed. Seven wondrous melodies must unite as one, in a single song . . . By you, Naia. By the menders who hear the cries of the Dark Crystal. This is Thra's answer."

"I will do it," Naia said without hesitation. "Seven fires, seven songs—whatever Thra believes will save us, you can rely on me. I will bring the truth to the clans and unite the Gelfling."

Amri shivered. He could almost see her face, gazing fearlessly into Aughra's eye. He hoped she could feel him, standing beside her even if it was in a dream. She wasn't alone. He would be with her, and so would Kylan.

"All-Maudra Mayrin," the song teller said, "we came all this way to tell you what the Skeksis have done. To give you this dream in person. To show you the vial . . . but we didn't know if we could trust you. Now that you've seen what we've seen, seen what Rian has seen, tell us true: Do you believe?"

The All-Maudra's form came and went in the face of the Crystal, liquid and shifting until suddenly solidifying with clarity. Amri held his breath waiting for her answer.

"Yes," she said. "I see now it cannot be denied. Go forth, knowing the first fire already blazes . . . Ha'rar and the Vapra will stand against the Skeksis."

Amri's heart nearly burst with light. The words from the All-Maudra were like a salve on the ache in his heart. The worry that she would deny them as liars and traitors or, worse, that she might have already known and decided to look the other way. Maybe they had been wrong to doubt her. Even after seeing how she had turned Brea away.

Rian spoke up next, voice bristling with fervor. "And what about me? The Chamberlain drank the last of Mira's essence. The Skeksis have to pay for what they've done!"

Aughra was silent for a long time, and Amri thought maybe the dream had ended. When she replied, it was grave as the earth itself.

"Rian, you have a special task. One that can be done by your hand . . . or else by none. You must retrieve a sacred object. When you wake, you will know it."

"Aughra—wait—"

"*WAKE!*"

Amri bolted upright. A cold arachnid body huddled in the crook of his neck. Beside him, Naia and Rian stirred. The suns were setting. They hadn't been asleep for long.

"Was it a dream?" he whispered.

"I believe so," Tavra replied. So she *had* witnessed it. "And what a dream it was."

Naia shook out her locs and turned to Rian. "You all right?"

Rian sat up, a grim look on his face. His eyes were still red from the tears he'd shed over the vial of essence—the last remains of Mira, the Vapra from the memory. But the faraway look on the Stonewood's face was not all grief. It was also determination, and fury.

"Rian . . . ?"

"I have to leave." He stood, brushing off snow. He helped Naia and Amri to their feet. "I'm sorry . . . Thank you for getting me out of a bad place with the Chamberlain. But I have to go."

"What did Aughra tell you?" Naia asked. "Aren't you coming with us to light the fires of resistance?"

"No. I have a different task. Aughra wants me to get something. Some old relic . . . I don't understand."

"Don't be too surprised," Amri remarked. "This is Aughra we're talking about, after all."

Rian glanced his way and snorted. "Indeed. And even if I don't understand, I suppose I still have to try. That's the way this always goes, it seems. I'm sorry I can't come with you."

Naia fluffed her cloak. "It's all right. Do what you need to do, and so will we. I'm sure we'll meet again . . ." Naia trailed off, then bolted upright. "Oh, Rian! I nearly forgot—Gurjin is alive!"

Rian's whole posture changed from suprise to shock, then confused joy.

"What? I thought—I thought skekMal—"

"I did, too. But the Skeksis kept him alive. Something about us being twins. I sent him back to Sog to recover. No way the Skeksis will go all the way through the swamp to get to him . . . He's safe. I just wanted you to know."

The realization changed the Stonewood for the better. Amri was surprised Rian was able to smile after all that had happened to him. But he did at Naia's news, if only a little. He reached out and clasped Naia's hand.

"Thank you, Naia," he said again. "I'm indebted to you—"

"WHERE ARE YOU? RRRAUUGHHHH!"

They all held their breaths as a distant Skeksis scream echoed through the twilight wood. The freezing fingers of fear crept up Amri's spine, digging in and squeezing. It was the Chamberlain, down in the ravine. Amri felt the ground flinch beneath the snow, warning him.

"He's coming," Amri whispered. "The fire dust must have worn off. We should go."

Rian nodded. "Until next time."

He gave the rest of them a clipped salute, tossing his hair a last time before slipping away into the wood, heading south.

Tavra tapped Amri's cheek. "Quickly. Back to Onica's boat," she said. "We must tell her what we have seen, and we must not let Lord skekSil find us!"

The Chamberlain let loose another roar, shaking the trees with his essence-infused fury. Amri did not need Tavra to tell him a second time. He grabbed Naia's hand and headed back the way they'd come. As they hurried through the dusk, snow continued to fall, covering their tracks. Amri thanked it with every breath as they escaped the raging Skeksis, leaving him behind in the ravine.

CHAPTER 5

A chill wind blew as the moons rose, reflecting off snow. By the time the light reached the cliff along the coast, the mist had cleared. Below, the ocean appeared to bleed directly into the heavens with only the stars to differentiate the sky from what was the sea.

A bright light shone far to the north. Amri might have mistaken it for a star, or maybe even a moon, had he not already found the Sisters moving across the night closer to the horizon.

"The Waystar," Tavra said, noticing him looking. "A grove of star trees growing high on the Ha'rar cliffs. Along with the seafarer's lanterns, the grove lights the way for travelers coming to Ha'rar. Although it's not a real star, it's tradition for the Vapra to look to it in times of need."

Amri remembered the light he'd seen in the Far-Dream, when they'd been petals blowing into Ha'rar. The city of Silverlings and their All-Maudra were there. He shivered, but this time not from the cold. The first fire was lit.

"I wonder how many gaze on it now," Naia wondered aloud.

Onica was waiting for them on the deck when they arrived back at the ship, cheeks and nose red from the cold, crimson hair frothing around her face in the confines of her hood.

"Oh, thank the Sisters," she said. "After that dream, I wasn't sure if we would find you frozen to death in the snow. Come in, come in."

Amri let her pull them inside, let her wrap heavy quilts around his shoulders. Kylan looked up from the fire where he'd been stirring a pot of soup.

"Naia, Amri—Tavra! You're all right."

"And you," Amri said. "I was worried!"

"I had just made it to the top of the cliff when the dream-space happened . . . Afterward, I didn't know where everyone was, so I came back here. I'm so glad you're all right . . . But where's Rian? Did you find him?"

Naia told Onica and Kylan what had happened. With the Chamberlain and the vial. Rian's aloof goodbye. She ended with a sigh and a shrug, as if nothing else could be done for the Stonewood soldier. Maybe nothing could.

"I was able to tell him about Gurjin, at least," she said. "I just hope he doesn't do something brash and get himself killed."

"The two of you were there, too?" Amri asked. "I mean, in the . . . dream-space? I heard your voice, Kylan . . ."

Kylan nodded. "I think we all were."

"I wonder how many people saw it," Amri murmured. He had heard so many voices in the dream-space, and only some of them had belonged to his friends. How many had Aughra called? How many menders were there among the Gelfling clans, and how many of them were now waiting for them, to light the fires of resistance? Amri tried not to feel insignificant, thinking about it.

"I haven't seen the stone tree in Domrak since I was little."

"Domrak?" Naia said. "Is that how you saw it?"

"Yes . . . you didn't?"

"No. I was home in Sog, in the heart chamber of Great Smerth. Kylan?"

The song teller shook his head. "The meadows near Sami Thicket."

"And I saw the great ship *Omerya*, off Cera-Na," Onica said. "Hmm . . . not surprising. The dream-space is in our minds and our hearts, after all. Now, eat up while I take us out to sea. I fear the Chamberlain may come to the coast in his search for us, and I would like to be gone if that happens."

"So now the All-Maudra knows," Naia said as the ship drifted away from shore. Through the cabin windows, Amri could catch only glimpses of the Sifa Far-Dreamer bringing the boom around. The boat lurched when the sail bit the wind. Kylan served their supper, and Amri mulled over all that had happened.

"You think she's really with us?" Amri asked.

"Without a doubt," Tavra said. "She saw your truths and she will lead the Vapra—and the other clans—accordingly."

"*Accordingly*," Onica said, catching the tail end of their conversation as she returned to the cabin. Amri didn't love the idea that the ship was sailing out into the ocean with no one watching the helm, but he had to trust the Sifa knew what she was doing. And anyway, if the Chamberlain did come to the shore looking for them, he would rather be stranded on the ocean than trapped in the Skeksis' horrible claws.

"You still doubt her? Even after what she said?" Naia asked.

"All-Maudra Mayrin is the ordained ambassador between the seven clans and the Skeksis," Onica said with a shrug. "She speaks to Emperor skekSo himself. I find it hard to believe that in her position, she could have remained completely oblivious to what the Skeksis were doing. She is not naive. She is merely well practiced in turning the other way."

"But she said the fire was lit and that the Vapra will fight the Skeksis," Amri said, unsure. It was hard to misunderstand what she'd said, so forthright in the dream. Yet he felt like Onica's intuition was not to be dismissed. "Tavra, what do you think?"

"My mother will do the right thing," she said, but there was a hesitation. He wished he could see Tavra's reaction, but while she stood on his shoulder all he could sense of her was her voice. Almost as if she were speaking from inside his head, a constant sternness talking into his ear.

"The right thing, eh?" Onica said with a raised brow. "As she did when she found you were sneaking out to the wharfs to visit a Sifa Far-Dreamer?"

The hesitation grew. "That was a long time ago."

Onica sighed, as if the argument were old and tired. It probably was. "When your mother does the *right thing*, it will be what is right for the Vapra alone. She wears a heavy mantle in Skeksis colors, and it will not be easily changed for a suit of armor. Not everyone is like you, my love."

And to that, Tavra had no response. Through the porthole,

the light of the Waystar grove was nothing but a distant speck of light in the dark, icy mountains.

Naia pulled her locs over her shoulder and put both hands palm down on the table.

"We came this far to deliver our truth to the All-Maudra, and now we've done it," she said. "I don't have time to doubt her. We've still got to light six more fires, like Aughra said. She gave me that task, and I'm going to see it through."

There she was again. Fierce Naia, who had seen the cracked Crystal. Seen it, and lived to bear its pain, its call for help. Amri didn't know what to make of the dream they'd all seen. Not the one Aughra had brought to them, nor the strange image of the wall that Onica's Far-Dream had shown him when he'd asked a question too big to be answered.

Even so, he knew one thing.

"Us," he told Naia. "Aughra gave *us* a task."

Kylan nodded. "We're in this together."

Onica stood and withdrew a scroll from her vest. She set it on the table.

"Then I suggest we first go to Cera-Na," she said, gesturing at the scroll. "Shortly after the pink petals landed, Maudra Ethri called the Sifa to gather, but why, I do not know. She is usually not so secret about her intentions, so it seemed strange. I was planning to sail soon to find out what's going on."

"Cera-Na?" Amri asked.

"The bay where the Sifa convene, on the western coast of the mainland. It's only a day's journey by sea, and if anyone is brave enough to light a fire and rise against the Skeksis, it will be Maudra Ethri."

Naia smacked a fist into her palm. "Then it's decided. We'll go to Cera-Na first and meet with the Sifa."

CHAPTER 6

Amri woke in a corner of the cabin under a pile of cushions and quilts. Something crawled across his face, and he took a swat at it—then yelped when it pricked him.

"Wake up. Up!"

Early-morning light glowed from the colored glass that filled the porthole windows. Another blinding day would soon begin. Amri wished he could sleep through it, until it was night again, but that was all it was—a wish—and he forced himself up.

"Why? Are we there?"

Tavra skittered up his sleeve.

"No. You have training to do. Up! Take my sword."

"Training? What are we now, captain and soldier?"

She laughed, though it wasn't joyful. *Joyful* didn't seem like a word that would ever describe her, though Amri wondered if that could change. "You're hardly a soldier. But we'll see what we can do, especially if you are all so set on becoming traitor rebels."

Amri took the sword and stumbled against the wall as the floor lurched one way, then the other. He resisted the urge to throw himself down onto the planks, lie as flat as he could, and hope the bobbing and rocking would just go away.

"Oh yeah. Boat."

"Straighten your posture. Tie your hair back. You're not in the caves anymore."

He braided his hair and tied the end in a knot, swallowing his indignation. The Vapra was only trying to help. Probably. Naia had said the same thing, back on the cliff, but in a kinder way . . . and having his hair out of the way did help in the whipping ocean wind. But he didn't need to give Tavra the satisfaction if she was going to be so bossy.

"Posture," Tavra reminded him. Even after Naia had coached him on walking upright, he'd already begun to return to his usual crouch. Determined to join the daylighters, he did as Tavra said, drawing his shoulders up and straightening his back. It didn't help his balance, especially not while he still had the sandals on, but he did it anyway. He stepped out of the cabin onto the deck.

Wind filled the fins of the ship, no longer biting and cold. In fact, the gusts that pushed them along were warm enough that Amri could catch the scent of the sea, salty and full of life. They raced atop the waves in an endless bowl of blue green, contained only by the white strip of light that sparkled on the horizon where the suns rose. He had never seen such unending space before. Looking out at it made him dizzy, surrounded by so much water and air instead of stone.

"Good morning!" Kylan called from above. He stood with Onica on the roof of the cabin, a bouquet of rigging in his hands. He listened intently as the Sifa pointed at the ropes and then to the sails. "What are you up to?"

"Apparently, Tavra's going to make me into a Vapra paladin," he declared with a joking flourish that ended with him almost dropping the sword. "Soon you will bow before Amri the Strong!"

"Amri the Strong, eh? Hope you're strong enough for me."

Naia stood opposite him on deck, dagger in hand. She grinned at him and twirled the thing so it shot rays of sunlight across the ship and in his face. Her locs were tied back, her feet confident and unwavering on the constantly shifting deck.

"Amri the Strong accepts your challenge," he said.

"Go on, to the foredeck, both of you," Tavra directed. The foredeck wasn't big at all, but at least they were out of the way of Kylan's sailing lessons. The nose of the ship jumped up and down on the waves, and Amri wanted to crouch on all fours to keep his balance. But no one else was, so he didn't.

Tavra took her place on his neck, where he could hear her over the roaring of the ocean waves and wind.

"All right, then. Naia, thirty lunges. Amri, thirty parries. Begin."

"Thirty! I don't even know what a parry is."

"If we're going to war with the Skeksis, Naia is going to need someone to watch her back, and you're not going to be able to rely on your strange Grottan tricks every time."

"I could if I had a bigger spice pouch."

"Come on, Amri the Strong!" Naia laughed, then struck a pose. She looked like she could take on anything, from darkened monster to cruel Skeksis. *Like a hero*, Amri thought. "It'll be fun! I'll try not to beat you too badly."

He glanced up at Kylan, who was tying off one of the sails, and wondered if he'd rather be learning to sail—but he knew as much about ships as he did swords. The Spriton boy gave him a little wave, as if to say, *Good luck. You'll need it.*

"All right. Here I come."

He held the sword and spread his feet like Tavra had told him to before when he'd faced the Chamberlain. Something about it did feel good, holding a sword as the ship raced across the open water. Even if he was sure that any moment he'd drop the blade and lose it in the depths.

Tavra showed him how to parry. Naia's blade was shorter than the sword, made for stabbing and cutting. Her thrusts were strong and to the point, and even when Amri successfully parried, he felt the jolt of impact where the blades collided. By the time the second Brother crested the horizon, Amri's entire body ached and the salty breath of the ocean coated his face.

"Are you sure you never trained to be a guard at the castle?" he asked.

Naia didn't seem winded at all, feet quick and bright eyes focused.

"Ha, I'm sure! But I win the hunting festival every season, in both *bola* and spear!"

Amri's arms jolted again as he barely knocked her blade's tip away.

"Like I said! Not fair!"

"Life won't always be fair, or kind!" The voice in his ear was like a conscience, reminding him of the things he would rather have not remembered: like that he'd never seen a *bola* or a spear before leaving Domrak, or that he'd never attended a hunting festival.

"Left!" Tavra ordered. "No, Amri, *left*. Don't—"

He thought he saw an opening in Naia's attack and reacted, flicking his wrist. The silver sword slid against Naia's dagger, her grip loosening as the blade twisted, and he stepped in. Too quickly, his blade was close, tilted up—and then she rammed her shoulder into his chest, knocking the air out of his lungs as he tumbled to the deck.

"I told you not to strike!" Tavra buzzed, like an incessant insect. "If this had been a real battle, you'd be dead."

"Well, it's *not*," he retorted. "I thought I saw an opening, so I went for it. What's the point of practicing if you're not allowed to take risks?"

"It wasn't a risk. It was a guaranteed failure."

"You don't know that."

"I did."

"Well, maybe I'm just tired of you bossing me around."

"I was trying to . . ." She clicked with frustration, ending with a final-sounding "Never mind. Do as you like."

Tavra hopped off Amri's shoulder and left them. He tried not to feel bad as Naia helped him to his feet and brushed him off. He didn't know if he was angry or glad that Tavra was mad at him. At least he'd told her to stop treating him like her personal puppet. Amri gingerly slung the sword at his hip.

"She's right. I could've murdered you," Naia said.

"It wouldn't have been a bad way for Amri the Strong to go."

She laughed and rubbed his chest where she'd shouldered him. The bruise ached less under her touch, though she hadn't used any of her healing magic. They took sips from the barrel of fresh water on the deck and found a place to sit.

"She's just trying to help, I get it," he added. "And that she's probably feeling helpless and everything, stuck in that little body. But I can't be her replacement. I'm Grottan. I can barely stand up straight on this boat, let alone do sword things."

"Don't worry about it. You weren't too bad, really."

Amri laughed. "You're just excited to have someone to beat up."

"Not true!" Still, she grinned. Then shrugged. "What I know about blades is from hunting. It's not really the same as combat, and definitely not the same as going up against . . ."

A Skeksis. Neither of them wanted to finish that thought. He could still see the snow melting on the Chamberlain's hot purple scalp, wrinkled from trine and trine of rage. How vindictively he'd drunk the last of the essence, just to spite Rian. And how it had *changed* him. Youth and fury rushing back into him, making him three times the monster he'd once been.

If those tiny drops in the vial had transformed him so dramatically, what could more of it do? How many Gelfling would it take to feed all the Skeksis, and what kind of unimaginable demons would they become, wild on the life essence of the Gelfling?

No, fighting a Skeksis would not be the same as hunting. The Gelfling had grown in the world as hunters and gatherers. Farmers. Scholars. Song tellers. Even the sailing Sifa clan, as ruthless as they might be to take on the wind and sea, had been raised and nurtured by Thra to be in communion, their voices one with the great song.

Why hadn't Aughra, who heard the song of the world, foreseen the Skeksis? If all on Thra was part of the song, then so were the Skeksis, as terrible as they were. So why hadn't Aughra prepared the Gelfling, the children of Thra, for such a great betrayal? Amri wondered if it was some sort of test. But he had heard real fear in even Aughra's voice, in the dream-space. If Aughra was worried, then how could this be part of Thra's song? She should already know the melody. The words, the harmony, and the outcome.

It had always been Amri's nature to be curious, and to ask. That was his role, as a Grottan. To ask the questions in the Sanctuary where the songs of the bell-birds that moved mountains still echoed. To find the answers and protect them in the Tomb of Relics. That was what Thra had charged his clan with, and yet even so, within days they had lost the Tomb and very nearly lost the Sanctuary to the Skeksis. But when he'd asked Thra how to stop the Skeksis, all it had shown him was a stupid wall.

The menders. That's what Aughra had called them. Amri glanced to Naia, who had turned to face the wind. Naia, who had seen the Crystal and lived. Naia, who had come from the farthest reaches of the Skarith land, who now feasted aboard a Sifa ship on the Silver Sea. Feasted with a Vapra, a Spriton, and a Grottan, no less! Who found friends wherever she went, who won respect with her unbridled bravery.

Perhaps Thra had a plan, after all. He just didn't know what it was.

They looked across the length of the ship, watching Kylan climbing the rigging as Onica directed him from the deck. The Far-Dreamer saw them watching and waved, her hair a tangle of red and chiming silver bells. She swung down from the rigging lines to join them, taking a sip of water from the flask at her hip.

"The song teller has a good hand at ropes," she said. "Where's Tavra?"

"Being Tavra," Naia replied. As much as it said nothing, Onica understood it all too well. She leaned against the taffrail beside them, watching Kylan handle the sails on his own. "How long have you two been together?" Naia asked.

"Together! My, what a relative term."

Amri tilted his head. "You mean because of her mother? Because you're Sifa?"

"My people come in and out of Ha'rar with the seasons. Tavra's mother never knew my face, only that when the spring and autumn came, her middle daughter was errant. Young and foolish." Onica shook her head with a wistful smile. "We thought we were getting away with something, meeting out at the seafarer's lantern. We weren't."

Amri almost said that he didn't see what the problem was, but he thought it through. Tavra was second in line for the Vapra crown, even if her older sister was the living heir. And the All-Maudra had to produce Vapra heirs—with pure Silverling blood, no doubt. Not a mix of snow and salt water.

"I'm sorry," he said.

"Don't be. In a way, for the first time in a long time, now we are together without Mayrin looking upon us with disdain."

Sadness pricked the Far-Dreamer's eyes, and Amri hastily changed the subject.

"So when we get to Cera-Na, then what? Do you know Maudra Ethri well?"

"I do. We grew up together. She is not a Far-Dreamer, but she has always believed in prophecy and the whispers of the wind. She sent out a call for the Sifa to gather, soon after Kylan's pink petals reached Cera-Na . . . It is possible she already knows, and believes, and is ready to rebel against the Skeksis."

It sounded like hope, and Amri decided to hold on to it, at least for a little while.

Onica showed them how to cast nets to catch their lunch. At least that was something Amri was good at. They brought in ocean clams and bits of floating coral. She taught them how to crack the spiny pink corals open, revealing the tender green core. They stripped the cores and made a cold salad of them, after Amri chopped the clam meat and seasoned it with more of Onica's fire dust.

As he stared at the two halves of the shells, joined in one hinge and mirroring each other in swirling abalone, he thought of the Skeksis. Fighting the Skeksis felt impossible. For all Amri or anyone knew, the Lords were immortal. And with the power of the Crystal and feeding off Gelfling essence, they might as well have been. But maybe . . .

"Do you think we should seek out the Mystics?"

"Mystics?" Onica asked. "The creatures in the dreamfasts?"

Kylan took his book out of his pack and paged through it.

"Their race are called the urRu," he explained. He showed Onica a drawing of one of the long-necked creatures, with four big arms and a long white mane. Now that Amri knew they were connected—somehow—to the Skeksis, he could see parts of the resemblance. But where the Skeksis were secretive and shrewd, the Mystics were wise and gentle.

"They're bound to the Skeksis, by some power we don't understand," Kylan continued. "We don't even know what they are, much less how to find them. We've only met them by coincidence. The Archer and the Storyteller."

"I didn't even know urLii was a Mystic until I met you two," Amri admitted. "I just thought he was a strange old sage. If you had come to Domrak and asked if I knew of any Mystics, I'm not sure I would have thought to tell you about him. It could be the same anywhere we go, and it could take forever."

"And we don't have forever," Naia agreed. She folded her hands. "I once thought meeting urVa and urLii was by chance, but now I'm not so sure. The Mystics are wise, but whenever we ask them questions, they never give us full answers. If we go looking for them, something tells me we won't find them until they're ready. If the Mystics are part of all this, they'll find us."

There was nothing else to say after that, and they listened to the sloshing of the waves against the hull.

A gust of wind blew, and Amri smelled earth. Onica stood, shading her eyes with her hand. A dusty red line had grown from the sea, far away on the horizon.

"Cera-Na awaits us," Onica said with a glint of pride. "Prepare for landfall."

Kylan put his book away and joined Amri and Naia at the rail. Together, they gazed out at the distant line of mountains that grew steadily closer. Any exhaustion from their sparring lesson earlier flitted away as Amri grew more and more excited to land.

"You think it'll be difficult to convince the Sifa to join the others against the Skeksis?" Kylan asked.

Amri glanced at Naia. The wind ruffled her wings like iridescent sails as she watched the land draw nearer, a more pensive look on her face. Determination, resilience, he figured. He tried to temper his own feelings to match hers.

"They're still Gelfling," Naia said. "I have no doubt we'll be able to bring the truth to them. Light the fires of resistance, whatever they are."

Mmmmmmnnnnnnnn . . .

Amri winced suddenly, pressing his hand against his ear. A low moan rumbled out of the ocean, like a deep voice trapped below the waters, calling for help. Then it was gone, lost again under the blustering of wind and sloshing of waves.

"Amri, are you all right?" Naia asked, putting a hand on his shoulder.

"I thought I heard . . ." Amri trailed off, scanning the waves with his eyes and ears. Nothing remained of the sound he'd heard. "A deep cry, like a creature in pain."

The sunlight set off the top layer of the seawater, a salty green blue capped with white. Below that, Amri realized, they could see nothing. He had no idea how deep it was, or what lurked below. He reached over the side of the rail, dipping his hand in the water. The ocean's voice was meaningless to him, its words dense and incoherent to his touch that only knew the language of stone. He wiped the salt water from his palm.

"I don't know what it was," he said. "It's gone now."

With the wind at their back and the tide rushing toward the cliffs, the Claw Mountains seemed to grow by the second. Just as the Three Brothers began their tilt in the sky, heading toward the other side of the ocean, Cera-Na came into view.

The mountains were huge up close, dense ridges of red and tan rock like a giant's hand resting in the shallow water near the cliffs. Among them, hundreds of ships docked along the rocky headland and sea stacks. With their battened sails in a rainbow of colors, they looked like a shoal of hooyim fish, gliding in and out with fins like colored glass in front of the light of the suns.

Amri gasped as they came around the main headland, then winced and had to shield his eyes from one vessel that rested in the arms of the bay. He squinted through his fingers at a magnificent ship that dwarfed all the others. It was not made of wood but *coral*; glittering white and pink at the keel, brilliant carnelian as its fronds reached higher. The masts were thorny spires, growing out of the coral body like trees and bloused with flowing anemone sails.

Onica, with Tavra on her shoulder, leaped down to the deck.

"The *Omerya*," the Far-Dreamer said. "Maudra Ethri's ship . . . Welcome, my friends, to Cera-Na."

CHAPTER 7

"Though Sifa ships may sail alone for many trine at a time, we always return here . . . and when Omerya is in port, we are all home once again," Onica explained as she brought them into port and tied the ship to one of the many white coral spires rising from the coastal floor. The water was clearer along the spires and near the headlands, in some places shallow enough to see the sandy, shell-littered bottom. Seabirds sang above them and Gelfling voices sang and yelled to one another from the decks of the ships and the planked docks. Amri caught sight of a pink petal on the air. A few danced along the waves near where the ocean met the land.

As the suns began to set, casting a cascade of blue and pink and gold off the cliffs and the shore, Cera-Na came alive with firelight. Torches burned where the docks entwined, and from lanterns dangling from ship bowsprits. As they followed the docks farther into the bay where *Omerya* rested, Amri saw what Onica meant. Cera-Na was a village that was forever changing, like a living body. The houses came and went as the ships did, the streets changing as gangplanks were set and withdrawn.

The Sifa roamed freely between the ships, looking like wind and fire themselves. Most had red hair like Onica, though sometimes it was streaked or dyed in black and blue and turquoise. Some did not even seem to be Sifa at all, or at least not full-blooded, though they were dressed like the Sifa in their seafaring clothing and jangling with charms and jewels. Had Amri seen them anywhere else, he would have thought them to be from other clans. One had long black hair like Kylan. Another looked Vapra, or maybe a mix of Vapra and Sifa.

One in particular caught Amri's eye. He elbowed Naia, and she looked up at the sturdy Gelfling with long, dark red hair in spiraled locs. His skin was the color of fresh grass, the striped markings on his cheeks dark black and blue. He watched as they passed below his ship, taking a sip of drink from a wooden flagon.

"Captain Staya," Onica said, tossing a casual nod hello in the captain's direction.

"Far-Dreamer," he replied, bowing low. Though it was respectful, Amri caught something like suspicion in the captain's eye.

"Is he . . . Drenchen?" Naia asked as they continued on.

"Sifa, with Drenchen in his family tree. Third generation, I believe. That ship has been in and out of Cera-Na since I can remember." Onica's smile twinkled as she looked back. "That is the beauty of Cera-Na, and Sifa tradition. We are bound together not by blood or by the confines of the earth. We are bound together by heart and by the changing wind. If the prophecies and signs say one must become Sifa, one does. We accept that."

Amri followed Onica, watching as the Sifa recognized her with warm smiles and sometimes reverent bows as they wound through the docks and makeshift bridges. Tavra looked like a piece of glass jewelry in Onica's hair. She shimmered, murmuring into Onica's ear, but she was too small and the air around too full of voices and music for Amri to hear what she was saying.

The *Omerya* was more impressive up close. Her hull was made of coral reef, and where it was submerged, Amri could see nooks and crannies where ocean life lived. Eels, fish, and water slugs and the like, swimming and darting in and out of the pink and peach fronds. Onica stopped at the gangplank, decorated with glittering hooyim scales, flags, and banners that caught the wind.

"Onica! You came!"

A freckled Sifa with golden-red hair leaned over the side of the *Omerya*, then hopped down, azure wings opening to slow her fall. She embraced Onica and nodded hello to Amri and the others.

"Tae!" Onica exclaimed. "I've missed you."

"As we have you! I was worried you would stay in Ha'rar after I heard about Tavra . . ."

Amri waited to see if Tavra would say something, but she didn't. He wasn't surprised; if he were in her position, he wasn't sure he'd want to reveal himself to old friends, either. It would be up to her when to share what had happened to her, in her own time.

"I need to see Maudra Ethri. It's important," Onica said.

Tae's eyes sharpened as she held Onica's arms. She glanced over Onica's companions, taking in the little group of Gelfling from across the land. She hesitated, as if reluctant to speak around them.

"A Far-Dream?" she asked.

"Something like that."

"I'll ask, but she may only be willing to see you alone. She's been preoccupied. There has been a thief on the loose, and on top of that there's Ethri's . . . guest." Tae tightened her lips. She put her hand on Onica's arm and turned her away, both whispering so Amri and his friends couldn't hear them. Naia crossed her arms.

"So much for that harmonious Sifa tradition," she said.

Tae stepped back from Onica and held her by the shoulders, then scampered up the gangplank and disappeared into the *Omerya* like a sun-colored fish into the reef.

"What's going on?" Naia asked. "What did you tell her?"

Onica waited at the foot of the gangplank. She gazed up at the ship, catching the torchlight in her eyes and said, "The truth."

"Do you know what she meant by *guest*?" Kylan asked.

Onica didn't answer. A porthole opened in the side of the ship. The coral curled away like a shutter until it was large enough for them to walk through. Tae stood in the entryway.

"Come," she said. She waved and added, "All of you."

The inside of the *Omerya* was a maze of passageways, splitting and rejoining organically, sometimes opening into chambers outfitted with seating cushions and lanterns. In other, darker places, the walls writhed with life, and Amri spied at least five glowing shrimp peeking out from their home-holes in the walls. It reminded him of Domrak.

But it wasn't Domrak. *Omerya* was a ship of the daylighter world, as were the coastal sands and the unending Silver Sea. He had to stop comparing things to the place he had left behind.

They followed Tae and Onica upward until the tunnel spit them out onto the deck, now overlooking all of Cera-Na. Much of the deck was natural coral, etched and smoothed so it could be walked upon, while other parts grew wild and rough as crystal. At the center of the deck was a round hearth. Despite everything being so different, here in the Sifa's bay, the hearth itself was the one thing that was familiar to Amri. The center of every Gelfling clan, whether it was aboard a moving coral ship or not.

Amri frowned as he neared it. There was no fire burning, and from the coals and ashes, it looked like there had not been one for some time.

"Onica!"

A Sifa came striding from an exit across the deck, every step jangling with metal chimes and bells. She had wild, dark crimson-and-black hair, accented with glittering beads and copper wire, ears strung with gemstone earrings. One of her green eyes sparkled more than the other, catching the light like a stone.

"Gem-Eyed Ethri," Tae said with a curt bow. "*Maudra* to the Sifa of Cera-Na."

"Welcome home!" Maudra Ethri crowed. She embraced Onica tightly, every bell on her sash ringing.

"She's so young," Naia whispered to Kylan and Amri.

Unlike old Maudra Argot, the oldest of the living *maudra*, or even All-Maudra Mayrin, Ethri couldn't have been any older than Onica or Tavra. Amri remembered what Onica had said, about growing up together.

Onica introduced them, and Ethri nodded at each of their names. Her eye glinted again, and Amri realized it was a gemstone set in her head. It didn't turn along with her other eye, its smooth surface seeming to look everywhere at once.

"I'm pleased to meet you, daughter of Maudra Laesid. Yes, very much indeed," Maudra Ethri said. "Now, tell me, what's brought you all the way from Sog and Sami Thicket, Domrak and the Caves of Grot. Eh? It must be good."

"It's not entirely good, but it is important," Naia said. "You've seen the petals? The dream within them?"

"Of course. I'd have to be much farther at sea to avoid seeing the blasted things everywhere."

"Everything you saw in that dream is true. It was Kylan's truth, on behalf of all of us who have seen the Skeksis' betrayal first hand. We've been tasked by Mother Aughra and Thra to bring the clans together. Ready to act when the time is right. Ready to fight against the Skeksis. So now we're here to ask: Will you join us?"

Naia's delivery was straight to the point, almost bluntly so. That was Drenchen hard-talk for you. Ethri crossed her arms, leaning on one hip.

"Join you?" the Sifa *maudra* asked, as if she didn't understand the question.

Naia frowned, taken aback. "If you don't believe us . . ."

"I believed the instant I saw the dream stitched in the pink petals. But you're asking me to pledge myself to . . . what, you? To Aughra and Thra? If I agree to join you, who am I even joining?

How will we know when the time is right—is it you who will tell us? Is this a war or an idea?"

Ethri didn't exactly laugh, though Amri felt like she might as well have. Just as he was about to say something he was sure they would all regret, Onica stepped forward.

"Ethri, I saw a dream myself," she said. "From Mother Aughra, and from Thra. All-Maudra Mayrin vowed to stand against the Skeksis."

"Mayrin, eh? Now *that*, I'm not sure I could believe. She would never resist the Skeksis, after all this time kissing their bejeweled claws! Do you have proof? No? And even if you did . . . If you have the support of the Vapra, then what do you need of the Sifa?"

"All the clans will need to stand together if we're going to stop the Skeksis from picking us apart," Kylan insisted. "We may not know exactly how, but we must heed—"

"I did not see that dream. Aughra did not speak to me and neither did Thra. Perhaps if I had seen it with my own eye, but I didn't . . . My friends, I thank you for coming all this way to bring the news to me in person. Be assured, I will do what is best for the Sifa."

"Be assured?" Amri cried. He bit his lip, trying not to speak out of turn, but he couldn't help himself. "The Skeksis are eating our people. That's the long and short of it! Devouring us like moss from the cave wall!"

His outburst was rude, but Maudra Ethri didn't seem to care about that. She merely waved her hand. "Then you ought to decide what to do that is best for your clans, as well. I have an important guest that I cannot keep waiting any longer. I trust you'll enjoy yourselves in Cera-Na. Take as long as you wish before you hurry on to entreat the other *maudra* to join you. Onica, a word?"

Maudra Ethri left them with the air of a parent dismissing a child's tall tale. Tae followed behind her. It was even more frustrating that the *maudra* was hardly older than they were. The only thing that kept Amri from shouting rude things after her was how tightly he bit his tongue. Beside him, Naia's fists trembled.

Onica frowned, the pensive look ill-befitting her usual features. In the short moment they were alone on the deck, she gently took Tavra from her hair and set her on Amri's shoulder.

"Something is not right," she said. "This is not the Ethri I knew. I will speak with her and see what I can see. I'll meet you back at my ship. In the meantime, Tavra can show you around Cera-Na."

Footsteps came, and Tavra scurried under Amri's hood when Tae returned to the deck. Her mouth was an uncomfortable, apologetic half frown.

"This way," she said with a little sigh. "I'll show you back to the dock."

The Sifa girl was silent about the exchange they'd all shared, eyes fixed ahead as if troubled or thinking or both. The longer they were in Cera-Na, the more Amri picked up the feeling Onica had spoken out loud: Something wasn't right. He wished he could ask Tavra more questions, but whenever they were around others, she wouldn't come out of hiding. Whatever she could tell him would have to wait.

Once, as they walked through the bowels of the ship, Amri thought he heard distant, throaty laughter. But the walls of the coral were too thick to make it out, and soon enough they were back on the docks.

"I'm sorry about Ethri," Tae said. "She's usually more hospitable. I would show you around myself, but I've got something I need to do. So please, make yourselves at home. Onica means very much to all of us here, and so her friends do, too."

"Not enough to make a difference," Amri muttered.

Tae looked down, opened her mouth as if to say something but didn't. She tossed them a simple salute and left them standing on the dock beside the *Omerya*.

"That could have gone better," Kylan said as the three of them—four if Amri counted quiet Tavra—walked away from the *Omerya*. More and more lanterns were lit as the evening settled in. Amri heard music and singing, smelled fire and smoked fish.

"Wonder who's the guest?" Naia spat. "Better be someone important. Aughra's Eye! It's like she couldn't care less. I didn't expect uniting the clans was going to be easy, but I thought the difficult part would be getting them to believe. But it's as if the truth doesn't matter. She knows, and she believes, but she's not going to do anything."

Now that they were alone, Tavra revealed herself on Amri's shoulder, moving down his arm.

"Why are you hiding? Don't you trust Tae?" Amri asked.

"I don't want people to know" was her simple reply. If she felt anything about it—pain, embarrassment, or otherwise—she kept it frozen under her usual ice. "Listen. I want the three of you to return to Onica's ship. Wait there. I am going to find out more about this guest that preoccupies Ethri. In the morning, we're going to force Ethri to commit to the Gelfling. It is her duty as *maudra*, to her people and the Gelfling as a race."

"Force her!" Naia exclaimed, surprised and impressed. "How?"

"You're not the only one whose mother is *maudra*. There is a reason the Vapra have led the seven clans since the rise of the Skeksis rule." Tavra leaped from Amri's sleeve onto the rope of the dock that snaked back toward the *Omerya*. She would be invisible as any other bug aboard the living-coral ship. As she left, she said, "Don't find trouble while I'm gone."

Then she scurried off, nothing more than a glint of starlight on the dock.

"Well, now what?" Kylan asked.

Amri looked down the dock toward the beach, where more and more fires appeared as the sky grew darker. Despite the orange and red flames, in his heart he knew none were the fires of resistance Aughra had spoken of. Still, he longed to be on solid land instead of the sea.

"Let's go to the beach," he suggested, hoping his real reasons for wanting to avoid the ship weren't obvious. "After all, we didn't come all the way here to sit it out on a boat while the princess does all the adventuring . . ."

Kylan tilted his head. "The beach? Why?"

Amri gestured, away from the *Omerya* and Onica's ship. "I think we should do what all good Gelfling do when something strange is afoot in a strange land. Seek answers."

Naia grinned in agreement. Apparently she wasn't eager to retire to the ship, either.

"Great," she said, leading the way. "Let's find ourselves some trouble."

CHAPTER 8

A light rain fell as they arrived at the beach, but the wide-leafed palms that grew in clusters out of the sandy earth protected them from the sprinkles. The air tasted salty with fish, and Amri's stomach growled. Naia must have heard it, or had her own talking belly, and said, "I'll get some food. Meet up over at the fire in a bit!"

After she was gone, Amri took in the stretch of white-and-coral sand, glittering in the light of the bonfires lit along the shore. The Claw Mountains, tall and red, blocked out the last remains of the sunlight with their pointed backs, giving Amri's eyes relief as night's tide washed over the land.

"Whew, it gets dark fast out here," Kylan remarked.

The two of them followed Naia down the dock at a more leisurely pace. Amri's ears perked up as he traced the lines of the headlands. Smooth, round openings riddled the rocky rises where they stretched out into the bay. Caves carved by the endless ebb and flow of the ocean, glowing dimly with bio-fluorescent life. Amri wondered what kinds of treasures might have been caught in the eddies and tide pools. Things lost overboard or from shipwrecks. Maybe even relics washed from across the Silver Sea, where no Gelfling had ever set foot.

"Hey, do you want to go check out the headland caves?" he asked, pointing.

Kylan followed Amri's finger, eyes unfocused. Amri frowned. All the song teller saw was darkness.

"I'd rather go sit by the fire," he said. "I don't really like . . . caves."

Caves. When Kylan said it like that, hesitant and fearful, Amri sucked in his disappointment.

"Oh, okay. Let's go, then!" he said, forcing some cheer and standing up straight. He didn't even look back over his shoulder as Kylan nodded in relief and led the way into the light of the bonfires on the beach. They found a place to sit and wait for Naia, and Amri tried not to squint in the light of the booming, crackling fire.

"Are you all right?" Kylan asked.

"Yep. I'm fine. Hungry. Hope Naia gets here soon."

Kylan glanced his way, then out into the dark, lips pressed into a line. Then he sighed and shook his head. "I'm sorry, Amri. I didn't realize. The light must be hard on your eyes . . . and here we've all been traveling during the day and sleeping at night. Why didn't you say something?"

Amri flushed. It was hard to get used to something difficult when someone else showed sympathy for the first time. There was some confidence in being alone with the problem; he could pretend it didn't matter if no one else noticed. He almost wished Kylan hadn't said anything, though at the same time his heart filled knowing the song teller had noticed.

"It's fine," he said again. "I'm adjusting . . . Don't tell Naia. I don't want to be a burden."

"Amri! You're not a—"

"Hey, guys. Look what I brought!"

Naia joined them, three splints of food in hand. Fish for her and Amri and a squash for Kylan. The splints were long enough for them to roast their food in the fire. Amri gave Kylan a gentle warning glance, and that was the end of it.

The three of them settled in with their supper. A Sifa group nearby scooted closer to the fire and took turns throwing handfuls of powders into the fire. The flames faded through jewel colors as the different spices ignited. The Sifa youth murmured in awe at the colors until one of them threw something in that caused a ball of white flame to spring from the fire, like a bubble in deep water.

The beachside quieted as the Gelfling watched the white fire dissipating into the night sky. The bright light of the fire against the dark of the night reminded Amri of their shared vision. He couldn't begin to understand what it had all meant, yet it had delivered them here.

The quiet brought Amri a wave of homesickness. Out under the open sky where he'd always dreamed of going, sitting on the beach while the ocean lapped at the bay. So far from Domrak and the Caves of Grot, and the Sanctuary where his clan kept watch over the remains of the place they'd promised to protect.

"Tell us a song, Kylan?" he asked. At first he thought maybe he'd embarrassed the song teller, but Kylan responded without hesitation.

"I'd love to," Kylan said, eager to make up for what he'd said and hadn't said before. "What song would you like to hear?"

"Do you know the song of the Three Sisters?"

Kylan withdrew his lute from their shared traveling pack. "Is that one of Gyr's? Was it written in Domrak on the walls?"

"Yes! It's about Gyr, and how one day, he was traveling. Or I guess it would have been night. Anyway, he found them crying. The two sisters. About the suns. I guess it would have been the brothers. No wait, it had to be day, not night, because . . ."

Amri stopped talking when he heard what he was saying. Naia laughed.

"Song-telling really isn't your strong suit, is it?"

"That's why I'm not Amri the Song Teller—come on, Kylan. You know the one, don't you?" Amri let loose a big grin. He reached out and shook Kylan by the sleeve. Even the song teller had a funny look on his face, trying not to laugh at Amri.

"Yes, I think I know the one you mean now," he said. He strummed the six strings of his instrument, tuning it by ear as he chuckled. The sound of the lute caught the attention of the Sifa nearby. Amri ignored them. This song was for him, and he would soak up every word of it.

Kylan cleared his throat and sang:

Gyr was a bard that traveled the seas

Oh li, oh la, oh lo

Told the songs of the rivers, the mountains, the trees

Oh li, oh la, la-lo

One long summer ago, the night stopped to come

The Sister Moons hiding, in fear of the suns

The daylight was endless, scorching the plains

So Gyr went to find them and bring night again

He found two of the moons at the edge of the sky

A lake at their feet from the tears they had cried

"The Brother Suns' fire for us is too bright

While they rage in the sky we cannot bring the night

So we Sisters take turns going first into dawn

To spy on the Brothers to see if they've gone

'Twas our second Sister Moon's turn to go

Oh li, oh la, oh lo

But the second Brother Sun ate her whole

Oh li, oh la, la-lo."

The moons were too fearful since their Sister's sad fate

To bring night to the sky, to bring nine to the eight

So Gyr left them to watch the Brother Suns from the land

He returned three days later and told them his plan

The remaining two Sisters scaled the edge of the sky

Their fingertips wet from the tears that they'd cried

From their lips came a song: a mournful, sad sigh

And from the belly of the sun came a lonely reply

For the second Sister was still alive

Oh, the second Sister was still alive

To this day, though she's hidden by Brother Sun's light

Oh li, oh la, oh lo

Her song tells her Sisters to bring out the night

Oh she, oh sha, she knows

To bring out the night

Oh she, oh sha, she knows

Amri and Naia clapped and whistled when the song ended. As they did, they were joined, slowly, by the cheers of the Sifa around them. Kylan's song had enraptured nearly everyone on the beach. Amri waved at Kylan to stand, and when he did and gave a little awkward bow, the cooling evening seemed a little warmer.

It was not to last. A commotion at the far end of the beach, where the sand met the dock, sucked the spirit from the air. The cheers turned to whispers as the Sifa stood, turning back toward the dock. Amri and his friends stood with them, the last notes of Kylan's lute dissipating as he slipped it hastily into his pack.

"What's going on?" Amri said.

Sifa gathered, murmuring, one chanting and waving his hands in sigils of protection over and over in the air. Naia pushed into the crowd and Amri followed quickly after her, Kylan on his heels. When they broke through the throng of sailors, Amri stumbled to a halt.

Tae stood at the edge of the docks, barely lit by one of the torches. Her posture was off balance, slightly tipped to one side. She gazed straight ahead, unblinking.

"What," Naia gasped. "What's wrong with her?"

She shouldered her way free from the crowd, the only one brave enough to approach the ghostly Sifa, who stood, unmoving, one foot in the sand and the other on the dock. She wobbled when Naia touched her shoulders, then caught her when her legs came out from under her. Someone in the crowd screamed. Amri helped lower Tae to the sand.

"A healer! Someone find a healer!"

"Where's Maudra Ethri? Fetch her!"

Naia knelt over Tae, pressing a hand against her cheek.

"She's cold as ice," Naia said. She was pale herself, out of fear. Though Amri had never seen it himself, he knew what she was thinking. The drained look, the soulless, open-eyed gaze.

"How is this possible?" Kylan hissed. "How can it have happened so far from the castle?"

The crowd came in, a thickening wall of voices and eyes. One of the Sifa captains pushed to the front of the line. He swept back his coat to make sure they saw the blade hanging at his belt. Like the captain Staya, he didn't appear to be a full-blooded Sifa, though from his thick black hair, Amri wondered if his ancestors had hailed from Stone-in-the-Wood instead of the Swamp of Sog.

"You, Drenchen! Spriton!" he called. "Who are you? Get away from Tae."

"I'm a healer, that's what I am," Naia shot back.

"Oh? Do you know what's happened to her?"

"Looks like poisoning," said someone.

"Her earrings are missing!" cried another.

Naia gently turned Tae's head to the side, where it fell without resistance. The jewels they'd so recently seen strung along her ears were gone.

"There's a thief, then, eh!" said the captain with the sword. He turned and glowered at Kylan, then caught sight of Amri and leaned in. "*You* wouldn't happen to know anything about that, would you? Say we search your pockets. We going to find Tae's pretties in there?"

"Absolutely not," Amri snapped. "I was over by the bonfire when she came here!"

The angry captain stood tall, casting about. "Anyone see this little Shadowling by the bonfire like he says?"

"*I* did!" Naia yelled. She shoved the captain aside. He was older, but not much bigger than she was. "All three of us were all the way across the beach. Kylan told a song and everyone heard it. Isn't that right?"

Amri looked over the crowd. Though he saw dozens of familiar faces, ones that had smiled and cheered at Kylan's song, none of them stood up to defend him. Amri wanted to sink into the earth, but Naia wasn't so quick to be discouraged. She ignored the silent bystanders, fixing her attention back on the Sifa captain.

"I'm a healer," Naia said. "Back off and let me help her."

"I'm not letting you anywhere near Tae!"

Naia held her ground, but even she was unprepared as the hollering around them intensified. The firelight grew brighter as others brought torches. Amri caught Naia's eyes in the commotion. Though they were surrounded, she wasn't afraid, and she had the angry captain's attention. Everyone jumped back when he drew his blade.

"What's going on here?"

Maudra Ethri stormed like thunder down the dock. The shouting ceased and the crowd backed down, spilling away from Amri, his friends, and Tae like a school of fish parting around a predator. Ethri glared at Naia first, then fixed her gaze on the angry captain waving his sword around.

"Put that blade away, Madso."

He did as she said, then he jabbed with a finger instead. "They poisoned Tae and robbed her blind! Look at her!"

"What is this?" Ethri asked lowly. "What's happened to her?"

"I think she's been drained," Naia said. "I don't know how."

Drained.

The word erupted through the Sifa like fire on oil. Ethri stood, back to the *Omerya*, casting an eye on each of the Sifa as if daring them to keep saying the horrible word.

Drained? Like in the pink-petal dream? But that means . . . How?

"That's impossible. If we're to believe the rumors of the petals, the draining is done far away. At the castle, with the Crystal!"

As Maudra Ethri knelt to examine Tae, Amri felt a familiar prickling on his neck. Tavra had gotten all the way up to his shoulder in the commotion.

"Be ready with that sword," she whispered in Amri's ear, voice hot like steam rushing through cracks in the center of the earth. "Maudra Ethri's guest—"

His heart raced. "Ready with the sword? But—"

Amri's Grottan eyes penetrated the night even the distance to the *Omerya*. At first he saw nothing but the ship's gently undulating sails, its hull glowing with ultramarine sea life. Distracted by the spectacle on the beach, no one else noticed the huge shadow descending the gangplank, striding gracefully down the dock. Amri's hand sweated against the sword.

"No," he whispered.

Skeksis.

"What's all this, Maudra Ethri?"

The murmurs snuffed out like candles at the grand, rich voice. A tall avian figure, dressed in a salt-dusted brocade coat shining with embroidered green and gold, stepped off the dock and into the torchlight of the beach. She towered over them, half in serpent-scale armor and half in a ruffled gown.

"Lord Mariner," Maudra Ethri said, issuing a hasty bow. "I can take care of this. You didn't have to come down here to see this commotion . . ."

"And why wouldn't I? You are my little Gelfling, are you not?"

The Mariner doffed her black-and-green plumed hat. Beneath, her face was reptilian and blue, coiffed in a mane of black fur and streaming feathers. Amri's hand froze on his sword, his feet buried to the ankles in sand and unwilling to move. Naia reached for her dagger, moving in front of Kylan when he fell back in surprise. Tae was the only one who did not react, blank eyes staring straight into the sky.

"And please," the Skeksis purred, "call me *Captain*."

CHAPTER 9

"Skeksis," Amri stammered, though all that came out was a breath. "Why's a Skeksis . . ."

The Sifa around them bowed, hushing in the presence of the Mariner. They weren't surprised to see the Skeksis there. They'd known. They'd all known, the whole time. Maudra Ethri waved them away, even as their necks bent to the Skeksis Lord.

"Everyone, go back to your ships. Leave this to me and Lord skekSa. Go on, get out of here."

Amri gripped the hilt of his sword as the Sifa murmured, heeding their *maudra's* orders. Some threw glittering fish scales and jewels at skekSa's feet as they left, giving her wide berth on their way back to the docks. Within moments, it was just Amri and his friends on the beach, their shadows tiny in comparison to the fearsome silhouette of the Skeksis that stood over them.

Naia was the first to turn on Ethri. "Explain yourself!"

Maudra Ethri's fists clenched, her whole body overcome with annoyance and defensiveness. She wasn't used to being questioned, Amri realized. That was about to change. He stood beside Naia, drawing strength from her despite how nervous he was challenging a *maudra* and a Skeksis.

"So this is why you turned your ear against us?" he asked.

"Because it was already owned by a conniving Skeksis?"

skekSa snorted. "It's rude to talk about *a conniving Skeksis* while they stand right in front of you."

Amri tried not to buckle at the Skeksis's deep, velvety voice. skekSa elbowed back her coat, kneeling. Where the Chamberlain's joints had creaked with age, skekSa was limber and graceful, though up close Amri could still see the wrinkles between the metallic scales on her cheeks.

"Poor little Tae. Let us move her to somewhere more comfortable. It is unsettling to see her in a pile like this."

She easily scooped Tae's body up in one arm, cradling her like a youngling. Her tenderness made Amri wriggle with discomfort. He wanted to run, either at skekSa to tear Tae from her claws, or to flee the place entirely. But he couldn't do either, not without abandoning his friends or challenging a Skeksis.

They followed skekSa to an abandoned quilt that had been laid out on the sand near the biggest fire, and skekSa gently lowered Tae to rest there. She sat on a makeshift throne of stacked logs, swinging one boot over her knee and arranging her coat and skirts. The tide was coming in, eating the sand and transforming it into ocean.

"Now, my dear Drenchen girl. Explain what has happened," skekSa said.

Naia drew herself up, still clenching a fist around her dagger.

"Don't call me your dear, Skeksis," she said. "I know about you and your kind. I know what you've done."

So much for not challenging the Skeksis.

skekSa placed a hand against her breast, leaning back and raising her brows as if scandalized.

"You know what I've done! So then, you know that I left the Castle of the Crystal hundreds of trine before you were born, when I was disgusted with the way skekSo chose to rule? Hmm? You know that I've spent the last seventy trine alone on the Silver Sea, as far from the land as I can sail? Only returning to Cera-Na to gift my little ones with the treasures I've found abroad?"

Amri felt the sarcasm thick as salt air. He didn't feel bad for her, and she was probably lying, anyway. Naia's cheeks twitched where she clenched her jaw. She was angry, too, but like Amri, she held her tongue.

"That's enough," Maudra Ethri said. "Please, Lord Mariner. Do you know what's happened to Tae?"

"She's been drained, that's what," Naia said. "Just look at her face and her eyes, the way they see nothing. This is exactly what it looked like when I saw the Gelfling in the tower of the castle. After they'd been drained by the Skeksis Scientist."

Amri felt ill watching skekSa brush Tae's hair back with her talons, then touch her cheek. It was eerily gentle—more deceit, as sweet as nectar and deadly as poison.

"She hasn't been drained, little Drenchen. Look closer. Look at her eyes. If she'd been drained by skekTek's diabolical machine, you'd see the milk of death upon them. Isn't that so? But not here. No, she's been drugged. By what, I'm not sure, but she can be cured if we can find out what has poisoned her. But we must be quick. The toxins are taking their toll, and she may become very ill if we don't find an antidote soon."

skekSa held Tae's hair away from her face, beckoning them closer. None of them moved, until Naia stepped bravely into the Skeksis's reach. She knelt beside Tae, almost touching skekSa's leathery claw, daring her to make a move. In the face of the fear pinching all his insides, Amri joined Naia. He was afraid, but he refused to let her stand before the Skeksis alone.

"I hate to admit it, but she's right," Naia said. "Look."

He'd seen the milky blue haze on Tavra's eyes, when she'd been controlled by the spider. He'd seen it in Rian's dreamfast, overtaking Mira like a frost. But Tae's eyes were clear and bright, reflecting the starry sky and the fire that roared nearby.

Still, this had to be the work of the Skeksis. It couldn't be a coincidence.

"How can we know what poison?" Maudra Ethri asked. "If we don't know and give her the wrong antidote, it could make her condition worse."

skekSa leaned one aristocratic elbow on her knee, tapping a talon against her snout.

"It would be quickest to simply determine who poisoned her," she said. "That person would be in the best position to know which poison they used. Who here in Cera-Na has motive to poison your dear Tae?"

Ethri paced, kicking up sand in her distress. It was not the stoic countenance of a *maudra* but the worried agitation of a friend. Though it betrayed her inexperience as a leader, her concern for Tae was the first thing that endeared her to Amri.

"I don't know! Everyone loves Tae. She has no enemies, makes friends wherever she goes. I can't imagine who would want to do this to her."

"She said she had to meet someone when she left us on the docks," Kylan said. "Whoever poisoned her must have done it after she left us. It wasn't that long ago."

"But she didn't say with who, so all that does is tell us it's a poison that works quickly," Amri added. He thought over every poison he had learned of, smelled, and even tasted in the Tomb of Relics. There were herbs and venoms that could cause the cold skin or the paleness, or even the waking sleep, but none could account for them all. And who was to say what he'd found in the Tomb was exhaustive? More likely it was just a tiny collection representing an infinite world he'd never seen.

skekSa didn't seem concerned about any of this, but then again, she was a Skeksis. She snapped a claw, waving Naia closer.

"Drenchen girl. Do you possess the healing talent of your clan?"

Naia glanced at Kylan and Amri, then nodded.

"Some," she replied.

"Then come closer. Use your Gelfling magic. Use your *vliyaya*. Tell me what you sense about her. Perhaps you can unearth a clue that will help us save her."

Naia was wary, and Amri almost told her not to do it. Using her *vliyaya* in the presence of a Skeksis was dangerous. *Vliyaya* meant *flame of the blue fire*—the blue fire of Gelfling essence. What if it piqued skekSa's appetite? But Tae was dying and they needed answers. Amri shouldered his coat back, the way he'd seen angry Captain Madso do, to make sure skekSa saw the hilt of the sword at his hip.

skekSa took note of it, sniffing as if he'd said something amusing. But all she said was "Go on, then. Hold out your hands. Sense it."

Amri nodded to Naia and she nodded back, releasing her grip on the dagger. She settled closer to Tae, holding her palms out, and Amri waited for the blue glow. Before it came, Naia wrinkled her nose. She leaned in and gave Tae a big sniff.

"She smells like Drenchen nectarwine," she said.

Amri frowned. "That doesn't sound like a poison. That sounds like the opposite of a poison."

"It's made from fermented sogflower nectar, used in recipes for healing and merriment."

"Hmmm!" skekSa crooned, stroking the feathers under her chin. "And here in the north, there must be so many other *merriment* potions that are easier to come by. Only someone with a taste for sogflower would make the effort to have it on hand."

For an uncomfortable moment, Amri envied the Skeksis captain's knowledge. She had lived for so many trine and traveled so far and wide. Her mental compendium of medicinal knowledge had to be staggering. Maudra Ethri's gaze narrowed, her gem eye glinting.

"Staya."

She turned toward the docks and put two fingers in her mouth, signaling with a series of short, ear-piercing whistles. Moments later, two Sifa alighted, sounding of bells and chimes. They bowed to Ethri and to skekSa.

"Find Staya," Ethri ordered. "Bring him to me, now."

"Grand, simply grand," skekSa said. "Our first clue. Perhaps Staya could bring some to share. I could use some potions of merriment m'self."

Amri regarded the Skeksis, thinking about Tavra's warning. The Vapra on his shoulder had gone utterly silent, hidden in his hair. The Skeksis Lords would all know the names of the All-Maudra's daughters. Perhaps even their voices. What problems could it cause if one of them found that Princess Katavra lived? How easily did the Skeksis communicate with one another? Dozens of questions Amri had never even thought of sprang up as he stood on the beach, paralyzed by circumstance.

Kylan caught his arm, squeezing gently.

"Don't panic," he whispered, surprisingly calm. "She won't do anything in the open with so many Sifa about, so long as we don't give her a reason to. Act like everything is normal and don't challenge her."

Amri gulped and tried to calm himself, told himself Kylan was right. It was the song teller who had faced down skekLi the Satirist, had told songs before the Skeksis Lords when they'd visited the Spriton village. The Spriton, the Stonewood, the Vapra—and apparently the Sifa, too, were used to the Skeksis. Respected and revered them. Even if Lord skekSa were part of the Emperor's scheme to harvest Gelfling essence, it would be foolish for her to betray the Sifa so publicly. And if the

Skeksis were anything, it was not foolish.

Act normal. What was normal, anyway?

"Let go—Ethri! What's all this about? Lord skekSa—"

Staya yanked away from the Sifa who had brought him and dropped to a deep bow. As soon as his formalities were complete, he strode toward Maudra Ethri, sand spraying from his boots. The two met almost nose to nose, Ethri with a cool gaze, though Staya was taller and broader. Ethri stared the Drenchen down, then turned to the side and pointed at Tae.

"You'll answer my questions first, Staya," Ethri said. "What do you know about this?"

Staya took in the scene, unconscious Tae resting under the silent gaze of a Skeksis. "What's happened to her?" he asked.

"You tell me. She smells of nectarwine, and you're the only one in a day's flight who drinks the sweet stuff. What've you done to her?"

"I didn't do anything."

"It's unbecoming to lie to your captain *maudra*," skekSa reminded him mildly. "Even by omitting the truth. Especially a truth that may save little Tae's life."

Staya gulped audibly, then tossed his hair back.

"Tae came to me this evening. She wanted to talk. We drank. That's all."

"And then?" skekSa asked.

"And then she left! Not long ago. She must have come straight here. She was wobbly when she left, but I only thought she couldn't hold her nectar!"

"Did she leave with all her jewelry intact?" Ethri asked.

"Her jewelry? Ethri, now you call me a common thief? What need have I for her dainty lassywing metals?" That much was plain. Staya was laden with twice the number of bangles and jewels Tae had been. He didn't need any more.

"Her pulse is growing weak," Naia said. "If we don't find out what's poisoned her"—she shot a look at skekSa—"or *drained* her, soon, I don't know if she's going to make it."

"Staya, if you know anything . . . !" Ethri warned. "At least, think of Tae!"

"And the penalty for deceit," skekSa added, narrowing her diamond-shaped pupils. Staya turned away, clenching his fists, and Naia shouted,

"Out with it!"

When Staya turned back, the apprehension was gone from his face.

"I put zandir in her nectarwine," he confessed. "To make her tell the truth. And I'm glad I did, because she told me what you're planning, Ethri!"

Ethri went rigid like she'd been struck by lightning, every facet of her gem eye igniting with light and fire.

"What's he talking about?" Naia asked lowly.

"Ah, the truth, the truth," Captain skekSa sang. She rose and swept closer to Tae, stooping to once again lift the unconscious Sifa into her arms. "It all comes out in the dark."

"Staya, that's not—" Ethri was on her back foot now. She watched skekSa wrap Tae in her coat. "Staya, I'll explain. Lord

Mariner, where are you taking her?"

"Now we know what is wrong with her. Come, quickly. To my ship."

"Why do we have to go to your ship?" Amri cried.

"I have the means to heal her there. More reliable means, that is, than burning colored dust and reading bones over her slowly dying body. If this little Drenchen healer comes with me, we'll have Tae back on the wing in no time."

Amri didn't want Naia or any of them to go anywhere with the Mariner, especially not some Skeksis ship where they'd be trapped, floating out on the wide sea. skekSa could do whatever she wanted to them there, and no one would notice. They'd sink to the bottom of the ocean, forgotten as the Grottan clan, nameless to history and remembered by no one.

But Tae was dying, and Naia wasn't afraid.

"I'm not letting you take Tae alone to your ship, that's for certain," she said. To Ethri, she added, "And you. After this, I want to know exactly what Staya is talking about."

Maudra Ethri pinched her lips, indignant as a seabird trapped in a net.

The five of them followed skekSa down the dock, Maudra Ethri and Staya in the lead while Amri and Kylan held closer to Naia, who marched ahead, shoulders squared and jaw set. Amri tried to be like her. He hated being afraid. As he watched skekSa's massive shoulders swaggering ahead, he tried to grab his fear in the hands of his heart. Squeeze it like clay, molding it into something else.

None of them spoke; the Skeksis ahead seemed to hear all that happened around her. Even Tavra was silent, though Amri felt her holding his shoulder as tightly as he gripped the hilt of his sword.

skekSa led them down a long dock that stuck straight out into the ocean from the end of the headland, far away from any of the other Sifa ships. They gazed out into the open, endless water, and Amri remembered the moan he'd heard when they'd first arrived in Cera-Na.

"I don't see any ship," Kylan said.

"Surely, you wouldn't let your eyes deceive you."

skekSa held out the claw that wasn't cradling Tae. A smaller hand emerged from inside her coat—one of her four. It dropped a shining metal pipe in her other palm, and she lifted it to her mouth. A long, high-pitched, almost inaudible note rang out over the ocean. Amri's sensitive ears flattened on the sides of his head, and Tavra latched on to his neck in pain.

When the note ended, a rumbling, low moan replied.

"That sound . . . ," Amri gasped.

Waves churned in the deep water off the end of the headland. Under the pale light of the two Sisters shining above, the ocean split across the spined ebony back of an enormous beast. They all watched as the thorny shell of the biggest creature Amri had ever seen rose from the water. Its carapace glistened in the moonlight as the ocean water streamed down its sides. Its shell alone was as large as the *Omerya*, though its obsidian color stood in contrast to the brightness of the *maudra*'s coral ship.

The moaning grew louder and louder until the behemoth's cavernous head breached the surface of the sea. Waves sloshed against the dock. It groaned again, the sound so loud, Amri felt it rattle in his chest.

Moments later, a small boat detached from the great beast's shell, pulled by an armored, spiny fish with glowing spots along its back. The fish brought the boat to the dock.

skekSa gestured casually, taking care not to jostle Tae.

"All aboard."

CHAPTER 10

A mri did not want to board the ship.

It wasn't even a ship. It was a living, breathing, heaving, groaning monster. But he didn't have a choice. Before he knew it, the small boat thunked against the side of a scaly dock carved into the creature's thick, barnacle-covered shell. Kelp and seaweed were strung from every prickling spike that jutted from the enormous thing, and in some places fish flopped where they'd been marooned as the creature had surfaced.

"This way, my dears," skekSa said. She pushed open a scale, revealing a doorway big enough for her not-insignificant figure. In the Skeksis went, leaving them little choice but to follow.

The passageway inside was a slope reinforced with metal and shell, and Amri committed the path to memory in case they needed to escape. The flesh that made up the artery twitched and spasmed underfoot and all around, circulating the fluids in the wall and giving off the occasional draft of tepid, thick air smelling of fish and blood. Glass lamps filled the passage with an ethereal, mysterious gold light. As reluctant as Amri was to be treading inside the behemoth's body, he couldn't help but stare as he passed.

"It isn't far," skekSa called over her shoulder. "We'll bring Tae back to her good health soon enough. Watch your step here, looks like the cleaners have not reached this far up the corridor, hmm . . ."

skekSa took a wide step over something that lay across the way. It was a big bloodred worm, its slick skin drying up even in the damp air. It twitched, nearly dead, as they stepped over it, one at a time.

Aside from the dying worm, they saw no crew or accompaniment aboard the dank, dark ship. skekSa reached a widening in the tunnel and blew a series of chirps on her whistle. The flesh in the wall trembled, scales folding back and spines retracting to reveal a chamber.

"Welcome to my laboratory."

They must have been deep under the behemoth's shell, for the ceiling was high and structured with beams and rods and poles. A large chandelier of the golden lamps glowing with a fireless light hung from the center of the ceiling, illuminating a long row of shelves stacked with bottles and jars and flasks, and on the other end an expansive library of books. Crystals, looking glasses, lenses, and other objects littered every surface.

skekSa found a table stacked high with scrolls and cleared it with a single swoop of her free arm.

"Come, bring that cloth. Make a pillow for her sweet flutterling head."

Kylan and Ethri did as she asked, and they gathered around Tae. The Sifa girl's skin was nearly white now, her breath so shallow, Amri couldn't tell if she was breathing at all.

"Will she live?" Staya asked, almost equally as pale with guilt and worry.

"She needs cleansing and hydration," skekSa said. "Water to flush the toxins from her body, and life to replace that which has been sapped away."

"Zandir wouldn't have caused this," Amri said. "It's a truth dust. It—it doesn't have this effect, and neither should nectarwine."

"Astute, my little Grottan apothecary. However, the zandir flower, known to unlock the mind, is less commonly known to be a distant relative of the sogflower. When taken together, the fruit of the sogflower is awakened by the zandir pollen. It results in a spore that causes the worst effects of both plants: dehydration, loss of blood pressure. And of unlocking the mind, yes—to a degree most severe. Had Staya known this, surely he wouldn't have given both to Tae in one cup."

Staya looked away, ears flattening. "I didn't know. I wasn't trying to hurt her."

"So she wasn't drained," Kylan said, eyeing the refracting lenses that rested on a tray nearby. Even though the contraptions all around them had the sophistication of Skeksis design, there was no way skekSa could harness the power of the Crystal. Not from here, so far from the castle.

"I told you that already, little Spriton," skekSa said as she brushed through her equipment. She found a large, bubble-shaped flask with a stopper, then kept rummaging until she procured a long tube, pulling it from under a pile like entrails from carrion. skekSa noticed the others standing around the table and barked,

"It's too crowded in here. Ethri, take them out! Except for you, little apothecary. The rest, get out. Give us room to work."

"Yes, Lord skekSa," Ethri said. "Come on, Staya. Spriton."

Amri tried not to shake while he stood beside the table, watching Maudra Ethri lead Staya and Kylan away. He didn't want to remain in the room with skekSa, but then again he would rather have stayed than left Naia alone. At least skekSa hadn't noticed Tavra hiding on his shoulder.

"Drenchen girl," skekSa said. "Do you have a name?"

Naia paused. She had not given her name to the Mariner yet—the name that had been attached to the word *traitor* by the Emperor skekSo himself. Amri tensed, wondering if he could possibly defend them with Tavra's sword in these quarters, buried deep in the behemoth ship's belly.

"Naia," she replied boldly.

"Yes. You have the gift, Naia, do you not? Come over here."

No recognition salted skekSa's command. Naia passed a glance back to Amri and did as the Skeksis directed, moving so she was under skekSa's arm beside Tae. Amri hated how close they were to the Skeksis, but there was nothing that could be done now. Not if they wanted to save Tae and escape the living ship alive.

"Hands here. Yes. Close your eyes and focus . . . And you, Grottan. You'll be our assistant. You must have a name as well?"

"Amri."

"Amri, then. Fetch water from the spigot."

In a cluster of steaming pipes near an iron woodstove was a pair of spigots. The pipe leading to one spigot was perspiring and cold, the other snaking from out of the stovepipes hot to the touch.

"Hot or cold?" he asked, picking up an empty basin.

"Warm. But not hot, or her skin will burn. Once you've filled that basin, grind some soothing salts into it. From the rack, something for hydration. Figure it out yourself, I've got to help your friend now."

Amri wrenched on the spigot knobs, which were made for a Skeksis-size claw, not Gelfling hands. While the water trickled into the basin, some from the hot and more from the cold, he climbed onto the shelf under the apothecary rack. skekSa's inventory was overwhelming, with everything from hooyim roe to nulroot powder. If Tae was suffering from a spore infection, with cold skin and pale face—

"Hold your hands here. The spores gather in the lungs . . . yes. Oh, you're a quick study, my girl. It seems you've trained. Under Maudra Laesid, perhaps?"

skekSa's crooning voice was like a wash of ink, filling in the fibers of a raw sheet of paper. Naia was reserved with her answers, though her hard-talking upbringing made her awkward with lies.

"Yes," she said.

"The Blue Stone Healer. Her name is well-known. I heard from Lord skekZok that she had twins, one a son who went to serve my kin at the Castle of the Crystal, one a daughter who inherited her abilities with healing *vliyaya*. Oh, what I'd give to meet the two of them. Twins being so rare among Gelfling and all."

Amri's skin crawled. skekSa *knew*. Of course she did. They had been stupid to come here and stupid to trust her. Now they were trapped in her laboratory, deep in her disgusting behemoth ship and surrounded by water. They would disappear into the endless sea and never be heard of again. The fear in his gut writhed, trying to escape his grasp, trying to eat him from within.

"What are we going to do?" he whispered to the spider on his shoulder. For once, he wished she would tell him what to do. Anything to get them out of this awful place alive.

"We're going to wait," Tavra said, so quietly only he could hear her. "Right now the only thing we can do is to hope she truly can cure Tae and that we have an opportunity to escape."

Her stoic voice calmed the panic. He browsed the jars and canisters, trying to both stall and hurry at the same time. There were endless containers of spices, dusts, and potions, some marked and some so old their labels had dissolved in the tide of time. Amri had no idea if they were all scents and salts, or if some contained poisons. Yet others could most certainly be both, given the right circumstances and time.

Like the Skeksis, Amri thought. He recalled for a moment the words of days past relived in countless songs: *The Skeksis Lords gathered in the Castle of the Crystal, radiant in their decadence. They had been born to the world already godlike, with knowledge about the stars and the earth, equipped with the technological magic of science. For hundreds of trine they had watched over the Crystal and the castle. They had cared for the Gelfling, their favored wards. Cared for them even when Mother Aughra had disappeared.*

Hundreds of songs over hundreds of trine told of their glory. All lies.

Amri plucked a jar from the wall and opened the lid. A sweet, warming scent wafted out of it, calming and tingling a place in his forehead. It flooded his mind with the memory of Domrak—a dust made from the moss that grew under the roots of the Sanctuary Tree. The Grottan had lived since the beginning of time in the shadows and caves, making the dust and poultices. Alone in the dark. And look what it had gotten them. Forgotten and neglected, the first to fall to the Skeksis. The Shadowling way had failed them.

Now here he was, doing as skekSa told him without protesting. Despite the lies the Skeksis had told them all, despite how the Lords of the Castle had begun plucking from the Gelfling as he was about to pluck from the scented salts. He would never become a hero if he kept doing things the Grottan way. Alone and hiding in the dark.

So this time, Amri asked himself what a daylighter would do.

The room glowed blue. Naia was working her healing *vliyaya*, intently focused as skekSa put a hand on her shoulder, crooning into her ear. Amri hastily shook the moss dust into the warm water, letting the scent waft throughout the chamber. He wanted it to overpower everything else, especially the stench of the behemoth's pulsating insides.

"What's going on over there, assistant?" skekSa called.

"Coming," Amri said. He didn't pick up the basin. Instead, he drew his sword.

Tavra pinched him, hissing in his ear, "Amri, no. Don't be a fool!"

"There are only so many Skeksis," he whispered. "After tonight there could be one less."

"She'll kill you. She'll kill us all!"

He looked at skekSa. Her back was to him, in between him and the table where Tae lay, guiding Naia's hands and speaking gently in her ear. She was distracted, focused. Ignoring him, as everyone always did. He had to strike now.

"Amri, no!"

Tavra pricked him, then pricked him again when he ignored her. Each time it felt like a tiny sting, numbing his movement. But it wasn't enough, and he didn't need her telling him what to do. Heart pounding, he crept toward skekSa's back on silent feet, hand sweating. She wouldn't see him, and if he was quick, he didn't have to be good with a sword. He just had to be fast.

"Assistant?" skekSa asked, turning. "Where's that water?"

As skekSa moved her shoulder back to look for him, he lunged toward the Mariner's fleshy neck, bracing himself for contact—

"Amri, stop!"

His blade tasted nothing but air. Every muscle in his body was rigid, unresponsive, held immobile by the tiny words echoing through his mind. Tavra had done it. His neck throbbed from the eight needles driven into his skin.

The blue light from Naia's hands died as she yelped and jumped back.

"Amri—what in Thra's name—"

skekSa grabbed the sword by the blade and, in his surprise, yanked it from his grasp. Quick as an eel snatching a fish, she plucked the spider from Amri's neck and dropped her on the table beside Tae.

CLUNK.

Down came a bottle, swiftly containing Tavra in a thick glass prison.

Amri's mind flooded back to him, regaining control of his body, but all he felt was sick. He pressed his hand against his neck where Tavra had let blood. His heart pounded faster than his lungs could keep up with. He faced the Skeksis he'd tried to kill—tried, and failed. Now they were all going to die.

"Interesting," skekSa said. She turned away from him as if nothing had happened. "Ah, there she is. Good evening, my dear."

Consumed by his attempt to kill the Mariner, Amri had failed to notice that Tae was awake. Naia grabbed her shoulder and helped steady her as she sat up. The paleness was fading from her cheeks. She coughed, then wheezed, then spat when Naia held out a pail that had been waiting below the worktable.

"Where am I?" Tae mumbled, holding her head.

"Take it easy. You're still weak."

Naia rubbed Tae's back and stared at Amri. He didn't know how to explain what he'd done, what had happened, so he kept his mouth shut. He wasn't sure who he was angrier with, himself for what he'd tried to do or Tavra for stopping him.

The Mariner stood back, pulling a lace handkerchief from her coat. She handed it to Amri and gestured.

"For your neck," she said. "Now fetch that water, will you? Then we'll discuss your little spider problem."

CHAPTER 11

While Tae soaked her feet in the basin of water, skekSa left Amri and Naia to bring the others back in. Amri kept the cloth skekSa had given him pressed against his neck until the bleeding stopped, avoiding eye contact with the spider in the jar.

"I have a headache that's something terrible," Tae grumbled.

Naia moved her hands, blue light filling the basin and soaking Tae's ankles and legs. "You're dehydrated. I was able to remove the spores . . . or most of them, with skekSa's help. You might be coughing up flowerets for a few days, but you should keep feeling better as time passes."

"Tae!"

The laboratory warmed with life and noise again as Maudra Ethri, Staya, and Kylan reentered. While Ethri clasped Tae's hands, Kylan pointed at the turned-over jar.

"What's going on?" he asked.

"We need to talk about that," skekSa agreed. "Among a great many other things."

She found a chair hidden beneath a pile of furs and scrolls, clearing it so the pile was on the floor in a heap instead, and took a seat. She stretched one arm to snatch a dusty decanter from where it was half-buried under books. The cork popped out between her teeth, and she took a long glug of the burgundy liquid. With a free hand, she gestured.

"Go on, then. Let it all out. All the pieces are here. I will preside, to make sure no one gets untoward . . . or tries to kill me."

The last she tossed like a stick on the fire in Tavra's direction, though the spider had retracted all her legs so she looked like any other gem resting inertly on the table. Amri soured with guilt. He had been the one who'd tried to kill skekSa, not Tavra. And after seeing how easily the Mariner had torn his sword from his hands, he realized the Vapra soldier had been right. There was no way he was going to put an end to skekSa, especially not here in her laboratory with a blade with which he had no skill.

He wanted to tell them the truth. Wanted to apologize to Tavra for putting her in this position, to Naia and Tae for endangering them, but held his tongue. skekSa had not retaliated. So long as she thought it was the spider's idea, perhaps they could escape with their hearts still beating. He wished for everything this hadn't happened, but it had. He only hoped they could survive long enough for him to make up for his foolish mistake.

But skekSa ignored the spider and Amri. She waved at Staya, inviting him to speak.

"First matter. You had a grievance, I believe? I bid you air it."

The captain trembled and hung his head. Before responding to skekSa's invitation, he turned to Tae, and Amri saw honest regret in his pinched cheeks and wrinkled brow.

"Tae, I didn't mean for this to happen to you. I didn't know. I wanted to ask you about the rumors I'd heard about Maudra

Ethri. The zandir pollen was a mistake. If you had died, I would never have forgiven myself."

"Then you are quite lucky, aren't you?" Tae quipped, though it lacked energy. skekSa coughed loudly, waving her decanter so the drink inside sloshed impatiently.

"Enough apologies. I want grievances!"

Staya hesitated, eyes shifting to skekSa and then over to Maudra Ethri. Like the other Sifa on the beach, he was reluctant to confront her. No wonder the *maudra* wasn't used to being challenged.

"Come on, out with it," Naia said.

"There's been a rumor adrift in the bay," Staya began. "That because of the message in the pink petals' dream, and the growing whispers that the Skeksis have betrayed us, you called us all here not to rally us to rise against the Skeksis, but to gather us to flee."

All eyes went to Maudra Ethri. Amri thought she might lie, or at least speak another truth. One less cowardly than running away. She didn't.

"It's true. We sail tomorrow at sunset."

Staya gasped, as if he hadn't really expected to hear the truth.

"How could you," he whispered.

Naia's reaction was more intense. "What!" she exploded. "You mean you plan to sail out to sea and leave the rest of the Gelfling to fight the Skeksis?"

"You will restrain your tone with me, Naia," Maudra Ethri bellowed. "If I choose to lead my clan out from under Emperor skekSo's claws, that is my choice to make."

Staya found his footing, raising his voice against his *maudra*, though not so bluntly as Naia. "But, Maudra, you ignore the signs! The wind is against us. The tide is against us. With every limb of its body, Thra pushes us back toward the south, yet you'd sail in the face of that? You'd trust a Skeksis over the signs of Thra?"

"I don't need the wind or the tide! The Lord Mariner has looked after the Sifa since we first touched toe to the sea. Has sailed with us far from the Castle of the Crystal and the traitor Skeksis. We have our Sifa charts and navigators, and skekSa's ship will break the waves for us. She has promised us this, and I believe her."

skekSa's only response was to take another swig of her drink, as if she were watching a performance and was pleasantly entertained. Staya turned, cheeks red, to the Sifa girl recovering on the Skeksis's worktable.

"Tae, what do you make of this?" he asked.

Tae paused. Whatever she was going to say died in her mouth when Ethri spoke first: "Tae is my first-wing. She has known of this plan since we began making it."

Amri's mind reeled. They had come all this way to win over the Sifa, to bring their torch to the hearth fire, and only to find this. A Skeksis, and a plan to abandon the other Gelfling and save themselves.

Naia faced Ethri.

"Onica believed you were brave," she growled. "I wanted to believe her. But now I know you're nothing but a coward and a traitor."

For a moment, Ethri looked her age. Only slightly older than Naia, maybe even as lost and confused as Amri felt himself.

"The first to stand are the first to be struck down," Ethri said.

"But the All-Maudra—" Amri began, but Ethri would have none of it. Even if they'd had proof, Amri guessed it wouldn't have changed her mind. The youth vanished, and she was bold again, the *maudra* of the brazen, wild Sifa.

"Staya, you are welcome to remain in Cera-Na if it pleases you. Stay here and die. But if you will choose wisely, then you will set sail with the rest of the clan tomorrow night."

Ethri helped Tae down and bore her weight as she left. Staya hesitated, glancing to Naia and then to skekSa. For a moment, Amri thought he might continue to fight—that he might take a stand for what he believed in. But instead, he looked away, shaking his head slowly before striding after his *maudra*.

When they were gone, skekSa joined the others around the jar on the table.

"Now then, on to other matters." In a single garish movement, she lifted the jar and flung it over a shoulder so it crashed against the wall. She leaned in and sneered. "Tell me what you want, Arathim. *Spider.* Have you reported all this to the Emperor, then? Shall I expect he and General skekUng will arrive shortly to dispatch me? Or will it be skekMal, your mad pet?"

Tavra did not respond. If she spoke, her nature could be revealed—or even worse, her identity. Amri floundered as skekSa rooted through her tools and finally lifted a pestle from a granite bowl and cried, "Let's see how well crystal-singers grind to dust!"

"No! She's not Arathim!" Before she could bring the pestle down, Kylan scooped Tavra up and held her close.

"Of course it's Arathim," skekSa retorted. "It's a spider, isn't it? Sworn to Emperor skekSo. The crystal-singers, the silk-spitters, the whole squiggly lot of them. Make my scales crawl, they do." She eyed Kylan suspiciously, but tossed the pestle over her shoulder to join the broken jar. "What's going on here?"

Amri gulped. They couldn't tell skekSa about Tavra, but if the spider race—the *Arathim*, was that their name?—were sworn to the Emperor, then surely skekSa would force them to explain what one was doing on her ship. Wouldn't she? But what could they say that wouldn't reveal Tavra to the Skeksis?

When no one spoke, skekSa shrugged. She reached down, plucking the sword she'd yanked from Amri's grasp off the damp floor. She held out the sword to him, hilt first, and as he grasped it, she looked him in the eye.

"Try as you might to keep it to yourself, one day you will tell me," she said, almost as a threat. "I will wait. After all, I have eternity."

She let go, and Amri gingerly took the sword. If she believed Tavra was not Arathim, then she knew it was he who had tried to kill her. Not the spider.

"Why are you giving this back to me?" Amri asked.

"A reminder of my generosity," skekSa said. "Come. I reckon you all believe any moment I'll strap you down and have you attached to some infernal contraption. I will call a boat and return you to shore."

By the time skekSa left them on the lone dock in the bay, the suns were rising. Watching skekSa's ship submerge under the pink-tinged sky, Amri suddenly felt as if every bone in his body were made of stone.

Onica was waiting for them wrapped in a quilted shawl.

"Ethri told me what happened. We need to talk."

"About that, and other things," Naia said. "I think whatever you learned talking to Maudra Ethri, I just made it worse."

Onica took Naia's shoulder and said, "We will persevere."

As they followed Onica to her ship, Amri stole one look back. skekSa's ship was nothing but bubbles.

Onica's cabin was more welcome than Amri could have imagined, dim and warm and dry. Even if the ship creaked with the sound of wood and water, it was not the constant deep burbling and breathing of the behemoth ship. It was a boat, but at least it was a familiar one.

Onica nodded solemnly when they told her what had happened.

"Ethri told me as much," she said. "I stayed to speak with her crew, to see if I could learn how we might change her mind, but they were all close-lipped. Even to me. I fear too much has changed, and too quickly, since I last had Ethri's confidence."

"Staya said the signs were against her," Kylan said. "Against her plan to leave and cross the Silver Sea. Is that true?"

"There are many signs, all with many meanings. What I know is that the tide is against a northward journey, and the wind this time of season would make it impossible if it weren't for skekSa's promise to help. And aside from that, no one even knows what's across the Silver Sea. Ethri is well aware of all this, yet she plans to defy the signs . . . It is not the Sifa way. Something has come over her. I don't know if it is the fear of the Skeksis, or that she is being manipulated by Lord skekSa." Onica sighed and pushed her fingers through her hair before adding, "Worst of all, I fear she is no longer the Ethri I knew."

Tavra stepped out of Kylan's hands, approaching Onica.

"Then we must accept her for who she is now," she said. "Tomorrow, we will speak with her. She will change her mind . . . I will make sure of it. What happened tonight is proof of our dire circumstances." Next, she turned toward Amri. His neck hurt where she'd drawn blood. He tried to shrug it off, though he couldn't shake the feeling of her voice driving itself through his body, controlling his limbs with crystal whispers.

"Amri, I'm sorry."

"I don't know what you're sorry about. I'm the one who tried to do something stupid that almost got us all killed," he mumbled.

"I didn't do it on purpose. I just didn't want you to—"

She reached out to him, but he pulled his hand away. It was still sore from gripping the sword. In his mind, he saw a different night unfold: one where he struck skekSa with the tiny blade. She didn't die, not that way. She was only enraged, snatching the weapon from his weak grasp. Flinging it across the room and bringing her other claws across Naia's neck. All because he'd tried to be a hero.

"I'm tired," he said.

He took the sword from his belt and set it on the table beside Tavra. He found a darker corner of the cabin among the cushions and quilts, wrapped his cloak tight around his shoulders, and pretended to go to sleep.

CHAPTER 12

While the day outside awakened, soon the cabin was quiet with the gentle sounds of sleep. When he heard snoring, Amri quietly pushed the quilt away, sighing. His body was exhausted but his mind refused to rest. So while the others slept, he silently crept out onto the deck.

The sunrise was a lovely one. Only the Rose Sun was up, not bright enough to hurt his eyes yet. Perhaps he was finally becoming accustomed to the daylighter sky. He found a spot on the bow and huddled in his cloak, watching the ships bob in the bay, backed by the sweeping headlands of the coast.

A sight that, only a single trine ago, he would never have expected to see for himself. Had a Far-Dreamer come into the deep Caves of Grot and told him that he would soon leave the caverns he'd lived in all his life on a journey that would take him to every reach of the Skarith Land, he would have laughed. He'd studied every apothecary tome available, tasted every old musty spice in the Tomb, even if they'd gone bad. He'd never thought he would step foot on the snowy ridges near Ha'rar, nor ride aboard a Sifa soothsayer's boat.

But now, looking out on the bay, he only felt an intense longing. As if he'd reached for the branch of a tree, only to find once he grasped it, the rock he'd been standing on had fallen from under his feet. He missed the caves. He missed the Tomb of Relics, filled with promises of the mysterious, strange daylighter world without the dangers that pervaded it.

How easy would it be, he wondered, to hop onto the dock and head inland? He would have to cross the Claw Mountains, but mountains were full of tunnels and caves—terrain he understood. If he traveled under the highlands, he would land in the northern pass of the Dark Wood, where the Black River cut through. Follow the river and in another two days' time, he could be back in the Caves of Grot. Back where he belonged.

"Thought I heard you come out here . . . Are you all right?"

Amri looked over his shoulder as Naia joined him. She sat close enough to him that they could share warmth in the chilly morning.

"Just thinking," he said.

"About what happened last night?" she asked gently. "Do you want to talk about it?"

"I don't know what there is to say."

Naia nudged him with her elbow. "Just start talking. Words will come . . . If you want to, that is."

He had plenty of feelings but he balked at saying them out loud. He tried to come up with something lighthearted to say, but instead of the usually endless-seeming well of quips, all he found was an empty pit of embarrassment and weariness.

Naia put her hand on his shoulder and squeezed.

"Amri. It's all right. No one got hurt last night, you know? And it's not like I don't understand what you were feeling. I thought it was pretty brave what you did, actually."

"Now you're just saying things to make me feel better."

"No, really! I remember how scared I was the first time I faced a Skeksis. I didn't think I could do it. I thought Gurjin was dead, and Tavra . . . I'll never forget. It takes a lot of guts to do what you did."

Amri scoffed when he felt his cheeks warm. "We're just lucky the only Skeksis I decided to attack ended up being the one that was willing to forgive me. Can you imagine what would have happened if I'd actually stabbed her? She could have . . ."

"But she didn't. And I won't forget what you did back in the snow. You really gave the Chamberlain something to remember."

She grinned and Amri smiled a little, thinking back on the look on the Chamberlain's face. But then he remembered what Tavra had said when she had decided to teach him to use her sword.

You're not going to be able to rely on Grottan tricks every time.

His smile faded.

"I just don't know what to do." He noticed he was wringing his hands and made a fist instead. "I'm trying so hard to do things the daylighter way, but I'm not very good at it. I can't see very well, and I don't know anything about anything . . . I can hardly walk upright without tripping on my own feet."

She hesitated, then put her hand on his clenched knuckles. Her silence filled Amri's heart with a fragile feeling, like he'd shown her something by accident. Something he hadn't even known was there himself, and now that he was telling her, it all came spilling out.

"I just want to be good at something, you know? You're so strong. Fierce Naia. And Kylan, the song teller with the magic *firca*. Tavra, soldier daughter of the All-Maudra. The things I'm good at don't matter up here . . . I'm probably going to end up being Amri the Forgotten. Like the rest of my clan."

Naia caught her breath in her throat. "Oh, Amri . . ."

She didn't try to untangle his fists, didn't tell him not to be sad. Didn't scold him or tell him he was wrong for feeling the way he felt. She just rested her hand on his, and at that moment, it was all he needed. She was with him. Straightforward and truthful, and still sitting beside him despite what he'd told her and what they were up against.

The loneliness clenching his heart loosened.

"Augh!" he cried. "I thought the problem was going to be getting people to believe. I thought once they believed, they would know the right thing to do! But Maudra Ethri still plans to sail *tonight*. We only have a day to figure out how to stop her. And then there's skekSa—I don't know what to do!"

"I'm disappointed, too," Naia admitted. "Nothing is simple anymore. But it's not your responsibility to figure this out on your own. We all need to be honest with each other, and rely on each other. If we do that, we'll figure it out. After all, the whole point of this is for us to trust despite difficult times. Come together as Gelfling . . . all of us. Including you. Including the Grottan."

He sighed. Wanted to believe.

"You think we can?" he asked.

She grinned. "I promised I'd bring you home to Great Smerth, didn't I? We'll have to find a way, if we're going to make it all the way south to Sog! Then you can meet Gurjin, too, and my sisters and my parents. They would love to meet you."

Amri badly wanted that. He let the idea, that hope, lighten his heart.

"You think Gurjin made it back all right?"

Naia rolled her shoulders and tilted her head. There was no way for them to know for sure, and they had been traveling for so long, it was doubtful even a messenger swoothu could find them. Even if it brought good news. Naia leaned back and faced up into the sky, wiggling her feet back and forth while she thought. He worried he'd asked a question that would make her worry, but she was nodding, a little smile on her lips.

"You know that place in your mind, right before you wake up? In between your dream and the waking world? Like in a dreamfast, almost . . . When I'm in that place, sometimes I can smell Sog. Feel it, all around me. Like I'm sleeping in my hammock back home. But it's not me. It's Gurjin. With Neech, and . . . I can't explain it, but somehow I just know he made it back."

She looked at him, and it was the closest Amri had ever been to seeing the southern wetlands, full of life and green and hope. He wanted to believe that they would go there together, one day. Reach Great Smerth and meet Naia's mother. Proud Maudra Laesid, who would surely join her eldest daughter to the beating of the Drenchen drums. He tried to imagine who Maudra Naia would be, one day, and whether she would be different from the friend who sat beside him, watching the Rose Sun's gold melt away the edge of the sky.

Naia's eyes drifted away from his.

"Is it just me, or is *Omerya* moving?"

Amri stood with her to look across the bay. At first it seemed perhaps the coral-tree ship was only dancing on the changing morning currents. But then the anemone sails unfolded, blooming like night flowers. Within moments, it moved away from its dock. All around it, the Sifa ships came to life, sails dropping.

"Oh no," Naia breathed. She leaped to the top of the cabin, scaling the mast and dropping the sails. "I thought we had until sunset—quickly, get Onica! We have to catch them before they make it out to sea!"

Amri dashed to the cabin, slamming the door open and waking everyone inside. Onica had heard Naia's footsteps on the cabin roof already, swinging out of her hammock.

"What's going on?"

"Maudra Ethri's taking the *Omerya* out. They're leaving!"

Onica's untamed hair cascaded around her face, and she quickly wrapped it back with a sash. Tavra was on her shoulder. Onica pushed past Amri and out onto the deck, swinging up into the rigging. Kylan followed quickly after. The ship caught the wind and swung out to sea, heading a course to intercept the *Omerya*.

"Can we catch them?" Naia called. Onica's boat was small and fast, but once the *Omerya* hit the open ocean, it would be unstoppable. They had to catch up before Ethri cleared the bay.

"I don't know," Onica said. "But we must try."

Kylan grunted, pulling on a rope with all his weight. "And once we do, then what? How do we convince her to join us when she's made up her mind to leave?"

They raced toward the *Omerya* as it broke away from the docks, the dozens of Sifa ships coasting on its typhoonic wake. The coral ship had not reached its full speed yet, its enormous body blocking out the sun with its sparkling coral hull and flowering sails. Amri could barely make out Ethri standing at the bow, Tae at her side.

"Wait!" Naia called. "Maudra Ethri!"

Only Naia's voice could rise above the crashing of the waves on the bow. Amri clung to a rope to keep from being thrown from the bucking deck. Ethri saw them and exchanged a word with Tae, then raised a horn to her lips. The ship slowed, though it did not stop altogether, and the Sifa ships flocked around it.

When the waves subsided, Ethri leaned on the coral taffrail.

"If you're here to try and convince me again, save yourself the effort!" she shouted. "But if you're here to apologize and come with us, you best hurry up. That little ship won't make it across the Silver Sea, even with skekSa's help!"

Amri gulped, glancing out to sea. In all the chaos, he'd forgotten about the gargantuan ship, hiding somewhere beneath the waves. With one blow of skekSa's whistle, it could be right below them, a huge monster ready to swallow them all.

Onica leaped from the deck with surprising swiftness. She didn't even use her wings, one moment airborne with only ocean below her, the next grabbing hold of the ropes and lines that laced the hull of the *Omerya*. She untied one of the lines and threw it to Kylan, shouting orders. He obeyed and quickly tied the rope to their smaller ship's prow so they were pulled along by the *Omerya*.

As soon as Kylan finished the knot, Naia jumped from the boat. She snagged the ropes and climbed up after Onica.

"Are we really doing this?" Kylan asked, eyes wide.

Amri grabbed the song teller's shoulders.

"Yes!" he cried. "We are!"

Salt licked their heels as they leaped. The rope netting was thick in his hands, easy to grab on to, though the rough coral scratched his knuckles and arms as he crashed against the hull. He worried at first Kylan wouldn't make it, but within moments he was close behind, clambering up the netting. Together, they pulled themselves against the wind, finally toppling over the taffrail onto the deck.

Dozens of Sifa were staring, some aghast and some, Amri pretended, in awe. He didn't try to guess how many captains and crew had forsaken their ships in Cera-Na to join their *maudra* in her quest to escape upon the Silver Sea. He recognized Captain Staya, and the other Sifa who had called him a thief on the beach.

By the time Amri got to his feet, Naia and Onica had already found Maudra Ethri on the deck. The *maudra's* dark hair whipped like a storm around her face.

"Ethri!" Onica cried. "You must stop this. You must heed the signs. If you have any faith left in me, as a Far-Dreamer—as your friend!"

"Faith has nothing to do with this, Onica," Ethri said. "A

storm brews in the Skarith Land. That is the sign I'm heeding. The pink petals with their song. The rumors of the Skeksis at the castle, feeding off the Gelfling. I can't be reckless anymore, not with the lives of my clan at stake. I will do what must be done, winds and tides be damned."

She said it all with the force of a gale, but Amri saw the flicker of doubt across her face. He saw the clouds that arced toward land, blowing against the sails even as the *Omerya* struggled to continue out to sea. The cold hearth on the deck, where he imagined the Sifa once lit the fires of prophecy every night.

Onica saw it, too.

"I know you are only afraid," she said. "Please do not let fear change who you are, Ethri. Who I know you to be."

Tae looked between the two Sifa who commanded the attention of all that stood on the deck. She took Ethri's arm in her hand a moment, and Amri remembered when she had begun to say something before, in skekSa's lab. But once more, Ethri brushed her aside, striding forward to meet Onica eye to eye on the lower deck.

"You and Tae trusted me once," Ethri said. "And you alone paid a terrible price."

"In exchange for a wonderful gift, worth the price I paid. One I am grateful for every day."

The Far-Dreamer's soft reply was like the ocean, passionate and eternal. Even Amri felt swept up in it, and he was but a silent witness to her truth. Onica took Ethri's shoulders in her hands, and this time the *maudra* did not protest.

"Ethri, we cannot know the future," Onica said. "We can only heed the signs when Thra whispers. But there is no need to be afraid. Not when we gaze upon the stars with open hearts together. I remember an Ethri who looked into the future with me, unafraid. When is the last time you looked into the Sifa fires? Where is that fearless Ethri I once knew?"

Ethri looked down, shaking her head. "Gone."

"I don't believe it. And I can't be the only one who remembers, and who will challenge you to remember who you truly are."

Onica turned, seeking the eyes of the Sifa who watched her from the deck. One by one, they looked away. Amri remembered what Ethri had said to Naia on the ship: *The first to stand are the first to be struck down.* What a defeating superstition.

Amri jumped when Tae stepped forward. Her hair was a brilliant gold in the rising sun, rippling with pinks and reds. She touched Ethri's shoulder, this time holding her fast with a gentle hand.

"Onica is right," Tae said. "How long has the hearth been cold? Ethri, please. Light the flames of the old ways there. Look into the fires as we used to."

Ethri opened her mouth to protest but stopped when Staya stepped forward.

Then the Sifa to his left. Then another, and another.

"Come, Ethri," Tae said. "Just one last time, unafraid. Let us at least know we asked. If you ask the flames, if you listen, we will follow you to the ends of the earth."

Ethri became young again—became herself for just a

moment—as she watched the Sifa join hands before her. One green eye was weary with fear, the other a crystal stone shining with hope.

"And if the flames say we flee?" she whispered.

Onica approached the fire and held out her hand, beckoning.

"Then we will heed the sign," she said. "And we will heed it together."

The Sifa parted around Maudra Ethri as she walked to the hearth fire. Onica waited for her, hands open and palms filling with sunlight. Ethri took the Far-Dreamer's hands and sighed, as if she'd come home after a long journey.

"Then join with me, my beloved Sifa," Ethri said. "And you, who carry out Aughra's task. Let us see what the future brings."

CHAPTER 13

Amri stood at Naia's side as they joined Onica. Feeling
something greater than himself begin to overcome the
rushing of the wind and the crashing of the waves against the
Omerya's hull.

Ethri stood at the hearth in the center of the deck. It was made
of the same coral as the rest of the ship, reinforced with stone and
black from ages of use. But the coals had been cold for a long time
and Ethri knelt to touch the black dust that coated it.

Tae came to her shoulder. She had a small bundle of herbs in
hand, tied with miniature versions of the knots Amri had seen
everywhere on the *Omerya* and even on Onica's ship. Ethri took
the bundle and split it, giving half back to Tae. She held her own
half against her palm, closing her eyes until her hand glowed blue.
Smoke wafted from where the bundle touched her skin, filling the
air with the savory scent.

Onica took her own bundle from within her cloak. She and
Tae followed Ethri, and soon three blue-gray trails of smoke cut
like pathways into the sky. Onica led them in the ritual, raising
her hands over her head and drawing mystic symbols in the air
with the smoke of the smoldering herbs. Triangles and spheres,
spirals and many other shapes. Amri saw the signs of the moons

and the suns, the sigils of the wind and fire, earth and rain. Ethri and Tae mirrored Onica, the *maudra*'s motions reserved at first but warming with every passing moment.

"Deatea. Deratea. Kidakida. Arugaru. We open our souls to the fire. We open our minds to the wind. We open our hearts to the water. We open our hands to the earth."

Onica lowered the smoldering herbs, drawing a line of smoke from the four directions down into the hearth. She let go, and the bundles lit up in flame, falling like three comets. When they touched the ancient kindling at the bottom of the hearth, all went silent.

Amri held his breath. He wondered if the prayer had failed.

Smoke rose from the depths of the hearth. Fragile at first, like a dying whisper.

Then heat. The smoke blew away, replaced with the clear, hot air of a growing fire. Within moments, the hearth beat again. The hearth of the ship, the heart of the Sifa. Amri joined them as they gathered closer, taking in the warmth, holding out their hands as if they might grasp the radiant flames themselves.

The scent of the herbs was deep now, consumed by the flames. Amri breathed them in, his head filling with space. Stars and suns and moons, the sigils Onica had drawn, drifting in and out of his mind. He closed his eyes and breathed, feeling Naia's hand in his.

Onica's voice rose from the quiet, one with the crackling fire. She did not speak words. The song from her throat was wordless, harmonious. Amri opened one eye to see her, head tilted back, crimson hair alight with the red of the fire. Her song changed, as if she herself were transformed—one moment a Sifa, Gelfling as the rest of them—the next, a different being, made of dreams.

She bowed her head to face the fire, eyes open, seeing all and nothing. All were silent.

"A hero stands before the hearth fire of the Gelfling. But not alone. From the darkness that surrounds him comes . . . Wind. Lightning. Light. Earth, Shadow, Water . . . Fire."

Onica's brows crinkled in pain, a tear escaping. Her voice was transparent, rippling, not her own. Amri listened, rapt. Saw Ethri and Tae, Naia and Kylan doing the same, every breath hanging on the Far-Dreamer's words.

"Great trials face us. Pain and loneliness, I see . . . Seven *maudra*. Seven of seven. Bearing the fires. Wind, Lightning, Light. Earth, Shadow, Water, Fire. In this way, the Seven become One. By Gelfling hand, or else by . . ."

The fire heaved. A vision consumed Amri like a living creature, swallowing his mind. He saw the hearth fire, the silhouette of a Gelfling standing before it, something glowing white from within his fist. The fire of the hearth flickered, struggling to push back the darkness.

From beyond came voices. Voices in song, like instruments. Wind and lightning, a blazing star in the sky. Out of the shadows came Gelfling, bearing torches against the shadows.

And behind them all was a wall, engulfed in flame.

Amri gasped when the vision faded, mind reeling. The flames receded, and Onica opened her eyes. She had returned to herself, swaying slightly before righting, drawing in a deep breath.

"I was there . . . We all are," Ethri murmured. "At the hearth fire."

They had all seen it, then. The Gelfling emerging from the dark, joining before the hearth and thrusting in their flames so the fire blazed brighter. Amri couldn't shake the vision from his mind. He didn't want to. He'd heard those voices before, in the dream-space. When the fire had brightened, he'd seen some of their faces. Recognized them, though he'd never met them. At least not in this life.

Hand upon hand linked together, and Ethri closed her eyes, pulling a deep draw of breath.

"My Sifa," she said. "My heart breaks with grief that I nearly let you down. Forgive me . . . I will stay, if you will stay by my side. So that we may stay by the side of the others who stand against the darkness. For Thra."

Tae lifted her hand to the sky, Ethri's fingers entwined in hers.

"For Thra," she said.

All at once, the hands of the Sifa rose like wildfire.

A pillar of flame exploded from the hearth, sparks showering in a rainbow of colors. The fire burned in every color under the three suns, the whistling and howling of the air as it fed the flames resonating with a familiar, bone-deep song. Kylan's *firca* rang on its own as the wind tore around the deck, sucked up into the brilliance of cascading colors.

Light melted across the deck below their feet, carving and etching the forms of letters and images. Amri saw the ship *Omerya*, a Sifa with wild hair and a crystal eye. A Far-Dreamer and a storm, a behemoth ship lurking below the waves. It was the story that had brought them to this place, to light this fire. The song of the Sifa fire, lit aboard the living coral tree in the bay of Cera-Na.

When the fire calmed, turning orange and red again, the deck was stunned to silence. Amri's face still felt warm where it had been bathed in the light, though his eyes hadn't stung in its brightness. The ring of Gelfling broke hands, the Sifa in awe of what had happened and the proof that remained all around them.

"Fires of resistance," Onica whispered, reading the dream-etchings on the deck. "Gelfling, made of *vliya*. The blue fire, the life essence of Thra . . . We have seen this fire in dreams."

Ethri looked upon the etchings, understanding them. She saw herself in them, and the recognition lit something within her, even brighter than the flame in the hearth. A gust of wind blew her hair back, fanning the fire in her eyes.

She strode back to the foredeck, giving orders to bring *Omerya* back into the bay. Though the ship had barely tasted the waters of the Silver Sea, it heeded commands without complaint, as if relieved. Tae commanded the crew, flying high into the sails and lines. As the *Omerya* came about, it picked up speed, rushing back into the arms of the land it had never wanted to leave.

"First the Vapra and now the Sifa . . . ," Amri said. "That's two of the seven clan fires lit already. I can't believe it!"

"Only five more to go," Naia agreed with a grin.

They looked up as Ethri joined them. For the first time since they'd been in Cera-Na, she seemed like two halves made whole: a *maudra*, proud and valiant leading her clan, and her youthful self. The Ethri that Onica had known and brought back to life.

"Maudra Ethri," Naia said, stepping forth. "Thank you."

They clasped hands. For a moment Amri saw two *maudra* standing on the deck. The faces of the new leaders that might be able to save their world. He wondered what Maudra Argot would think, if she had been there.

"The Sifa flame warms your back," Ethri said. "When it is time to rise against the Skeksis, we will be ready. Ready to heed your call, to join against them wherever that battle may take place. Where do you travel next?"

"I don't know yet. Where the wind takes us."

"Then may it fill your wings."

"And yours. I know you were afraid of being the first to rise. But what we were trying to tell you is that the Vapra fire is already lit. By All-Maudra Mayrin, in Ha'rar. And now there are two fires burning . . ." Naia glanced at Amri, then back to the Sifa *maudra*. "You know, Maudra Argot of the Grottan was actually the first to hear our story and believe. And because of it, they *were* struck down. They lost their home. They've been in the dark and cold, alone. Waiting to know the other clans are out there . . . and now, you are part of their hope. Your fires will guide them . . . You are not alone, and now, neither are they."

Amri shivered. Ethri took in what Naia had said, then looked to him, understanding falling on her fair face. Almost like in a dreamfast, she realized who he was. Where he'd come from, and why. Perhaps she'd mistaken him for a Vapra, or perhaps he'd been invisible to her altogether, but now she looked right into him, and her brow cracked with remorse.

"You have a name, Shadowling?" Ethri asked.

"Amri."

He stiffened when she held her hand toward him, then swallowed the ball of emotions in his throat as he took her palm in his. With her free hand, she pointed at her gem eye, then the other.

"I see you now, Amri. And I will remember."

"Thanks," he said. "I mean, thank you, Maudra."

She chuckled.

"Please. Call me Captain."

As they said their other goodbyes and made their way to the gangplank, Amri stole a last look out into the ocean. Somewhere beneath the waves, Lord skekSa captained her terrible behemoth, overwhelming even the dark of the sea. Soon she would realize the Sifa had changed their minds—if she hadn't already. What would she do when she found out? Would she be angry, or would she show nothing on that shrewd face of hers? If she were truly separate from the rest of the Skeksis, prepared to live out her life beyond the shadow of the castle, perhaps it wouldn't matter to her if Ethri and the Sifa had decided to resist the Skeksis.

Either way, there was no way for Amri to know. Ethri would be the one to face skekSa, but if there was anyone now who could, it was the Sifa *maudra*.

They descended to the main dock. Sifa deboarded around them, breaking out into song and dance with torches in their hands, alight with colored dust.

Onica guided them down to the dock and paused when Kylan cleared his throat. In the rush of the growing celebration, Amri had almost forgotten that they had one more farewell to make. Onica was Sifa. She had only been their guide to Cera-Na, yet Amri's heart ached at the thought of saying goodbye, of returning to their journey without her.

Kylan held Tavra out. Her arachnid body twinkled, blue the color of an unspent tear.

"I must go with Naia," she said. "But I will not forget our promise—"

Onica interrupted her with a sweet laugh. "Don't be daft, my Silverling. You think I would let you go to light the seven fires of resistance without me?"

Onica's grin was contagious. For a precious moment, their daunting task of uniting the Gelfling clans against the Skeksis and the cracked Crystal were nothing but wisps of clouds in the sky. Amri looked across his friends' faces—Drenchen, Spriton, Sifa, Vapra—then down at his Grottan hands. Five of seven.

As they stepped off the dock and onto land amid the throng of celebrating Sifa, Kylan grunted as someone barreled into him.

"Watch it!" Naia shouted, but the hooded figure slipped into the crowd. Kylan pushed his cloak back, patting around his shoulders and neck.

"Tavra?" he stammered. "Tavra!"

Amri leaped into action before he fully knew what he was doing, Naia close behind. He shoved Sifa aside as they caught sight of someone darting up ahead. When the thief glanced back and saw them in pursuit, he broke into a run for the trees that skirted the beach. Amri and Naia left Kylan and Onica behind as they raced after him.

"Why would someone steal Tavra?" Naia asked.

"I don't know! She's tiny, and shiny? You know, we never did figure out where Tae's stolen jewelry went! How are we going to find him in all this?"

"I don't know! But we have to!"

They crashed into the brush at the edge of the beach. There was only a narrow, dense strip of tropical foliage before the ground rose into the Claw Mountains that protected the entire bay. Within moments they were clambering up an incline overgrown with thick-husked trees and vines.

Naia was a strong climber, though Amri was faster than both her and the thief on the sheer rock. He caught glimpses of the thief climbing through the ledges and vines up ahead, every sighting charging his body with urgency as he sprang up the incline. Tavra could only take care of herself to a point—what if the thief put her in a bottle? Thought she was a crystal-singer and crushed her, not knowing she was one of the daughters of the All-Maudra?

Amri vaulted over the side of a steep boulder and leaped, tackling the Gelfling in the hood.

"Gotcha!"

They rolled to the ground and wrestled until Amri came out on top, yanking back the hood. Beneath was the tattooed face of a Dousan boy. His face was pale and sand colored on the left, fading into a deep, glittering indigo on the right.

"Give her back! We know you took her!"

"Her?!" sputtered the boy. "Fine, fine! Just get off me!"

Amri backed up enough for the boy to grapple at his belt where he had a pouch. Inside was a glass jar big enough to keep a spider in. Amri reached for it, taking his attention off the Dousan for a moment too long.

"Fool!"

Amri saw stars, falling back and holding his head where the Dousan had struck him with a stone. The boy leaped to his feet, only to be shoved against a tree by Naia, dagger drawn.

"Don't move," she growled. Then to Amri, "You all right?"

"Yeah, I'm great."

Amri got to his feet as she pressed the flat of her blade against the Dousan's neck.

The boy sighed and raised his hands, and Naia reached into his belt pouch and took out the jar. She pulled the cork with her teeth, and Tavra scurried out. Amri panted in relief when he saw she was intact.

"He has Tae's jewelry in there, too," Tavra said, voice clipped with anger and frustration. "He must have taken advantage of her while she was suffering from the spores."

"You speak well for a crystal-singer," the thief said.

Naia stepped back, now that she had Tavra.

"So, what? You've just been sneaking about Cera-Na filling your pockets. What do you have to say for yourself?"

He shrugged. "It was worth it?"

"We'll see if you still think that after we bring you to Maudra Ethri," she said. She grabbed him by the collar.

"What's a Dousan doing so far from the Crystal Sea?" Amri asked as they made their way down. It was difficult with a captive, but the wiry Dousan didn't seem like a fighter. He did what Naia told him to, eyeing her dagger as a bead of sweat rolled down his temple. If he was a thief, it was probably more likely he'd try to slip out of their grasp when they weren't looking, and Amri wasn't about to let that happen.

"I could ask the same of a Grottan and a Drenchen," the Dousan said, raising a brow and running a hand over his shaved head. "And a pretty trinket with a Vapra accent. Sorry about that, little one. I thought you were a jewel. If I'd known, I never would've—"

"Move!"

"Hey. Hey! Wait a minute."

When they reached the jungle below and Naia walked them out onto the beach, the Dousan turned, hands still up in surrender. Kylan and Onica were waiting for them where the sand met the trees. They nearly melted in relief when they saw the spider on Naia's shoulder.

The Dousan saw he was even more outnumbered than before and waved his hands.

"Maybe we should start over with a proper introduction, eh? My name's Periss. I'm a Dousan. Obviously. And you are . . . ?"

"None of your business," Naia said. She pointed with her dagger toward the *Omerya*. "Let's go."

"Wait! I heard what the Far-Dreamer said down on the beach. About seven fires of resistance, or whatever. And of course I've seen the pink petals. Does that have something to do with the seven clans?"

Naia hesitated. "Yeah? And?"

"Well, I couldn't help but notice you arrived on a sea ship."

"So?"

"So . . . how are you planning on reaching the Dousan clan in the Crystal Sea? Without a, you know. A sandship, and a Dousan to sail it."

Amri hated the smug twinkle in Periss's eyes. Naia crossed her arms.

"No way. I'd rather walk the whole way than go with a thief."

Tavra sighed. "Naia, wait. He's right. We'll never make it without a sand skiff. The desert's sands shift as constantly as the ocean. It's a vast place, dangerous and full of ruthless creatures. And even if we found a way to survive, the Dousan are nomadic. Tracking them on our own could be impossible."

Amri looked up at the Claw Mountains that rose south of Cera-Na's sandy shore. He had never seen the Crystal Sea in person, of course, but he'd seen maps and drawings. On the other side of the Claw Mountains spilled a vast desert of golden and white sand. The desert sprawled southeast, stopping only where its waves of sand lapped the border of the Dark Wood. Between the Claw Mountains and the Dark Wood, it was a world of light and constantly changing terrain. Desert creatures roamed the dunes. It was somewhere out there, navigating the constant storms, that the Dousan Gelfling had made their home.

"I think Tavra may be right," Amri said.

Periss's hands had drifted from the air to his belt, his expression of surrender transforming into a pompous smile. He adjusted his cloak and brushed the dirt and leaves that had stuck to his jerkin when Amri had tackled him.

"So, have we an accord?"

Amri had never seen Naia so reluctant to put away her dagger.

"Let's see this sandship of yours," she grumbled.

South of the bay, through the brush that ringed the beach, was a rocky pass into the Claw Mountains. A sand river cut the ravine like a slow-moving knife, and waiting there was a low-lying craft the size of Onica's ship, made from the skeleton of some flat, wide beast. Periss gestured grandly as they approached.

"I promise my fee will be fair," he said.

"We're not paying you," Naia retorted. "Your reward for helping us is knowing you took part in saving the Gelfling race."

"I'm afraid good feelings don't make my heart as full as a pocket of pretties. So, show me what you have to give, and I will tell you if you've come up short."

Amri wanted to tackle the Dousan again and take his sand skiff as their own. It wasn't right, of course, and he didn't know how to sail the thing at all. But the thief's attitude was so grating, it almost felt like it would be worth it. He didn't want to give up anything, especially not if it was going into the thief's pocket.

But if they were going to reach the Dousan, it was the only way.

"Well?" Periss asked. "Do you want to get going or not? If we leave today, we might reach the Dousan and light that fire by tomorrow morning. Wouldn't that be worth all this?"

Amri frowned. He had his own pouch, but it was filled with spices and dirt, twigs and berries and roots he'd found on their way north. But to a Dousan with an eye for what glittered, Amri's treasures were good as hollerbat dung.

Naia clutched the hilt of her dagger. It had a stone in the handle, and it was Skeksis metal, made in the Castle of the Crystal for her brother. Periss's eyes drifted to her hand, then to Kylan. The Spriton had unconsciously put his hand on his own most precious object, the *firca* hanging at his neck.

"I'll take the dagger and the *firca*," Periss announced. "And, Far-Dreamer, you'll read my bones, once we're asail. Give me those things three, and I'll give you as many days as it takes to find Maudra Seethi and my clan."

Naia gulped. Amri wanted to tell her no, that they would find another way, but he wasn't sure there was one. They had only reached Cera-Na thanks to Onica. Without her help, he wondered how they might have arrived. They would likely have been too late, getting to the bay only in time to see the ships sailing off on the horizon, flanked by skekSa's behemoth ship.

What if it were the same with the Dousan?

Teeth clenched, Naia nodded at Kylan. He closed his eyes and looked down, but he knew it, too. Together, they handed over the dagger and the bone *firca*. Periss stuffed them in his traveling sack and yanked on the line. The sails, made of thin white leather, dropped and the skiff lunged, held in place only by stakes driven into the sand.

The Dousan gestured with a broad smile.

"Congratulations, my friends. You've just bought yourselves a one-way trip into the desert of death."

CHAPTER 14

Sailing on the river of sand was rougher than on the ocean.

The skiff itself was an oval body kept upright by two floats on either side, each balanced by several webbed fins roughly the size of a Gelfling's wings. The rigid parts of the ship were all bone, light and hollow, with leather and woven fabric attached with hardened sinews. Black sand snakes raced alongside the skiff as it cut atop the sand river, all of them carried by the current and propelled by a strong wind that howled along the bottom of the ravine.

Still, Amri preferred the skiff to the ships on the sea. Though the sands were ever changing, they were still of the earth. Still rock and dirt and crystal, and he could just make out their whispers. Like a million voices, speaking all at once, resonating against the deep tones of the red cliffs.

Periss handled the ship alone, leaving the rest of them to sit, holding on to the rope loops knotted into the deck.

"At this speed, we'll cross the Claw Mountains and reach the desert within two days' time," Onica said. "At least our guide wasn't lying about the integrity of his craft."

"Then it's worth it," Naia said, hand on her belt where her dagger used to sit.

Kylan hadn't been able to give up his part of the payment as easily. From Naia's dreamfasts, Amri had seen her let go of her brother's dagger once before. But Kylan had created the bone *firca* from his bare hands, and performed perhaps the single most rebellious act against the Skeksis with it. But Periss didn't know that, and Amri hoped he never would. It would make getting the instrument back all the more difficult.

Periss tied the sails off as they entered a long, straight stretch of the ravine. The immense cliffs cast a shadow that flooded the gorge with blue, highlighting the wedge of gold light at the far end where the river would eventually empty into the desert. Periss swaggered back to the deck where his passengers sat, easily keeping his balance without holding on to the many rope loops that flopped about the ship's architecture. He dropped down, cross-legged, on the open end of their circle.

"You've made a good investment, so let's make merry." He gestured to his shaved head, covered in tattoos. "Since I'll be your guide and protector as we make way into a dangerous landscape, I should know your names, eh? So I can shout them before you make any stupid decisions that will get us all killed."

"We already met. I'm Naia."

"Drenchen, yes. I've got waterskins belowdecks for you; you'll need them and I'll sell them to you at a good rate. You're the leader of this little crew?"

The question had never been asked. Amri had always assumed Naia was their leader, though Onica and Tavra were both older. Not to mention that Tavra was the daughter of the All-Maudra.

Despite her station, though, she was also a spider now, and it was Naia who had seen the Crystal and led the charge on every other account.

"Yes," Naia said.

"And you're one of the Gelfling the Skeksis are after, eh? Along with the Stonewood, what's his name. Rian?" Periss lifted a finger, scanning their faces for the sign of a woodland Gelfling. "Hm, so he's elsewhere. Then you, Spriton, must be Kylan the Song Teller. Who bewitched the Sanctuary Tree that grows near the Grottan Tomb of Relics."

"You're surprisingly well-informed," Kylan muttered.

"My father always told me I have many knives. And you— you're Onica. I've heard your name around Cera-Na. Saw what you did aboard the coral ship. They say you're a talented Far-Dreamer."

Onica was the least perturbed by the ship's turbulent shaking, kneeling casually with one rope loop nearby in case of rough sand. "They aren't wrong," she said.

"And what about you?"

"Amri." He was really starting to hate that question. "The Mysterious."

"I've never heard of Amri the Mysterious."

"That says more about you than it does about me."

Periss snorted. "All right, Amri the Mysterious. Naia, Kylan, Onica. That leaves one piece I haven't got figured out . . . the spider with the Ha'rarian accent. Speaks like a princess, that one. I'd heard one of the All-Maudra's own daughters got caught up in this mess with the Skeksis. Disappeared in the Castle of the Crystal.

There was a reward for songs of her whereabouts, though I think by now many believe her to be dead. You all wouldn't happen to know anything about that?"

Amri had lost track of Tavra, though he guessed she wasn't invisible by accident.

"Nothing indeed," Onica said, mildly changing the subject. "As for you, Periss. I agreed to read your bones. I expect you have some? I don't lend my own to read for thieves."

Periss grinned broadly and tilted so he could reach into the small of his back, under his cloak. He must have had a second pack there, a slim one hidden by the folds of red fabric. Out came a pouch, and then a soup cup carved from another piece of bone. He handed both to Onica.

"Have you ever had your bones read?" she asked, tossing the pouch in her hand. Over the roaring of the sand below the skiff, Amri heard dry jangling.

"Never. I'm quite intrigued!"

Onica poured a handful of tiny bone fragments into the cup. Holding the cup in one hand and placing the palm of her hand over the top to keep the contents inside, she shook the bones. Amri had never seen bones read and wished it were under different circumstances. Then again, if Onica had bad news to tell, he would rather it were to Periss than any of their friends.

"I stole those from a Sifa soothsayer," Periss remarked, ill-placed pride poking at the corners of his smirk. "They're authentic."

Onica smiled her usual mysterious smile, as if everything Periss said washed off her like ocean wind. With a swift motion, she plunged the cup, upside down, onto the toughened leather of the deck. She leaned over the cup and fixed Periss with an electric, turquoise gaze.

"Love, life, or death?" she asked.

Periss returned her smile. "I'm Dousan, sweetling. I don't need to know about my death. Tell me about love."

Onica pressed her hands against the cup, holding it down on the skin of the deck. She closed her eyes and drew in a deep breath. As she let it out, her shoulders drooped and her head tilted back.

"Hmm . . . Your heart yearns. I see a plant . . . No, a tree, growing in rich soil. Hands reach down, grasp the stem. Pull it out, roots and all. There's a hole left, but the hole goes deeper than the tree ever grew . . . No matter what you pour in, it never fills."

Periss's face didn't change, still set with that smug smile. Trying not to be vulnerable, Amri thought. Trying not to appear intimidated by the Far-Dreamer's words. Onica tilted her head to one side, moving her hands along the cup without lifting it.

"Yet you try . . . Restless and unrelenting. You seek love, but cannot find it. You believe it is because you don't deserve it. But the truth is, love is the only thing that can heal the wound. You are looking in the wrong place. Outside, when you should be looking within. You look to what you can take from the future, instead of mourning what you've forsaken in the past."

"All that without even looking, eh?" Periss said, resting one elbow on his knee and his cheek on his fist. "Impressive. Can't wait to hear what you can read off the bones themselves."

Onica opened her eyes, gaze falling from the skies down to

the Dousan in front of her. She put a hand on the cup.

"The bones say . . ."

She lifted the cup. The wind rushing along the deck blasted through, scattering the bones in a cloud of gray shards. Periss yelped and grabbed after them, but they were already lost to the wind and sands.

". . . That you shouldn't ask for bone readings on a moving sand skiff."

Periss growled in frustration. He snatched the cup from Onica, then realized he'd shown a real emotion, even if it was anger. He coughed and put the cup away, reabsorbed by his nonchalant arrogance.

"I suppose I deserved that," he said.

Onica shrugged. "Now I've told you your fortune. You can tell us ours. What will we face in the desert, and what can we do to be sure of our success?"

She leaned back, and Amri felt a swell of respect. Tavra couldn't have chosen a more formidable partner, and now she was his friend and ally, too. Periss accepted his chagrin with surprising grace, spreading his hands.

"As you know, there is a great desert that fills the space between the Claw Mountains and the northwestern border of the Dark Wood. My people call it many things, but the name that has stuck is the Desert of the Dead."

"Sounds promising," Amri said under his breath.

"On the northern edge, where the desert pools in mountain bays, there are four seas. The Crystal Sea is where we head. During the season of storms, my people gather there until the winds are less fierce."

"The Crystal Sea is deep inland," Amri said. He'd seen many maps of the area in the Tomb. Although he knew there were also similar maps in Kylan's book, he didn't want Periss to know about any more of their precious possessions. "Is your ship durable enough to weather the storms?"

"This ship is made from the bones of my ancestor's Crystal Skimmer. It will outlive us all. It is we mortal folk who will need to prove ourselves."

"And how do we know you're not just taking us out into a wasteland to leave us, after you steal every last thread from our hems?" Kylan asked.

Periss snorted. "I may be a treasure seeker, but the Dousan pride ourselves on our word." Periss paused. He looked like he wanted to spit. "Words are the only thing worth keeping in this world, or so says Maudra Seethi." This statement sounded well rehearsed, as if he'd been forced to repeat it many times.

"Treasure seeker? What a fine way to say thief," Naia said.

"Call me what you like. We've made a deal, and I'll honor my end of it if you honor yours."

The Dousan boy stood, brushing himself free of the sand that had gathered since he'd sat, and waved over his shoulder as he left them to stand at the bow of the skiff. Naia rolled her eyes and touched the sand in her own lap. They had only been sailing for half a day, and she was already looking pale, as if the color were being drained from her by the bone-dry air. Amri hoped it wasn't a bad sign. He gestured with his chin.

"Are you going to be all right?"

She looked at her fingertips, lips quirking.

"I'll live. Even if I have to pay for those waterskins he mentioned."

"If he's wise, we'll travel at night and rest during the day, once we reach the basin," Tavra remarked. It was one of the first plans she'd had that Amri wholeheartedly liked, but he didn't say so. He was just glad when Onica replied,

"And if he's not wise, I will educate him."

"Did you really read his bones through the cup?" Kylan asked.

The Far-Dreamer's smile was mysterious and misleadingly demure.

"Oh, I read his bones," she said. "Just not the ones in the cup."

CHAPTER 15

When night fell, Kylan mildly suggested that Amri take the first watch. At first Amri thought it was a rude thing to volunteer for someone else, but then he realized that first watch meant *night watch*. So, while the others went belowdecks to rest, Amri sat on the bow of the ship, watching the desert basin draw slowly nearer. There he sat all night, hand on a rope loop, the subtle thought of kindness from the song teller keeping him warm.

Later, as the sky lightened, Naia joined him. Her eyes were red and her cheeks wan.

"Are you all right?"

"Had a bad dream. I'll be fine."

"Want to talk about it?"

She sat beside him. "I dreamed I was in Sog again . . . as Gurjin. A windsifter came with a message for my mother. I . . . Gurjin . . . went to my mother's chamber to hear what news it brought, but all I saw was this horror in her face. And then I woke up." Naia groaned and rubbed at her face with her hands. "I don't know what the message said, but it was bad. Very bad."

"Do you think it's an omen? Maybe you should ask Onica."

"She's sleeping. I'll ask her when she wakes . . . You should rest, too, nightbird."

Amri stood and yawned. Then he added, "Birds die in caves."

"Night*worm*, then."

"They're called nurlocs."

"Go on!"

Before he left, he put a hand on her shoulder.

"It was just a dream," he reminded her, even though he knew they both had the feeling it wasn't.

The lower deck was cramped, but there were woven hammocks hanging from the ceiling, and Amri climbed into a vacant one. The bumping of the ship was absorbed into the gentle swinging of the hammock, and his exhaustion overtook him in moments.

"Amri! Get up, hurry!"

Amri tumbled out of his hammock, hitting the tough underdeck. He didn't remember falling asleep, but he must have. Daylight burned through the slats of the deck above. Kylan pulled him up as the floor tilted and lurched, then slammed down with a bone-jarring crash. Amri scrambled to grab hold of one of the many lines strung along the ceiling.

"What's going on?" he shouted as they clawed their way above deck.

"There's a storm—and Crystal Skimmers—"

Bright chaos blasted his eyes.

The ravine was gone. In its place was unending white and gold sand, reflecting the light of the Three Brothers like fire. To their right, the sky ended in a cloud of gray dust crackling with lightning rolled like a monster with fire in its teeth. It boiled, unleashed and unconstrained like a whirlpool, in the wide desert.

Amri peered the best he could into the raging storm. The approaching sand clouds teemed with horrific golden creatures. Their diamond-shaped bodies were bigger than the skiff, the size of the three-masted Sifa ships, with rough, ragged manes and long barbed tails. The creatures crashed out of the sands turned up by the storm to the left and the right and all around them, snapping with enormous gaping mouths. It was only Periss's and Onica's shouting and pulling against the skiff's side floats and boom that kept them upright.

"They're darkened creatures!" Naia shouted. "Look at their eyes!"

As one of the Crystal Skimmers shouldered against the skiff, shrieking in a rage, Amri saw its eye—violet and electric, lens scarred by the crystal sands. Infected by the darkness spreading from the Crystal, even in such a remote place as the Crystal Sea.

As much as Periss pulled against the sail, the storm grew. Soon it would overtake them.

"But how? From the storm?" Amri cried.

"They came busting out of the sand-shield when we passed," yelled Onica. "We would have made it around the storm if they hadn't been in there! What were they doing?"

Periss stared into the flashes of magenta and purple lightning that cracked through the dark clouds. "This is no natural storm! It must have caught them by surprise, too—these are darkened beasts?"

There was no time to answer. A Crystal Skimmer rammed alongside the starboard float. The skiff shuddered, and Amri clung to the ropes and prepared for the small ship to capsize. Instead, the skiff took an unexpected and stomach-turning swing. Something dragged on the port side while the starboard float hoisted high in the air. Amri gasped in horror when he realized what had happened.

"The ropes are caught on the Skimmer's . . ."

On the Skimmer's *what?*

Periss raced upward, climbing the deck of the near-vertical skiff like a wall. The others wrapped their arms through the hand lines.

The Crystal Skimmer shrieked, jerking and bucking while racing along the top of the sand. As Amri squinted against the sand, he realized the Skimmer had a structure strapped to its back. Although mostly destroyed from the mad Skimmer's thrashing and the storm, the parts that remained were clearly Dousan handiwork.

"Is that a harness attached to the Skimmer?" Amri shouted as Periss made it toward the top of the skiff.

"I know this Skimmer!" Periss said. "Hanja, listen to me! Calm yourself!"

"You can't reach her, she's seen the darkness!" Onica climbed swiftly past Amri, reaching the top of the skiff and making her way out to the float. She pulled a dirk from her belt. "We have to cut the skiff loose, or she'll drag us to death! Amri, stay there! I'll need you to grab me when we're cut free. Kylan, you wait for Periss—Naia, hold the mast!"

Onica's command was sterner than the storm, pushing aside

all of Amri's fears of the raging storm that had infected the Skimmers with its darkness. He focused on what she'd told him to do, hooking his feet in the rope loops and grabbing hold of the starboard side of the skiff. Onica dragged herself out to the float. Periss did the same on the bow end of the skiff, and Kylan struggled to make it to the edge so he could grab the Dousan when it was time.

Onica worked quickly, cutting away at the Skimmer's harness where the float intertwined with it. As she reached the last strap and put her blade below it, she shouted at Periss,

"Ready?"

"On three! One—two—THREE!"

Their blades cut and the straps snapped. The Skimmer jerked away and the skiff shook, for a moment standing on its port side and skidding along the sand so quickly and wildly, Amri was sure they would tip or splinter into a thousand pieces. He reached for Onica and grasped her hand, pulling her toward him as Naia worked the sail, and the starboard float started to head toward the sand again.

Amri grabbed both of Onica's hands in his.

"Gotcha!"

Just as the starboard float glanced off the racing sand below, another Skimmer burst from below them. Amri felt Onica's fingernails rip against his palm as the Skimmer snagged her in its enormous mouth, tearing her from his grasp.

"ONICA!"

The skiff balanced, and Periss lunged at the boom, helping

Naia turn the sail to whip back toward the Skimmer that had taken Onica, but the beast was already pulling away.

"Follow it!" Naia bellowed.

Through the wind and sand, they could see Onica dangling out of the Skimmer's toothless mouth. She struck at its lips with her knife, but the thing was so mad, it didn't seem to feel the pain. Periss threw himself against the boom, and the skiff whipped in an arc, nearly a tailspin, in its pursuit.

"I'm trying!"

The Skimmer raced through the sand, diving and leaping in massive, air-bound swoops as it circled the horizon of the storm. Periss wrestled with the ship, holding it as steady as he could against the buffeting, searing wind. The Skimmer lanced through the dunes like a fish bouncing through choppy water, in higher and higher bounds, riding the storm winds with its enormous fins.

"She'll have to fly down to us," Periss shouted as they flanked it, falling under its silhouette as it leaped overhead, crashing down into the sand only to shoot higher the next time. "It's too high!"

"She can't fly."

The tiny, numb voice came from the folds of Amri's cloak.

"What?"

"She lost her wings in a storm," Tavra said. "She can't fly."

Amri stared up at the Skimmer and the Sifa girl in its mouth. Her efforts to pull free of the creature's mouth had eased, one of her arms slack. Every time the Skimmer dived back into the sand, he expected it to leap out again with Onica lost down its throat.

"She can't fly," he told the others. There was no way they could hear Tavra over the storm. Naia's face paled, and she tore off her cloak.

"I'll go."

"No! Naia, you can't—the desert air will destroy your wings!" Kylan cried, grabbing her arm. She whirled on him, knocking him away.

"What am I supposed to do, let her die? At least I *have* them!"

But Kylan was right. Naia's Drenchen wings, usually lustrous and shimmering, were dull and thin from the dry desert air. There was no way she would be able to hold a current.

"I've got it," Amri said.

"But, Amri—"

Amri ignored his friends' protests and raced to the floats, climbing along the arms that held them to the deck. He landed on the shuddering float and tugged, snapping off two of the guiding sails of bone and skin. In the ravenous storm, the two missing fins hardly made a difference. He slipped his arms through the first two rope loops so they fit along his shoulders and elbows, leaving the last loops for his hands.

"Tavra, do it! Do what you did before on skekSa's ship. Take over my body so we can save Onica!"

Amri yelped and fell to all fours as the Skimmer thundered down beside them, nearly tipping the skiff on the wave of sand that flew from under its fins. The wind was so strong, it almost knocked him off the float as it hit the sails strapped to his arms. Amri grabbed the third rope loop on the sails, bracing himself.

No, not sails—*wings*.

"Amri, I didn't do it on purpose before," Tavra protested. "It was an accident! I don't know how!"

"Well," he growled, "you're going to have to figure it out!"

He leaped and spread his arms.

The wind picked him up like a hand, thrusting him into the sky. The gusts were like waves, coming from every direction, knocking him and twirling him higher and higher. He had no idea how to navigate, how to fall—how to *fly*. All he could do was try to keep his arms from breaking as the wind battered and beat him.

"You and Onica made a promise!"

"But I can't—"

"Are you going to break your promise?"

Amri's scream tore through his lungs, all the air evaporating from his body. He lost himself in the moment, blinded by the storm and the wind. Then a different kind of storm overwhelmed him as Tavra's dreamfast crashed into his mind.

He saw Onica's eyes, deep and green as the sea, wreathed in fiery hair thick with salt wind. They were in a storm, at sea this time. Onica clung to the little ship as it broke into pieces around her. Her wings, once green and amber, were in shreds at her back, pierced and battered by pieces of the ship and the unforgiving hail.

Protected below her was another Sifa with golden-red hair. Tae, safe in Onica's arms, even as the wind and the sky drove lances of ocean water against them.

Amri was Tavra in this dreamfast. Prevailing against the storm. Untangling the two Sifa from the wreckage, spreading her wings just enough to ride the violent wind. Up and away, leaving the tiny vessel to be ravaged by the jaws of the storm . . .

Promise me, someday we'll sail away.

Tavra and Onica sat together on a misty shore, watching the tide bring in shards of crystalline ice. The seafarer's lantern glowed nearby, dimly lighting the fog that surrounded them like a protective blanket. They were hidden there, by the silver mist. Or at least they could pretend they were, just for this moment.

To a place where no one can find us. Where there are no Sifa . . . no Vapra . . .

Their hands touched palm to palm, fingers weaving together.

Where it doesn't matter. Where we can just be . . . one.

Amri gasped, thrown from the dreamfast. He squeezed his eyes against the sand and wind, but the barrage had weakened. He wondered at first if the storm had let up, and opened his eyes.

The storm winds raged as angry as ever, but his arms moved as if he could anticipate them, flitting up and down along them as easily as slipping down a riverbed.

They were flying. He and Tavra, swooping and diving, racing along the invisible currents, light as a moth and fierce as a Vapra soldier. He barely felt Tavra's legs where they pricked his skin, driving in, whispering to his body how to move: how to see the wind as a terrain like any other element.

"There!"

The Crystal Skimmer leaped through the sands just below them. Amri's arms folded, and they dived . . . then Tavra spread their skiff-sail-wings and banked at the last moment, popping up on the draft that rolled off the Skimmer's fins. Amri caught sight

of Onica, hanging limply out of the Skimmer's mouth.

"No!"

The willpower that had flooded his body with the wisdom of flight vanished. He grappled at the fur around the Skimmer's mane, barely taking hold of it before his wings were ripped away by the sand and wind.

"Tavra, get it together!" he groaned. Hand over hand he climbed through the Skimmer's mane toward its mouth. Onica was unconscious, one of her arms badly misshapen, blood streaking across her face and body where she'd been struck by the millions of grains of sand. Amri buried his face in the Skimmer's mane as it dived, nearly losing his grip as the sand crushed over them, then gasping for air as it surfaced. He grabbed Onica and pulled her from the Skimmer's mouth. Holding her tight and hoping for the best, he kicked away just as the Skimmer neared the sand again.

Every bone ached as they rolled to a stop. The storm roared above and all around them, geysers of sand popping up where the Skimmers charged in an uncontrolled stampede. Amri held Onica in his arms, unable to tell in all the chaos if she was even breathing.

He stood, tried desperately to find Periss's skiff, but it was impossible. All he could see was gold and black, the storm and the din and the deafening howls of the Skimmers. He pulled Onica with him, trudging—any direction, it didn't matter, he only wanted to be anywhere else. The sand burned his eyes, washed against his ankles, then his knees. He tried to listen, but its voices were too many. Millions of screaming sand-crystals, earth moving like water, singing in a tongue he couldn't understand.

He turned as the ground shook. A Skimmer erupted under his feet, and Amri's own scream was lost as the beast's black maw swallowed them alive.

CHAPTER 16

Amri woke floating in a calm darkness and wondered if he was dead.

He saw lights. Little gold ones, flitting inside glass jars strung up by rope. Dousan rope, he noticed, and then he sat up. The ground under his hand was soft and damp, and it moved slightly when he touched it. The air was dank and smelled of fish and dust, and there was a distant groaning coming from somewhere.

The first person he saw was Periss, who said, "I guess you're alive."

"You did it!"

Amri grunted as Naia threw her arms around him. His body ached everywhere, like it was one big bruise, but the Drenchen girl's embrace soothed the pain as quickly as if she'd used her healing *vliyaya*. Next to him, Onica was wrapped up to her chin in cloaks and blankets. Tavra held fast to a lock of her hair, dangling like an earring.

"Oh no . . . is she . . ."

He suddenly remembered the dreamfast he'd shared with Tavra. The memory of Onica and Tae in the little boat torn apart by the storm. How Tavra had saved them, fearless and strong.

Naia shook her head, and his heart calmed.

"She's fine. She's just resting now. She took a beating from the Skimmer, but I was able to heal her . . . Amri, you were amazing. Sandmaster Erimon said he's never seen anything like it!"

"Sandmaster who?"

She pointed. Another Dousan, taller than Periss but with a familiar brow and similar tattoos, watched from nearby. Other Dousan lingered near the wall, curious but quiet. Amri rubbed his eyes and tried to stand. Erimon broke away from where he stood with Periss and the other Dousan to meet Amri. He clasped his shoulder.

"I'm glad you survived, my friend," he said. "I saw what you did, out in the storm. It would have been a tragedy to lose someone with your courage. Where did you learn to fly?"

"It's a long story," Amri said. He blushed and wriggled out from under Erimon's hand. "Um, so where are we, anyway?"

"Tappa," Naia said with a broad grin.

"What's a Tappa?"

A big gurgling groan rippled along the slightly shiny, viscous walls of the chamber, and Amri got a bad feeling. The surface under his feet shifted, and Erimon chuckled.

"Tappa isn't a what, she's a who. Come on, I'll show you."

Naia and Amri followed Erimon to a row of tall, narrow windows near the front of the chamber. The living chamber, Amri noted, as he watched the slick surface undulate with more and more fingerling cilia the closer they got to the doors. The exit holes themselves were lined with spongy frills like a mushroom. A rope net was tacked inside the chamber wall, folding out of the exit passage and onto the hull of the vessel's—of *Tappa's* exterior.

Amri grabbed the net and followed Erimon out into the open air. They climbed up the rigging to the platform lashed onto Tappa's wide back. Other Dousan minded the rigging, one driver up at the front near Tappa's nose with a long cane that he used to gently punctuate his shouted orders.

Tappa, the Crystal Skimmer, swam across the intolerable heat wafting from the sands, like a leaf on a river. The storm was behind them, rolling across the desert like a herd of great black beasts. Half the sky was light, the other dark, and it seemed no matter how fast Tappa raced toward the red mountains in front of them, the storm was gaining.

Erimon looked at the storm wall with them and grimaced.

"Our clan is divided into twelve groups—xerics—each led by a sandmaster. We rarely gather in one place, but Maudra Seethi summoned us. My xeric and I were headed to the Wellspring when the storm hit. A tail of it rose up from the sand and cut us off from one of the pods . . . the Skimmers spooked and dived. The ones swallowed by the storm must have seen something below the sand. It drove them mad." He peered at Naia, then Amri. "But if your Spriton friend is the one who sent the dream on the pink petals, then I presume you already know this."

"The darkened veins must have reached the desert," Naia said quietly. "The Skimmers saw the pain of the Crystal and were consumed by it . . . This is horrible. I can't believe it's already spread this far."

"So you received the message, then?" Amri asked Erimon.

"Indeed. It explained many of the dark days we have seen, here in the crystal sands. The storms, which once followed trails as regular as the stars and have coexisted with the Dousan for generations, are erratic and unpredictable. It is still difficult to believe the Skeksis are to blame, but there are few alternate explanations. It can only be darkening, as you said. Caused by what the lords have done to the Heart of Thra."

Despite the fact that the darkening had even reached the desert, Amri felt a spark of optimism. The darkening might have come this far, but perhaps hope had, too.

"So you believe?" he asked.

"Yes, my friend. And I'm honored to have been the one to rescue you from that storm. I'm just glad Tappa was strong enough to look away from the darkening and endure so we could find you in time."

Erimon glanced over his shoulder where Kylan and Periss were surfacing to the deck and added, "Periss can sail and read the skies, but not as well as he should. Our father always said he has many knives, but none of them are sharp."

"Your *brother?*" Naia exclaimed. She coughed. "You two are day and night."

"I'll take that as a compliment," Erimon said. Amri wondered if Periss would have said the same. As if summoned, the younger of the Dousan brothers joined them, arms crossed and a grim knot in his forehead.

Kylan was with him. He clasped Amri's arm and squeezed.

"I'm so glad you're safe," he said. "You saved Onica's life, you know. When we're done on our quest, I'll sing your song over the flames of the seventh fire."

"I had help."

That was an understatement, but there wasn't time to explain everything. Amri looked back at the storm wall behind them, cutting them off from the rest of the desert like a black-and-gold curtain. He could hardly believe they had survived crossing through. Then again, they wouldn't have if it hadn't been for Erimon, and Onica could have died from her injuries if not for Naia.

"We'll reach our destination soon," Erimon said. "Up there, where the mountains come close like a hand, there is a pass. On the other side is an oasis valley."

Amri squinted at the clouds and lightning. After how far they'd traveled, and at such speed, he felt as if it should have been farther away.

"The storm wall won't enter the valley?" he asked.

"It never has before."

"But the darkening—"

"It never has before," Erimon repeated, with a hard look that dared Amri to ask again.

"Is the oasis where you were taking us?" Naia asked Periss.

"That was the plan," Periss replied. All of his arrogance was strapped down, now that he was around his older—and much more likable, in Amri's opinion—brother. Amri glanced out over the desert and realized something.

"But you only got us halfway," he said. "Erimon and Tappa are doing the rest. I'd say we paid you more than you earned. How about you give Kylan back that *firca*, and we'll call it even?"

Erimon arched a brow. "You made them pay you to bring them here?"

Periss shoved his hands into his elbows, crossing his arms tightly as if it could lock away the *firca*. But he soon crumbled under his brother's disapproving grimace. With a huge grumble and sigh, he took Naia's dagger from his belt and thrust it at her.

"But I'm keeping the *firca*. My skiff will need repairs, and I know someone who will trade his services for it."

Then he stomped away and ducked belowdecks again. Naia made a rude gesture after him.

"It's all right, Naia," Kylan said. "Really. The *firca* was made to send the message with the Sanctuary Tree. It's done its duty. I'll make another one. After all, there seem to be plenty of bones around."

"He's such a . . . !" Naia growled. Still, she sheathed her dagger at her belt and turned to Erimon. "What's his problem, anyway?"

The Dousan sandmaster shrugged one shoulder.

"He ran away three trine ago. He'd always been discontent with the Dousan way, but we never thought he would leave . . . then one morning, he left without a note. The only reason we knew he hadn't been eaten by a pit-shark was that my skiff was gone."

Amri snorted. "His first theft?"

"And apparently not his last . . ." Erimon's pointed ears perked up when the crew hollered. "We're arriving. Hold on to something and enjoy the ride."

The ruby facets of the mountains were suddenly upon them, rising up on either side like the claws of a giant. Erimon took a whistle from his pocket and blew a chattering signal, sending the crew rushing to action. Tappa crested a dune, and Amri caught a glimpse of green and blue, nestled in a deep valley of sands like an emerald. He grabbed one of the hand-loops on the rail as Tappa went into a near free fall, gliding down the steep dune toward the oasis. Erimon shouted orders, calmly monitoring the Skimmer's speed and strength.

"All tilt, spiral descent! Nice and easy for our guests, eh!"

The driver tapped at Tappa and clucked to her. She sang a deep *MNNNUUUUU* in reply and tilted, ever so slightly, and her course warped into an easy spiral descending toward the bottom.

Amri couldn't take his eyes off the lush oasis waiting below, except to grin at Naia and Kylan, who returned the expression with eager excitement. The waters in the long lake reflected the sky, topaz and indigo. Growing along the waterfront, trees in amber and red and gold sprouted and bloomed, crowned with the roosts of flying creatures. Though the storm wall lingered behind them, Amri tried to put it out of his mind. At least for now.

The air was sweet with the scent of fruit as Tappa slowed, big body gently plowing into the soft sand that was prepared for her on the bank. While Erimon helped the driver with the reins and rigging, Amri, Naia, and Kylan climbed back belowdecks to find Onica was awake.

"How are you feeling?" Amri asked.

"Grateful to be alive. Naia, is this your work?" Onica ran her hands along her arms, where all the scratches and bruises had been healed. All that was left was dirt and dust from the sands. Naia helped Onica to her feet.

"For a friend, it's never work," she said. "Amri's the one who saved you."

Tappa groaned and opened her mouth, filling the chamber with light. The Dousan sailors tossed rope ladders out. As they climbed down and on to the sand, Amri wondered how Tappa felt about carrying passengers in her mouth. He saw Tavra on Onica's shoulder and imagined what it would be like if she rode around on his tongue all day like they'd done to the Crystal Skimmer. *Blech.*

Amri lingered behind with Onica when Kylan and Naia went ahead.

"Thank you for coming after me," Onica said. "Tavra told me what you did. It sounds quite amazing."

Amri shook his head. It had been thrilling when it had happened, but now that it was over, all he could think about was how he wouldn't have been able to do anything if it hadn't been for Tavra. Her knowledge of flight and navigating the air. It was a daylighter's skill in the daylighter world that had saved Onica.

"It wasn't really me. It was Tavra. If she'd been able to do it herself, she would have been able to rescue you faster . . . Maybe you wouldn't have gotten hurt." He coughed awkwardly. He felt as if Onica should know the part of the dreamfast Tavra had shared with him, even if by accident. "I saw what happened. In the storm, when you were with Tae . . . I'm sorry about your wings."

Onica stood and put herself together. She'd lost her cloak in the storm, and now, through the opening on the shoulders and back of her jewel-tone tunic, the truth was painfully obvious. Where her wings would have been, there were only scars and uneven, long-healed ridges. She sighed, not in sadness but in remembrance, as if recalling a loved one who had died. The grief was still there, but she had accepted it.

"I had a dream, before I met Tavra. That a sun and a moon would eclipse over a storm at sea. In the dream, Tae was the sun. A silver-haired Vapra was the moon. Tae was excited to go, to find the Silverling to whom she would be bound. I was worried, that we would find danger by running off to follow my Far-Dream. But she and Ethri told me not to be afraid. Tae and I went in search of bad weather near Ha'rar . . . we found a storm indeed."

Onica smiled, and the two of them followed Erimon's crew down into the oasis below. Amri shivered. He could imagine Tae as a sun, with her radiant red-and-gold hair. And the other, a Vapra soldier, silver as the moon.

"I lost my wings that day. Tae thinks she is responsible even now. But she often forgets that it was because of the storm that I met Tavra." Onica finished the thought as they stepped out into the light of the day. Shielding her eyes, she added, "Dreams do not always end as we expect. End and beginning are one and the same. That is what I learned that day, and a lesson I relearn every day since."

Amri looked down, absorbing the Far-Dreamer's words.

"Did Tae ever find her Silverling?" he asked.

Onica shook her head and replied, "The reckoning of that eclipse has yet to come."

The Wellspring looked as if a part of the jungle had been plucked up by a big bird and deposited in the middle of the otherwise empty-seeming crystal sands. Had the storm wall not lingered so close over the shoulder of the mountains, Amri pictured it being nothing less than a verdant paradise.

Erimon led the way with Periss at his elbow. The two brothers captured the attention of the red-cloaked Dousan they passed. In Erimon's case, the greetings were warm, followed by bows of respect. Periss followed, jaw set tight, trying to ignore the surprised gasps as he was recognized.

Tents and canopies built from bones and hide were set up along the shore of the lake, temporary but sturdy shelters that Amri imagined could easily be dismantled, rolled up, and carried by only one or two Gelfling. In Grot, there was shelter everywhere, and one was never far from the trickling of fresh water coming down from the Sanctuary. Even on the ocean, there were storms and drinkable rain. But here the nomadic life was the only way to stay alive.

A row of Dousan bearing bones etched in patterns that matched their tattoos walked by. Out of the tops of the bones wafted a silvery smoke that filled the air with an earthy, woody scent. They did not look up as they passed, not even to acknowledge the visitors. Erimon stepped aside and bowed his head, the entire exchange transpiring in complete silence.

When the incense bearers had passed, Erimon continued down the footpath.

"The Wellspring is the only place where water flows in all seasons, and the mountains protect this haven from storms," he explained as they walked. "It is here where the Dousan gather in times of trouble."

"It is truly a time of trouble," Kylan agreed.

"Indeed. Since receiving your message, and seeing proof of the song it told, Maudra Seethi summoned the sandmasters of the twelve Dousan xerics. We gather here in the Wellspring to meditate. The Skeksis have long ruled Thra, and their ways have become our ways in many regards. As a clan we must reflect on how we are to respond. How to change our rituals of the present and of the future."

"Does this mean you've lit a fire?" Amri asked. He could hardly believe it, but maybe it was true. If the Dousan had already decided to stand against the Skeksis, then it would have been worth all the danger they'd overcome to get here.

Erimon tilted his head. "We light fires every evening. The desert is very dark at night."

"No, not that," Naia said. "We were asked by Aughra to travel to the clans and light the fires of the resistance. But it sounds as if you've received our message, and you believe the Gelfling must rise up against the Skeksis."

"Indeed. We have heard of the troubles and seek answers."

"That's not what she means," Periss interrupted hotly. But Erimon gave him such a cold look that he didn't elaborate. The sandmaster warmed his expression when he turned to Naia.

"The Gelfling are in peril, that much is true. The Skeksis

can no longer be trusted. The Dousan have always believed the answers are in Thra's eternal song. An ancient sage brought us these traditions, when the Dousan first found the Wellspring. He taught us to meditate, to guard the rituals of the earth and the song of Thra. It is our way to guard those rituals as well, in his absence. In the tranquility of that meditation, if Thra wishes to speak to us, it will. It is all we can do, to surrender to that wisdom."

Amri didn't know what any of that meant, but Erimon said it so solemnly that he didn't feel there was room to ask any questions. The Dousan sandmaster cleared his throat and broke the strange silence. He gestured at a tent nearby, a larger one without a torch lit in front. When Amri leaned down to peer through the front flap, he saw it was empty.

"Now! Night falls soon, and the desert is more dangerous then. In the morning, meet me at Tappa. I will take you across the sands again so you may continue your journey, knowing the Dousan are with you in spirit. In the meantime, use this tent, and the Wellspring itself, as your own. I must go and meet with the xerics, to prepare for Maudra Seethi's arrival."

Erimon gave them a deep bow and left them, and his brother, behind. They watched another row of Dousan incense bearers pass. They wore simple robes, moving one slow step after another. They did not look at the Gelfling strangers who watched them. They seemed completely unaware of their immediate surroundings, much less the storm Amri could see over the tops of the mountains. Had it been that close before? He remembered what Onica had said when they reached Cera-Na.

"Something is not right," he said.

"Something, or everything?" Periss growled, as if the words were rocks stuck in his throat. As he stomped away, Amri couldn't help but notice Kylan's *firca* hanging at his belt.

CHAPTER 17

Amri was the first to explore the tent. It was made, like everything in the Dousan world, of bone and skin, though after riding in Tappa's mouth and being inside skekSa's behemoth ship, it seemed less and less strange.

The tent was sparsely furnished, with only a circular straw mat ringing a firepit in the center. A chute of rolled bark allowed smoke to escape out of the apex of the tent. Everything was built to be broken down and folded, easily stowed in the cavernous storage spaces inside the Crystal Skimmers or under the decks of the smaller sand skiffs.

"Is anyone else starving for a soak in that lake?" Naia asked. Her Drenchen skin was paler by the moment. Amri felt dry and itchy from the desert, but he couldn't imagine what it must be like for Naia.

"I think I'd like to rest, if it's all the same," Onica said.

"I'd like to stay, too," Tavra said. She moved to Onica's knee as the Sifa took a seat in the cool shade of the tent. Amri imagined the two would like some time together, after Onica's ordeal.

The lakeside wasn't a sandy, shallow beach like the one in the bay of Cera-Na. As they neared, Amri saw that the basin was covered in tree roots. Ancient, huge, dried and woody, like a woven basket, with no shallows for wading. Instead, the depths dropped immediately into a deep, dark blue, the bottom of which couldn't be seen.

Down by the water, it was easier to ignore the storm that hovered so close by. All Amri could do was pretend it wasn't there and hope Erimon was right. The sandmaster had to be. He knew the Wellspring, knew the ways of the Dousan. Who was Amri to doubt him?

"This isn't an ordinary lake," Naia said, looking in. She sat on a root, dangling her feet in the water. The moisture crept up her legs, gradually restoring her natural greenish color. "But the water feels divine!"

Amri sat beside her. The water on his bare feet was cool. Now that he was closer, he could see cloud-jellies floating in schools deeper in the water, and schools of darting fish. Bubbles rose from below, big and voluminous, filling the water with minerals. The three of them soaked their feet and hands and sipped the lake's rich, fresh waters.

From the lakeside, they watched more strings of incense bearers. They came in sets of three, six, and nine, never looking up, some wearing veils or their cloak hoods over their eyes. They walked in short, even steps, eerily silent. Sometimes they stopped, using a long ladle to pour sand in swirling designs that were soon blown away by the gentle wind that caressed the valley.

"Looks like they're just going in circles," Kylan said quietly. "Do you think it's . . . normal?"

"Normal is a pretty relative term," Amri pointed out.

Naia slowly crept deeper and deeper into the water, until she was standing on a root in a place where the water came up to her chin. The gills on her shoulders and neck opened in the water, and a big sigh of relief bubbled out.

"The good thing is that they're gathering here," she said. "The Gelfling are banding together. Even the clans that rarely do, like the Dousan xerics."

"Don't forget that the Sifa only gathered to run away," Kylan said.

Amri jostled Kylan with his elbow, trying to get him to lighten up. "All the more convenient for us to reach them all at once and light that fire."

"But we still don't know what lighting these fires even means," Kylan said with a touch of frustration. "We don't know anything about that writing that appeared on the deck of the *Omerya*, or the colors of the fire. I don't deny that something special happened. But why there? Why then?"

"Because the Sifa decided to join our fight. Why else?"

Kylan sighed irritably. "Aughra said *fires of resistance*, but we don't know what that means, or why it happens. She just said things, as always, without *telling* us anything. Look around the Wellspring. Erimon may say the Dousan have joined us, but there's no fire. No dream-etching. Just like when All-Maudra Mayrin said the Vapra fire was lit in Aughra's dream-space."

As much as Kylan's over analyzing of everything could be depressing, something about what he said rang true. Erimon had no hesitation in believing and joining them, and even though they hadn't met Maudra Seethi in person, Erimon seemed to know what he was talking about. But the incense bearers were not preparing the Crystal Skimmers for travel into the central region, where the Castle of the Crystal was. The tents were not being taken apart and stowed for departure. In fact, as evening set in, more Skimmers arrived.

"They're not getting ready to leave," Amri realized out loud. He shook his head. "But neither were the Sifa. They're waiting in Cera-Na. For a signal."

"A signal we don't understand ourselves," Kylan sighed.

Naia swam in the lake while Amri and Kylan just kicked at the water. The suns descended, and the Wellspring grew cold with night. The fires Erimon had mentioned flickered to life in front of the dozens of Dousan tents. Amri imagined looking down into the Wellspring from the mountains would seem like looking into a basket full of stars.

The Dousan, like other Gelfling clans, had a communal hearth near the back end of the lake. Two Dousan stood at a long plank bench, cutting open a pile of leathery-skinned fruits. The others of the clan, including those wearing the same style of cloak as Erimon—other sandmasters, perhaps—and some of the incense bearers, took the fruit silently, giving only a bow of thanks.

When the fruit-cutters saw Amri and his friends, they waved them over and placed cuts of the heavy, juicy fruits in their hands. They even stacked an extra rind on top of Kylan's cut, knowing they had a fourth Gelfling guest back at the tent. All this without a word or sound. Amri tried one of the deep bows he had seen the others give. The Dousan bowed back in reverent silence.

They ducked into the tent just as Amri felt a spray of dust whip through the oasis. The wind picked up, moaning through the valley. The tent flap sealed it out, but he could hear the sand raining against the leather.

Onica had lit the fire, and together, the four of them sank their teeth into the sweet desert fruit. The rind was tough and thick and slightly hairy, but the yellow meat of the fruit was sweet with a green flavor at the back, like meadow grass. Tavra watched from Onica's shoulder, disinterested when Onica offered a bite.

Wind rattled the tent. As much as Amri tried to ignore the droning of the sand and the wind, he couldn't any longer. The sound of the tiny grains swarming in the wind told a song of its own, etching the shape of an image in his mind: the storm wall, pouring in through the narrow mountain pass and filling the oasis valley. It would destroy everything.

"That storm is coming into the valley," he said, breaking the silence. "Erimon says it won't, but I think he's wrong. I know a cave dweller like me is the last one you want to trust about the weather, especially desert storms, but I have a really bad feeling about it."

His friends listened, ears slightly angled, but none of them wanted to admit it.

"Maybe it's like this every night," Naia said. "They would know if the storm was coming into the valley, wouldn't they? And if it did, they'd . . . raise an alarm or something. They'd come and get us."

A gust of air slapped Amri in the face as the tent flap opened and shut. Periss sealed the flap again, then buried his hands in his cloak as they all stared at him.

"Are we evacuating?" Amri asked. It was half a joke. At least, Amri wished it were a joke. All he wanted was for Periss to laugh and tell him he was being a stupid Shadowling who didn't know a storm from a cloudy sky. It would have been a wonderful time to be wrong.

But it was not to be. Periss tongued his teeth and said, "The Dousan will never evacuate."

Naia leaned back and arched a thick brow. "Then why are you here? You want Onica to do more fortune-telling for you?"

"You're all here because I brought you here. And I did that for a reason."

Periss swept his cloak back. Naia rolled forward but didn't draw her dagger when Periss lunged at Kylan, pressing the point of a short, double-edged knife against the Spriton's cheek. Amri hadn't even thought to draw his sword and didn't know what good it would do now, anyway. Slashing around in the close confines of the tent would only be a disaster.

"Let him go," Naia said. "Just tell us what you want. Your . . . reason."

Periss grabbed Kylan by the braid, tugging him up. Still holding him at knifepoint, he backed toward the tent door.

"Come with me. All of you. And if you draw that sword or that dagger, I'll cut this song teller's tongue out of his mouth."

"Really not necessary. I'm sure we'll all be quite compliant," Kylan muttered, holding his hands up to illustrate his point. Periss looked them each in the face with nervous eyes, one at a time as they stood. Amri was especially careful not to make any quick moves, and he saw Tavra twinkle down the back of Onica's arm. Across the floor and then up his leg, finding her place at his shoulder.

A calm came over him. Now he could be ready with the sword, if he had to.

Periss lowered his knife but kept hold of the back of Kylan's hood.

"All right. No quick moves."

Out they went into the whipping wind. The sky was pitch-dark, though Amri couldn't tell if it was because of the clouds or because of the desert night. He could only see the silhouette of the mountains when lightning, purple and white, rippled across the sky. The storm was truly upon them, creeping over the valley in an unfolding mass of thunder, lightning, and ruining wind.

All the torches had blown out, and some of the tents were crumbling under the violence of the storm. Yet in spite of it all, there were no Dousan running about, trying to gather the Gelfling of the Wellspring and flee to safety. In fact, there was no commotion of Dousan at all. It was as if they had all vanished.

Something caught Amri's eye. He looked toward the lake and paused, a chill going down his back like cold water. In the dark and lightning, he could just make out figures, seated on the rocks and roots that surrounded the lake.

"What are they doing?"

Periss shoved Kylan ahead, and they followed him as he led them off the footpath. He didn't look back and growled, "Nothing."

"They're meditating," Onica said from beside Amri. The

Far-Dreamer was tense from top to bottom, and with the wind whipping her hair, she looked particularly fierce. "Come. Let's follow Periss before he does something he regrets."

The footpath quickly disappeared into the sand that surrounded the oasis, making it clearer than ever how small the pocket of life and safety was in the vast body of the desert. Sand washed around Amri's knees, and he tried to push back the all-too-recent memory of being stranded in this very storm, in this very desert. But this time Onica was on her feet beside him, and Naia was ahead keeping an eye on Periss. At any moment, Amri was confident, she could disarm the Dousan and end this. But she didn't, and so Amri trusted her. Maybe she'd caught the glint of the desperation in Periss's eyes, too.

"If I need it, you can help me with the sword?" he asked. No way Periss could hear him over the howling wind.

"Indeed," Tavra replied. "I will not allow Kylan, or any of you, to be harmed."

Thunder poured into the valley like a monster, shaking Amri's bones. A blunt gust of wind hit them so hard, they had to pause. When they could see again, the sand had blown away from around their feet, revealing a long stone walkway. The walkway stretched all the way to the mountainside ahead, ending in a gaping hole carved into the rock.

"Now, while the path is clear!" Periss ordered, waving with his knife.

He ran and the others followed, racing toward the mountain as the raging storm filled the valley.

CHAPTER 18

"Where are we going?" Naia shouted, and Amri remembered none of the others could see in the dark. "There's a cave," he called out.

The entire cliff face was etched in figures and pictographs, illustrating the passage of the stars and the sun, but he didn't have time to decipher them. Sand raked at his cheeks, and deafening thunder filled his ears.

Suddenly they were inside. The cavern was large enough that several dozen Gelfling could have fit comfortably. Red and gold ledges ribbed the ceiling, and Amri heard a trickle of water flowing underfoot, felt it when he knelt to touch. The heavy rock of the mountain enveloped them, and Amri's ears rang with the memory of the storm. It still howled out in the valley. He shuddered to think of the destruction that would befall the Wellspring.

"What were they doing back there?" he cried. "I saw them— the Dousan, all just . . . just *sitting* around the lake! While the storm destroyed the Wellspring! Why?"

"Because that's how they are."

Periss swore, fumbled in the dark, then struck a stone with his knife, bringing a torch to life. Naia, Kylan, and Onica took in what Amri had already seen:

On the walls, reaching up about as high as a Gelfling stood, were carved and etched illustrations. They showed Gelfling with shaved heads and tattoos, bearing incense, all standing in a line in sets of three. The row of Gelfling ended facing a beautifully articulated tree, with long gnarled roots surrounded by a pool of water. The tree branches and leaves spread wide and tall over the heads of the Gelfling. Above the canopy were the jagged depictions of lightning and storms, and at the tree's base sat a long-backed creature with a heavy tail. Four big arms and a mane tied in knots and braids.

"A Mystic," Naia gasped. "The ancient sage?"

Kylan walked right up to the drawing, and now that they were here, Periss let him go. He kept his dagger in hand as the song teller traced the pictures with his fingers.

"This tree, protecting the Dousan and the Wellspring from the storm. Where is it? In the picture, it looks like it should be at the center of the lake . . ."

Periss grimaced. "It was, once. Songs tell that it was so tall, it could be seen from every corner of the desert, guiding the Dousan to the oasis. But many trine ago, it began to dwindle. The lake, which once filled the entire valley, shrank. When I was a child, the tree was just a dried-up old trunk. I remember the day it fell . . . All it took was a gust of summer wind."

For the first time, Amri felt like he was seeing the real Periss. Under all the snide comments and thievery.

"So the tree . . . died?" he asked.

"No!" Periss's voice echoed with determination. "It's not dead.

Yet Maudra Seethi and the incense bearers gather the remains of its branches and burn them in an eternal funeral."

"I thought there was something strange going on, down in that lake," Naia said. "The water is so rich. You're saying you think the root of the tree survived?"

"I know it. If it hadn't, the lake would have dried up. The tree is the source of the water, not the other way around."

"And your *maudra* doesn't believe you?" Kylan asked.

Periss kicked a rock.

"Maudra Seethi was the first person I went to. She told me I had to let go. That clinging to things that have passed on will only chain me to an effigy of the past. She even gave me a part of it to burn. Can you believe it? A pyre for a tree that lives! That is the ritual taught by the sage, from hundreds of trine ago. But she wouldn't understand that rituals must change with time, and circumstance."

Naia crossed her arms, disinterested in the drawings. "All right, so you left in anger. Traveled the world looking for a solution. And you found us?"

Periss put his knife away, apparently realizing he wasn't going to need it anymore. He pushed Kylan's *firca* aside and opened his belt pouch, taking out a familiar pink petal.

"I found one of these on the wind. Saw your dream. Knew it was connected to the Wellspring Tree. I left to seek the All-Maudra's help . . . But when I saw you in Cera-Na, I recognized you. The song teller with the power to dream-stitch on the petals of an ancient tree, and spread a message like that . . . And you,

Naia. Who healed the Cradle Tree in the Dark Wood."

Periss plucked the *firca* off his belt and tossed it to Kylan. Secure in its master's hands again, the bone-flute nearly resonated with relief. Periss gestured sharply. Desperately.

"So now, do it. Revive the Wellspring Tree."

Kylan grimaced, hanging the *firca* around his neck so it rested where it belonged.

"Naia. When you were in the lake, you said you sensed something. Do you think the tree is alive?" he asked.

"Yes, I sensed something, but even if the tree is alive . . . Healing the Cradle Tree was one thing. Dream-stitching on the Sanctuary Tree's petals. But this tree has been below the water for trine . . ."

"Dying," Periss insisted. "It's been under there dying a slow death while all the Dousan turn the other way. You have to fix it!"

"I don't know that we can!"

"Well, we might as well try." Onica stood near where the cave opened back into the valley. The storm outside was so dense, it was like the fabric of a Skeksis robe. "If we don't, this storm will destroy everything. The Dousan, the Crystal Skimmers, the Wellspring. Even if we survive the storm itself, we may be trapped in this cave."

"Caves aren't really that bad, but I get what you mean," Amri said under his breath. Naia still looked unsure, and still a little angry at the way Periss had gone on about the whole thing, and Kylan was anxious as ever. No one was willing to make the first move. After all, Periss's task seemed impossible. How were they supposed to resurrect a tree that had gone from protecting the entire valley to being so ill, its Gelfling maintainers thought it was dead?

None of that mattered. What mattered was saving the Wellspring and all the Gelfling gathered there.

"If we revive the tree, you believe it will protect the valley from the storm?" Amri asked.

"I believe it with all my heart," Periss replied.

"Onica is right. We have no choice but to try. But let's make one thing clear"—Amri faced Periss and held out his hand—"we're doing this as friends. Not as hostages. Got it?"

The Dousan boy hesitated, but one glance out at the storm sealed his resolution. From the strength of his grip, Amri wondered if he would have preferred it this way from the beginning.

"Amri, still. I may have eased the Cradle Tree's suffering, and I can heal cuts and scratches, but . . . I don't know if I can do this," Naia said. "We don't even know where the tree is down there, and it's pitch-dark."

"And the storm is so loud, it will drown out the sound of the *firca*," Kylan added.

Amri ignored his friends' doubts for the moment. There was no point in arguing; they were right, after all. But what Onica had said reminded him. These were caves.

"Periss," he said. "I can feel water under the cave floor. Does water stream from the Wellspring into the cavern?"

"Yes . . ."

Amri nodded. Good. "Onica and Kylan, stay here, where

you'll be safe from the storm. Naia and Periss, come with me. We're going back to the oasis. To the lake where the tree is . . . or where it was."

"The *firca* definitely won't be heard by the tree all the way from this cave!" Kylan protested. Amri put a hand on his friend's shoulder and squeezed.

"Mountain water is full of minerals. You tasted them in the Wellspring. The minerals will have formed crystals around the underground rivers. Minerals like that will carry sound just fine. The clearer the better. That's how the Grottan speak when we're spread out among the caves."

"But I don't know if I can—I'm not a Grottan—"

"That doesn't matter. I believe in you!"

Kylan's shoulders tensed up, but when Amri shook him, he gave a dutiful nod and said, "I'll try to find a place where the *firca's* song will resonate."

"Play the song of life. Call to the tree. We're going to need your help if we're going to find it down there . . . if you can awaken the tree, maybe Naia can heal it."

Amri pulled his hood back over his head, trying to ignore the dread of going back into the storm. Naia stood with him, and then Periss. He didn't want to say goodbye to Kylan and Onica, as if they might not come back. So he didn't. Instead, he stepped out of the cave, feeling Naia and Periss at his back.

The return to the oasis was more harrowing than their departure. The storm was on top of them now, as if it had a mind and a sentience and wanted, more than anything, to devour the

Wellspring whole. They waded through the sand, climbing on top of it in intervals to keep from being drowned. He felt Tavra clinging to his neck and held his hood tightly around her to keep from losing her in the ravenous storm. He needed her with them when they went into the lake.

When they finally reached the grassy turf of the Wellspring, it felt like washing up on the shore of the ocean, but they couldn't rest. Amri tugged Naia along toward the lake. As its waters came into view, frothing with peaks under the pressure of the storm, he saw the statuesque shadows of the Dousan, still sitting around the lake. They were not trying to find shelter. They were not trying to escape. They didn't even seem to notice the storm that was bearing down upon them.

Amri couldn't think about them right now. He pulled off his cloak. Naia did, too.

"You're coming with?" she asked. "But you can't breathe underwater!"

"And you can't see in the dark," he shouted back. "You'll have to breathe for me!"

"What's going on?" Erimon, the only Dousan in sight besides Periss who was not immobile in contemplation, had found them. With the sand crossing between them in veils, it was hard to tell if his face was twisted in anger or concern.

"Could ask you the same thing!" Amri cried. "I thought you said the storm wouldn't come here!"

Erimon grimaced. "Where are you going?"

"Into the lake. We're going to revive the tree," Periss said, pulling Erimon away in defiance. "And you're not going to stop them."

"No!" Erimon shouted. He faced his brother. "Periss, listen to me! For once, just listen! The tree is dead. You have to let it go. This is out of our hands. There's nothing more we can do except surrender to Thra's will. Why can't you understand this?"

"You may not be able to hear its song, but I do. I hear it in my dreams and in my nightmares. My own clan won't believe me, so I brought someone who would!"

Erimon shoved Periss away. Next he tried to appeal to Naia and Amri.

"You could die down there, and for nothing."

"If we stay up here, we'll die anyway," Amri said.

He glanced at Naia. When she nodded, he grabbed her arm and jumped into the lake.

It was another world under the water. The booming of the storm instantly vanished, replaced by a droning, echoing noise of water against the ribbed, root-laden walls of the basin. In some ways, with its constant, thousand-voiced song, it reminded Amri of the sands of the desert.

Naia moved Amri's hand to her shoulder as her wings bloomed around them both, powerful as the fins on a fish. When he touched her skin, their dreamfast filled his mind.

Ready? she asked.

Did it not seem like I was ready when I pushed us both in? He blew a bubble at her, then glanced at Tavra. In the Sanctuary, when Kylan's *firca* had been but a bone shard, its song had brought the spider race to its defeat. They were a race close to Thra, sensitive to its song. Maybe even more sensitive than Gelfling. As keen as Amri's hearing was, it couldn't help them when his ears were full of water. They needed Tavra.

Tavra, can you hear it?

At first, she was hesitant, but after a moment she climbed down his arm so more of the lake water flowed across her body.

Yes . . . Yes. I can hear it. It is reaching the tree, I think . . . I can hear a song in reply. Something resonating . . . Distant. Down, to the right.

Glad you are with us, he thought to the Silverling.

Perhaps this spider body can be put to use, after all.

Amri held his breath as Naia pumped her wings and plunged, powerfully driving them into the murky deep. When his lungs screamed for air, Naia breathed life into him, gills open like lace around her neck. Tavra caught a bubble, holding it under her legs like a smooth, clear opal.

The lake seemed endless. It had been dark above, but as they dived, the lightning of the storm dimmed to a dull flicker. The sounds of the storm, the drumming, earthshaking thunder, died away, and as it did, Amri heard the sound of a flute. Through the underground streams and water it sounded like the eerie song of a ghost—transcendent and unending, calling out to something that might no longer be strong enough to hear. Surrounded by the song, it was as if they were floating through a dream.

Tavra pricked him gently. *There. I can hear it calling.*

They had reached the lake bottom. It was so dark, even Amri

could scarcely see the pit of roots that clustered there. He held on to Naia as they landed, feet easing into the thick mud that had pooled, grown over with slime algae and decomposing plant life.

Amri pushed at the mud with his feet, trying to find any sign of life.

Do you see anything? Naia asked, holding on to him while he worked.

He was about to tell her no, but the soles of his sandals knocked against something. Something that wasn't stiff and petrified like the rest of the roots that surrounded them. He knelt, using his hands.

Then they heard it.

Ringing, softly moaning in answer to Kylan's song. The voice of the mud was like that of rock, but faster, warmer. Wetter, mixing with the song of the lake water. Amri worked swiftly, lungs screaming until he had to ask Naia for another breath. And then, renewed, he gave the mud a last push.

Under the thick layers of silt and sludge was a bough of root that had not yet died. Amri pushed the decomposing bark away from it, finding a spot of green in all the black and gray. The place in the root where the tree still lived glowed in time with the song that saturated the deep water, a single pulse of light in darkness.

Amri tugged Naia down and pressed her fingers against it. She saw it and hunkered beside him, holding the tree root with both hands. She did not speak the language of the rock or the mud, but she did know the voice of the tree when she heard it.

The tree lives, she gasped. *Periss was right. They must never have seen it because they couldn't swim this far down.*

Can you heal it?

I don't know. I'll try.

The blue light from Naia's hands settled on the lake bottom. The tree's sorrowful song quieted at first. After a long moment, Naia shook her head, though she didn't take her hands away.

It's calling for someone else. I can't do this alone.

You mean me? Can I help?

No, it's . . .

Naia closed her eyes, focusing. She had a gift; he'd seen it before. To hear the song of Thra, to dreamfast with creatures other than Gelfling. He put his hand on her shoulder, lungs aching for his next breath.

It's asking for the Dousan, she said finally. She looked up at him. *Its people. Periss, Erimon. We need them here, now, or this tree will die, and the storm will kill us all.*

CHAPTER 19

Amri tried to stay calm. The faster his heart beat, the more air he needed, and Naia couldn't keep him alive at the lakebed forever.

I can't bring them all down here, he told her. *But I can bring them to the cave. Tell the tree I'll do that. Do you think it will be enough?*

Naia took her hands from the dying tree's root long enough to hold Amri's face.

It will have to be. I believe in you!

Their lips met, and she filled his lungs with air, more warmly than before, then thrust him away. He held the feeling in his heart, letting it buoy him toward the surface so far above. When he broke out of the water, the storm raged more violently than before, splintering the sturdy palms and blowing the Dousan tents to pieces. Still the Dousan meditated, clinging to the rocks and bowing their heads against the violent wind and cutting sand.

Amri coughed water as Periss hauled him out of the lake. The Dousan had to practically scream in Amri's ear to be heard over the wind.

"What happened?"

"We have to get all the Dousan into the cave," Amri said around the remaining mouthfuls of water. "The tree needs to hear your call. Naia is trying to heal it, but she needs to hear your song!"

"What are you talking about?" Erimon hadn't given up on Periss. The wind had torn away his cloak, and without the marker of his status among the xeric, the sandmaster looked more akin to his brother than ever.

Periss turned on Erimon, eyes wide with hope.

"Our people meditate, send thoughts and dreams into the universe, trusting Thra to send providence. But they won't take action—won't even lift a finger to save the gifts Thra has already provided! If they won't, then I will."

He tore from Erimon's grasp and ran to the nearest Dousan that clung to a rock in a steadfast, stubborn huddle. Amri followed him, but Erimon grabbed him and held him back.

"You say you saw it? The tree truly lives?"

"And can save us yet, if you'll believe in it!"

Like the living spot of the tree in all the dead, a spark of light flickered in Erimon's countenance. Like a wall breaking, like he was waking from a dream that he had been dreaming too long.

"Then let us gather the Dousan. We haven't much time," he said. He turned toward the lake and took a horn from his belt. Instead of blowing into it, he merely raised it into the wind. The storm rang through the horn, loosing a resounding note that filled the entire valley. Periss, whose efforts to rouse the Dousan had been either unheard or ignored, looked up at the sound.

Then, slowly, so did the bowed heads of the Dousan scattered around the oasis. They looked to the horn in Erimon's hand, blown by the storm itself.

"To the cloisters!"

Without looking back, Erimon took Amri by the shoulder and broke into a run. Periss joined them, and they hurried as quickly as they could down the footpath that would lead them out into the sands and, if it hadn't been destroyed, the promenade into the caves.

"Do you think they'll come?" Periss asked. "They're so deep in meditation already—they may not have heard the horn—"

"We must trust they will listen," Erimon said. "We can only lead by example . . . as you have, my brother. I will make proper amends when we survive."

The promenade was long buried below the shifting sands, but Erimon and Periss didn't need the stones to show them the way. When they reached the opening to the cave, Erimon took the horn out and thrust it into a crevice in the rock. There it stuck, the wind howling through it, sounding an unending wail.

Amri fell to his knees the moment they entered the protected cave, sand pouring from the folds in his cloak. The cavern was rippling with crystal light, reverberating with the sound of Kylan's *firca*. The Spriton had climbed to a pocket in the stone above, where he sat and played the little flute that sang with the enormous song. Onica rose from where she'd been waiting, helping them inside the cave and brushing them free of the endless sand.

"The tree?" the Far-Dreamer asked Amri.

"Alive." Then, to the two brothers, he said, "Go! To where Kylan is playing. His song reaches the bottom of the lake, where Naia is. Your song has to reach the tree!"

"But the others—" Periss began.

"You can't wait for them! If it's just you two, then so be it!"

Amri climbed to his feet as the Dousan brothers scaled the wall up to the ledge where Kylan played. They sat beside him, Erimon adjusting Periss's posture when they did. A moment later, the two brothers' voices filled the chamber, ringing in harmony with the *firca*'s melody. Their chant was a long, drawn humming that reminded Amri of the Mystics. Of Aughra's chant. Of the song they'd heard in the dream-space, the cosmic song of Thra.

"How will we know if it's working?" Amri asked. Onica gazed at the three, held her hands out. Amri tried, too, and when he did, he could feel the vibrations of the song filling his palms. It was almost tangible. His fingers grew hot, as if to dream-etch, but the language that whispered in the back of his mind was one he couldn't understand.

"If it works, the tree will rise and break the storm wall," Onica said. "And if it doesn't, we may be the only ones that survive this trial."

Commotion caught Amri's ear from outside. Three Dousan stumbled in, shoulders caked in sand.

"How did the storm get so bad?" they murmured. "Is this the answer Thra has given us? What shall we do?"

"We followed the horn. In my dream, I thought I heard a voice. The tree . . ."

"The tree lives," Amri said, helping them. "Now you must help it, so it can save us."

Just as the three left the doorway, two more came out of the storm. Then a sixth and seventh. In a long chain of hands, the Dousan of the Wellspring filled the cavern, coughing sand and shaking off the last tendrils of their deep meditation.

The Dousan fell silent, though at least this time they were awake. In their silence, they heard Erimon and Periss, the song of Kylan's *firca*. The doubt clouding their eyes faded as they looked upon the two brothers and the Spriton, heard the song that touched every rock of the cavern. Amri remembered what Periss had told Erimon. He stood aside and pointed at the etching of the tree on the wall.

"Thra has already given you an answer. To the darkening, to the Skeksis, to all the corruption that seeps into our world. Believe in the way Thra has shown us all along, even if it seems hopeless. In the tree. In the Gelfling. In each other!"

Amri held out his hands as the storm threw itself against the mountain, a monster knocking on the door. To his surprise, a Dousan stepped forward and took his hand.

"I will believe," she said.

Another followed her. Amri didn't know whether to laugh or cry. Holding the first Dousan's hand in his left and Onica's hand in his right, he knelt. The rest of the Dousan followed, bowing their heads toward the earth, where beneath them ran the waters from the Wellspring. Releasing their breath in the many-toned hum until it pushed back the roaring storm.

Hear us, Amri prayed. He remembered Onica's prayer as she'd stoked the hearth on the *Omerya*. *Hear us, Naia. Hear us, Tree of the Wellspring . . .*

A dreamfast rushed through his mind like a cold wind. A vision of the tree in its prime, huge fronds flocked with birds and ripe fruit. Moisture from the oasis condensing on the underside of its leaves, every evening showering the oasis with a light, sweet rain. The Dousan clan, coming and going from the sparkling oasis, finding their center before returning to the desert.

This song thickened the air, in the dreamfast and the chant. Vibrated into the earth and along the rivers that fed the lake. Amri could only hope they reached Naia and the weakened, dying tree at the bottom.

Amri . . .

Amri opened his eyes. The Dousan surrounded him like statues, as still as the stalagmites in the cave, their chant a roiling whirlpool of power. Beside him, Onica had awakened, too. He thought he'd heard Naia's voice. But from this far?

"Amri, look," Onica said.

They stood as the Dousan chanted. Outside, the darkness had lifted, revealing a gauzy pink and gold.

Amri stepped outside of the cave and gasped.

Still growing, at an impossible and rapid speed, a tree was unfurling from within the lake. Its spiraled shoot jetted into the sky, thick boughs with huge succulent fronds blooming like a storm of another kind.

The storm wall broke as the tree pierced it, scattering the lightning and wind. The clouds parted in a ripple, dissipating. Behind the black of the storm, the sky was light with morning.

A ray of light and color lit the cavern. In the center of the ring

of Dousan, a fire burst to life. As its ethereal, rainbow light burned into the walls of the cave, Amri saw the familiar etchings appear—the figures and words that he'd seen on the deck of the *Omerya*, but now they were joined with others. The picture of the Wellspring Tree and the Dousan. Of the two Dousan brothers, the first to join hands around a Spriton song teller playing a *firca* made of bone.

All the Dousan stared at the fire. Amri stepped toward it as it glittered blue, peering into its brightness. For a moment, he saw a shape—a ship made of coral. Cera-Na. Maudra Ethri's back as Tae handed her a scroll tied with a piece of silver twine.

"What is this?" Onica whispered.

Maudra Ethri and Tae turned toward them, as if they'd heard something . . . Then the fire turned gold again, and the vision was gone.

Amri swallowed the chills that crawled up his throat. "They saw us. What was that scroll?" Then he remembered what Naia had said, about her dream. A message, reaching her *maudra* mother in the Swamp of Sog.

Naia.

Amri ran from the cave, leaving the awakening Dousan behind. The promenade was still deep under sand, but in the brightening morning and with the storm broken by the tree, the way back to the Wellspring was clear and easy. Amri scrambled onto the solid turf and raced through the smaller palms toward the woody trunk of the giant tree that now grew from the center of the lake.

"Naia!" he shouted, looking for her. "Naia!"

The tree's bark was made of woody, layered diamonds like the scales of a lizard, pointing upward to capture what meager rain fell in the desert. Cradled in one of the shelves made of the bark, resting in a nest of lake weeds, was the Drenchen girl. Amri splashed through the water and climbed up the tree to where she lay.

"Oof," she groaned when he reached her.

"You did it. Naia, you did it."

She gave an exhausted chuckle. "It wasn't me. When I was down there, I could hear you. Through the water and the river. I heard Kylan's *firca*. I heard the Dousan singing the song of life." She looked at the palms of her hands. "I became one with the tree, in that moment. I felt as if my heart had grown wings. And then this miracle . . ."

Together, they looked up through the morning suns as they came through the tree's fronds, sparkling with the water that still dropped in pristine rain from so high above. Naia smiled and put her hand against the tree's bark.

"Oszah-Staba," she said. "The Wellspring Tree. Its tears have always filled the lake. But now they can be tears of joy instead of loneliness."

Amri looked out across the Wellspring. Everything had been destroyed by the storm. Every tent and torch, every stockade of supplies was gone. Not even rubble remained. At first he worried that even the Crystal Skimmers had been taken by the storm, but as he looked out into the dune where they'd left Tappa with the other Skimmers, the sands shifted. One at a time, out came the Skimmers, bellowing and wailing to each other as they surfaced.

They climbed down as the Dousan returned to the lakeside. Periss shoved his way through the throng to grab Naia by the waist. He hoisted her up.

"You did it! I knew you could!"

She pushed him away when he set her down.

"It was all of us. And don't do that again."

Erimon, less exuberant than his brother, stepped forth. They gazed upon the Wellspring Tree together.

"We were wrong," he murmured. "Periss . . ."

"Your sand skiff will make a fine apology," Periss replied.

Naia looked between Kylan and Amri with a blinding smile. Amri returned it, feeling it beaming from his core. The feeling was unstoppable, like the fire that burned even now in the cloister of the Dousan cave. The tree. The Dousan fire lit.

Even Tavra spoke kindly into his ear.

"You did very well, Shadowling," she said.

"And how are you, spiderling?" he replied.

"Tired."

In the past, her short answers had always seemed aloof, as if she didn't want to speak to him any more than she had to. But this time he heard something else. Not sadness, not reluctance; just exactly what she'd said. Tiredness.

With a start, he realized maybe this was just the way she was: not cold, but reserved. He remembered the dreamfast they'd shared, when they'd rescued Onica. Even then, with the one she loved, she had held back. Not to hide things, but because that was just the way she was. He shifted his weight, awkward with the forming idea. Remembering that ice was also water.

"Anything I can do?" he asked.

"I couldn't ask for more than what you have already done."

A Crystal Skimmer's bellow pierced the calm. The other Skimmers whistled in reply, rustling farther from the sands as the Crystal Skimmer came gliding roughly in from the desert. The deck strapped to its back was in shambles, the Skimmer itself covered in scratches and heavier wounds from the storm. The crew aboard was barely holding on as the Skimmer crashed to a halt.

"Maudra Seethi's Skimmer," Erimon gasped.

Amri and Naia followed the sandmaster to the Skimmer, which moaned in pain. Dousan bearing water from the lake tended it as Erimon leaped onto the Skimmer's harnesses, helping down the meager remains of a battered crew.

Kylan helped one of the crew to the ground, pushing a cup of water at him as he coughed dust and sand. Erimon leaped down to meet them.

"Sandmaster Rek'yr! What happened! Where's Maudra Seethi?"

The Dousan shook his head.

"We were caught by the storm wall. We backed off to the south, hoping it would break, but it never did. While we waited along the southern end, a windsifter came."

"From Ha'rar?" Naia asked. She looked at Amri.

"Yes. Tragedy has struck. Maudra Seethi left us to heed its call."

All the warmth drained from Amri's body, replaced with a

cold that he wasn't sure could be warmed. Rek'yr coughed again and groaned, producing a scroll tied with a piece of silver twine. He passed it to Erimon as proof. Amri waited while he read it, though with a horrible dread, he felt he knew what words would come from the sandmaster's mouth next.

"The *maudra* have been summoned to Ha'rar by Princess Seladon," he said. "All-Maudra Mayrin is dead."

CHAPTER 20

Amri felt like he must have misheard. Erimon passed the parchment to Kylan, who read it again. Amri didn't need to read it. He didn't want to. It wouldn't explain how or why or who had done it. Just that it had happened. He reached up to see if Tavra was still on his shoulder. She was where she'd been since they'd leaped into the lake, but she said nothing. None of them did, until Amri couldn't take it any longer.

"Do you think it's because of what she said in the dream-space?" he whispered. "Because she vowed to resist the Skeksis?"

Kylan crossed his arms, quietly twisting his ears back. He didn't show when he was upset like Naia did, but Amri was beginning to learn the Spriton boy's body language, and right now *upset* was putting it mildly.

"She said she lit the fire," the song teller said. "But when we lit the Dousan fire, we saw Ethri and Tae. The Sifa story was dream-etched onto the cloister wall . . . but we didn't see anything about the Vapra of Ha'rar. If these fires of resistance have to do with uniting the Gelfling and sharing the song that we are all telling— and if All-Maudra Mayrin truly had lit the Vapra fire—we should have seen it. No, this is not right. Not right at all."

"You think she didn't light the fire after all?" Naia asked.

"Maybe she thought she had," Onica said solemnly. "Maybe she died trying."

They had no proof except the feeling in their hearts. Amri didn't want to believe it, but he couldn't deny it either: The Vapra fire had never been lit.

Amri shuddered. If the Vapra hadn't been united, and the All-Maudra was no longer there to lead them—and not only that, but if she'd been killed for rising against the Skeksis—there was only one path before Amri and his friends. They were going to Ha'rar after all.

Erimon knew it, too.

"You can take Tappa," he said. He turned and blew his horn, shouting orders for his crew to prepare the Skimmer. Despite nearly being obliterated in the storm, the Dousan heeded his call.

"How long will it take to reach Ha'rar by Crystal Skimmer?" Naia asked.

"Tappa's the fastest in Erimon's xeric. She could make it to the mountains in a couple days, if we leave before the sands rise," Periss said. "Especially with Erimon in command."

"I trust you'll halve my time, then, my brother."

Periss coughed when Erimon pushed the command horn into his arms.

"Wait, what?"

"I must stay here. With Maudra Seethi on her way to Ha'rar, it falls to the sandmasters to lead the Dousan and to orchestrate our . . . resistance." Here he looked to Amri, Naia, and Kylan. "Now that the storm has broken, the xerics will continue to arrive.

I will tell them the song of what has happened here. And when the time comes, we will heed the signal of the flames. We will join the fight against the Skeksis."

"We still don't know what that signal will be," Naia said.

Erimon bowed. "We can never fully predict what form a sign will take. We only know it when we see it, or hear it, or sense it some other way. But I have faith in Thra, and in you. I will see to it the Dousan do not forsake the gifts we have been given. Not as we have in the past, nor ever again."

The crew shouted their readies from Tappa's back. Erimon wrapped his brother in a firm embrace.

"Deliver them to Ha'rar. Then return to us safely, brother."

Tappa had been fast in the storm, but she was even faster in open air and relieved from all the supplies she had carried for Erimon's crew. Unladen, she flew across the desert so quickly, Amri could barely see the glittering of the crystal sands; it was all a blur, a shine, and in some places, a wash of rainbows as the suns rose.

It was beautiful, but Amri struggled to enjoy it. While Kylan and Onica helped Periss maintain the auxiliary sails, Amri watched Naia pace.

"I really thought the All-Maudra had lit the fire," he said after he'd watched her cross the deck at least ninety times. "After what she said in the dream-space. She sounded so sure."

"How could this happen?" Naia asked. "How could she fail?"

"The Skeksis must have found out." It was the first thing Tavra had said since they'd received the news. She stood on the rail of Tappa's deck platform. "But there's no point making guesses out here. We must go to Ha'rar and reach someone who can tell us what happened. No more Far-Dreams or riddles from Thra. I want answers."

"How are you taking this?" Amri asked. Tried to keep it soft, to let her know he was asking her feelings and not her political opinion. She was hesitant in answering.

"I am worried for my sisters. I am worried for my people."

"Do you think Brea and Seladon are in danger?" Amri had no idea how the All-Maudra's death had come about, much less how the two Vapra princesses would react to the tragedy. After seeing them fighting in Onica's Far-Dream, he could only guess.

"They may be," Tavra said.

"Seladon will take care of Brea," he told her. He wanted it to sound reassuring but didn't actually know if that was true. He had no sisters himself, but older ones were supposed to look after younger ones, wasn't that right? At least, that was what Tavra and Naia had proven to him.

Tavra was quiet a long time, unmoving. She curled one leg in.

"I don't know that she will," she said. "That is my greatest fear. My mother put her duties first and her daughters second. It was difficult to find ways to earn her love. Because of our station. But we tried. For me, that meant becoming a soldier. For Brea, becoming a scholar. For Seladon, it meant becoming All-Maudra one day . . . but the pressure was often too much. She is not ready, and I fear the Skeksis know that."

"You should be All-Maudra," Naia said suddenly.

The idea brought a strange fantasy to life. Tavra, in her

Gelfling body. Sword in hand, draped in the silver cloaks with the living crown on her brow. She had traveled farther than any of them, knew more of the state of the world. Knew the Skeksis all by name, knew how the All-Maudra was expected to behave. Had the respect of her clan as a Vapra princess, but knew firsthand the hardships that had befallen the Gelfling who were so unlucky to find themselves in the Skeksis' crushing grasp.

If there was ever a leader the Gelfling could look to, Amri realized, it was Tavra. Tavra, who was locked in the body of a spider, whose voice could barely be heard even by those who knew enough to listen.

"That is impossible," Tavra said. She slipped below the rail and disappeared into Kylan's traveling pack.

True to Erimon's estimation, by the time evening descended, Tappa had taken them nearly all the way across the desert. Amri traced their path on one of Kylan's maps, finding the place where they'd cut through the mountains on the sand river from Cera-Na. From the land formations he could see, he found their course cutting along the inner bowl of the mountains, heading northeast.

"Is there another sand river that leads to Ha'rar?" he asked Periss as the sky darkened.

"Yes. I think we'll reach the snows by tomorrow at midnight. See the Waystar light?"

Periss pointed to the bright light peeking over the ridge of mountains. Amri remembered what Tavra had said about the light. That it was a grove of star trees, guiding travelers to Ha'rar as the seafarer's lanterns did. As they sped over the sands, drawing closer every moment to the mountains, the light shined brighter, white with a halo of blue. As he gazed upon it, Amri felt a strange, but welcome, sense of direction. As if just having a guide made the journey less daunting. Perhaps that was why the Vapra looked to the Waystar in times of need.

He wondered if someone tended the Waystar grove as someone tended the lanterns. Maybe the same someone. Someone out there, making sure travelers found their way. Making sure they had hope.

"Can Tappa travel in the cold?" he asked.

Tappa burbled with a high-pitched trill. Periss shook his head.

"I'll leave you at the frost line," he said. "But from there it will only be a short trek into the city . . . And anyway, if you enter on foot, you're less likely to be seen or noticed by the Skeksis, if they really have taken the city."

"How do you . . . Oh. Right. Thief."

"Your girlfriend is really something else," Periss said. He nodded at Naia, who was sitting up on Tappa's head, where the prow would be if the Skimmer were a ship. Her wings caught the wind like sails, though the air was growing less dry as they began their distant approach into the mountain region. "You really think you can light a fire with the Vapra?"

"I don't know if we can, but we have to try," Amri said. He tried not to let Periss's observation turn into doubt. Then he coughed, cheeks burning. "And she's not my girlfriend . . ."

"Have you dreamfasted together?"

Amri's ears went flat at the forward question. Of course he'd dreamfasted with Naia, but only to share memories that they'd needed to share, so the truth of the Skeksis and the message they carried would not be forgotten. But there were other memories, ones more secret and intimate. Private hopes and fears. Memories he had all to himself, beautiful things he'd seen when he'd been alone. Dreams he'd had, and nightmares.

Amri had always hoped one day to find someone to share those memories with. Someone he trusted enough and who trusted him to truly dreamfast. To share everything. It had never occurred to him that *someone* might be Naia. Until now, and only thanks to a wily Dousan thief. Periss grinned ear to ear, as if making Amri blush from embarrassment was his new favorite game.

"No. Not that way," he mumbled.

"Do you *want* to?" Periss asked.

"I *want* to change the subject."

The grin faded, and the Dousan looked north, toward the Waystar. The tattoos across his face shimmered under the moons and stars, growing serious as he contemplated the task ahead of Amri and his friends.

"Ha'rar is a big city," he said.

Amri nodded and replied, "Then it will have to be a big fire."

They slept and traveled another full day before reaching the edge of the mountains. Amri practiced his sword stances, parries and thrusts. Imagined striking down Skeksis after Skeksis as he charged into a citadel swarming with darkened beasts. It felt heroic in his mind, that part—the charge, the thought that he could single-handedly defeat the monsters that might have taken the shining city—but in the end, even in his fantasies, when he finally reached the throne, the All-Maudra was already dead.

No matter how quickly they arrived in Ha'rar, no matter how heroic they could be. No matter how much like a daylighter he became. No matter how many fires were lit and no matter how many Skeksis they might defeat, this one ending was already wrought. Their victories so far, and any that would come in the future, would always carry the weight of the tragedy.

They reached the mountains as the second night fell. Tappa had no night vision, but as she swam into the mountains, her trills turned soft and high-pitched, so high that even Amri could hardly hear them. The sounds bounced off the rock and mountains, even below the sand, guiding the Skimmer into a narrow pass. Her pace slowed as she found the sand river and glided against the current and upward. It would have been impossible to do it in a skiff, but the Skimmer's fins hovered just above the sands, coasting on the hot air that rose as the cold air poured down from the mountains.

Periss blew on the horn when frost appeared on the trees and rocks. Tappa lifted off the sand river and grounded herself on a rock. Her skin had changed from a deep gold to a pale yellow, her hide trembling from the cold.

"This is where we part ways," Periss said as they gathered on the deck, dressing in their cloaks and hoods as the cold air came down from the silver mountains. Naia clasped hands with the Dousan.

"Thank you," she said. "Safe travels back to the Wellspring. I'm sure we'll meet again."

"Be careful. With the All-Maudra dead . . ." He didn't finish. Instead, he took a string of jewels, tangled with metal bangles, from his pouch and handed them over. "These are Sifa's pretties. Now we're even."

They said the rest of their goodbyes, then stood on the frosted rocks and watched until Tappa's silhouette was swallowed by the shadows. Amri took a big breath of the calm air, listened to the rushing of wind in the trees. Here, the land was untouched by the darkness that was spreading. Amri wondered if the trees and rocks and the river of sand knew or cared that the All-Maudra had been killed. He had no idea what could have transpired in the time between the All-Maudra's death and now. He tried to absorb the last moments of peace, hoping they weren't too late.

"All right," Naia said after a moment. "Let's go."

The hike up the mountain was familiar, a steep and snow-covered slope bordered on either side by sheer, straight, crystalline cliffs. It was harder going than the path they'd followed when they'd first trekked to the coast to meet Onica. Steeper and colder, growing brighter as they followed the Waystar's distant light.

When they reached the top of the climb, their heads coming over the cliffs as if they were breaking the surface of a frozen pond, Amri stared.

A gateway rose from the gray and white rocks, like the entrance into the sky itself: two stone posts with magnificent open doors of swooping silver in the shape of wings. Amri touched the cold, shining metal. His fingers stuck for an instant where they rested, tickling with frost before it melted from the warmth of his hand.

They passed through the gates in silence, following the path as it changed from natural dirt to carved steps, and finally into a flat-stone path. They mounted the hill, and Amri beheld the crystalline, snow-coated city he had only seen in dreamfast.

They had finally made it to Ha'rar.

Like the crystals in a broken geode, the city of Ha'rar glittered in the protective shell of the mountains, covered in snow and glowing with moon- and starlight. At the far edge of the city, a majestic building stood with its back to the wide Silver Sea. It looked like an icicle, or one of the many crystal stalagmites in Domrak and the Caves of Grot. Every elaborately sculpted feature refracted the light of the moons and the Waystar, sending night rainbows across the city.

It was beautiful, but eerily silent and ominously dark.

"The lamps should be lit, shouldn't they?" Kylan asked, whispering intuitively. The streets were so barren and silent that even a soft voice would have carried to dangerous ears. "Where is everyone?"

Without the lamps and seafarer's lanterns lit, Ha'rar felt as cold as the wintry wood that waited in darkness beyond the gates. Amri's reflection warped and rippled off the stone and ice buildings, and wind blew dry snow across the motherstone pathways. The ice crystals sounded like the skittering of thousands of tiny feet.

"We cannot guess." Tavra had returned to Amri's shoulder, the air so still, they could all hear her foreboding words. "We must make our way to the citadel and find out what's happened. And above all else, if we encounter Skeksis, we must not be caught."

The path to the citadel was straightforward, though it seemed wrong to charge down the main road like an attacker on a castle. Instead, Tavra took them along the side paths, through alleys and under shadowy eaves drooping with snow. As they neared the citadel, Amri felt a trembling muffled by the soles of his sandals.

"Wait—"

The four of them ducked out of view just as heavy footsteps thundered down the street in wide, heavy strides.

"Oh no," Amri whispered.

Skeksis. Two of them, passing by on the street just in front of them. One wore broad-shouldered, black-scaled armor, covering his spiny back like the carapace of an armalig. Gray hair—or was it fur?—grew across his blunt forehead and cheeks, casting a hazy shadow upon his scowling lips and piercing yellow eyes. The other stood straighter in his crimson and black robes, armored and adorned in shining gold chains. He seemed taller yet, thanks to the fleshy spike that protruded from the top of his head like a horn.

"skekUng and skekZok," Tavra whispered. "The General and the Ritual Master."

The General. The one whose name skekLi had invoked as he'd challenged them in the Grottan Sanctuary. Even as they'd defeated him, though he and his minions had left Domrak and the Grottan clan in ruins. And the Ritual Master, who had told skekSa about Naia and Gurjin.

Wait to see what skekUng is making, he'd said. *The spiders were only a prologue.*

The two Skeksis paused, and Amri held his breath. Had they been heard?

"Did you hear something?" skekUng asked, squinting into the alley but seeing nothing. For once, the darkness was on their side.

"Probably just some stupid Vapra childling," rumbled Lord skekZok. "Ignore it. Focus on finishing our task and getting out of this stinking Silverling nest."

skekUng sniffed, then spat, curling his lip. "This is a waste of time. I say we kill the princess as we killed her mother and let the Vapra bow directly to us. As they should."

"My mother," Tavra whispered in Amri's ear as the two Skeksis lumbered again toward the citadel. "They murdered her, after all—"

As the lords passed out of earshot, Amri heard someone else approach from behind. Before he could react, a hooded figure grabbed him, jerking the cold flat of a blade against his neck.

"Wait!" Onica said.

"He's possessed by a spider," hissed a female voice, familiar in Amri's ear. "On his shoulder—quick, grab it and crush it!"

"No, it's not—" Amri's explanation was cut short, almost too literally, by his attacker's blade. He held out his hands and waved them as Tavra scurried into his hair. "It's not what you think!"

Onica stepped in, pulling her hood down to reveal her face.

"Put down the knife, Tae! It's all right!"

The familiarity clicked. Amri recognized the jewelry on the Sifa's hand where she clutched the knife.

"I've seen what those crystal-singers can do," she said. "Now take it and kill it while I hold him, before it's too late!"

"It's not what you think," Amri said, careful not to move. "Tavra . . . it's time. You have to tell her. Tae, no sudden moves, all right?"

Amri couldn't see Tavra as she revealed herself, but he could hear Tae suck in a breath and stiffen. Tavra let out a tired sigh.

"Tae, it's me. Katavra."

"Tavra? But how . . ." The Sifa girl faltered, letting Amri breathe without a knife in the way. He pushed the blade the rest of the way from his face and turned toward her.

"It's a song we must tell elsewhere," Amri said.

Tae couldn't look away from the spider on his shoulder. She nodded.

"Follow me," she said, then hurried away. They followed, putting the citadel behind them, though Amri could still feel it gazing down on their backs.

CHAPTER 21

At the far end of Ha'rar, the cliffs dropped away into the ocean. A narrow, carved stairway cut down the steep mountainside and deposited them at the wharf, a stretch of ice shelf held against the Ha'rar cliffside with stone pillars. Metal poles—used for docking ships, Amri imagined—stuck out of the ice and water like spines. But all were empty. What had probably once been a bustling marketplace and landing for the Sifa and other seafarers was now barren and silent.

There was only one ship in the harbor, a familiar Sifa craft with red, blue, and purple sails. Amri felt safer as soon as they were inside, cabin door locked and the cushions and quilts surrounding them with the scent of Onica's herbs and Sifa fernsage.

"Where's Ethri? Where's the *Omerya?*" Onica asked. "What are you doing in Ha'rar?"

"I accompanied Ethri when she responded to Seladon's summons. We didn't know what to expect when we came here, so we took your ship instead of the *Omerya,*" Tae explained. "I'll tell you what I know, but first, you need to explain what's happened to Tavra."

They sat at the table and Naia told the song of what had happened. About Krychk the crystal-singer, who had taken over

Tavra's drained body to infiltrate the Gelfling resistance. How Kylan had used dream-stitching to attach Tavra's soul to the spider's body when her physical one died. At last, how they'd sent their message of the Skeksis' betrayal with the Sanctuary Tree.

It was all just a beginning to the rest of it: their voyage to the Dousan Wellspring after they'd left Cera-Na. All of it. Although lighting the fire with the Dousan seemed to raise Tae's spirits, it was the fate of the Vapra princess before her that she returned to when they were done telling their tale.

"So you're still able to do as the crystal-singers do, and whisper songs in the ears of Gelfling," Tae said. "What's it like?"

Amri wasn't sure if the question was to him or Tavra. Tavra seemed hesitant to answer, especially since the occasions when it had happened hadn't been planned. In skekSa's ship and then in the desert storm.

"It's sort of like dreamfasting," Amri answered for them both. "You know how in a dreamfast, you feel like you're someone else, just for that dream? It was like that. I felt like I was her."

"And I was you," Tavra finished in agreement. "Yes, it was like dreamfasting. I was able to see through Amri's eyes. When we flew to save Onica from the Crystal Skimmers, it was as if for a moment . . ."

As if for a moment I was Gelfling again, she had been about to say. Amri frowned. He wondered how it must have felt, if even for a moment. To fly once more, only to have to go back to being a spider again.

"I can't believe this," Tae exclaimed. She pressed the heels of her hands into her eyes, as if she might rub the strangeness out of her mind. "All that time in Cera-Na. On skekSa's ship. When we lit the fires, you were there. Why didn't you say anything?"

"What was there to say?" Tavra asked with a spider-size shrug. "My own sisters do not know I am still alive. If this state could be called living."

Before Tavra could go too far down that depressing path, Onica spoke up.

"Tae, it's your turn. What has happened? We overheard the General saying the Skeksis killed the All-Maudra—is it true?"

"All anyone knew was that she had died—but I'm not surprised to learn it was the Skeksis that killed her!" Tae bunched her fingers in an angry fist, then sighed, shaking her head with a huff of frustration. "Seladon sent the windsifters with the pieces of the living crown and the message that Mayrin had passed. The *maudra* came to Ha'rar to bless Seladon's ascension as All-Maudra. Ethri and I attended the blessing, but it was . . . wrong. Now that I know it was the Skeksis that did away with Mayrin, it makes more sense."

"What do you mean?" Amri asked.

Tae rested her chin on her folded fingers. "In front of all the *maudra*, Seladon declared All-Maudra Mayrin a traitor. Refused to return her mortal body to Thra—disobeyed sacred tradition in doing so. Then, at the blessing ceremony, she invoked the Skeksis order. Declared the Vapra's loyalty to the Castle of the Crystal and Emperor skekSo. When time came for the *maudra* to bless her ascent, if anyone refused . . ."

"Then it was as good as declaring war against the Skeksis," Tavra finished. "This was planned by Emperor skekSo. A power play like this reeks of his manipulation. What happened when she asked for the blessings?"

"I thought with the Ritual Master and General so close at hand, the other *maudra* might be cowed into pledging anyway," Tae said. "Ethri didn't know what to do, so she blessed Seladon in the hopes that unity among the *maudra* might still support the resistance. But . . ."

"My mother withheld," Naia said. She looked down, lips pressed and pensive. Naia's mother, Maudra Laesid, whose two children had become targets of the Skeksis' lies of treachery. Of course she would withhold blessing an All-Maudra who would swear loyalty to the Skeksis.

Tae nodded. "As did Maudra Fara of the Stonewood."

"What about Maudra Argot?" Amri asked. "The other *maudra?*"

"Maudra Seethi and Maudra Mera blessed Seladon. Whether because they swear to the Emperor skekSo or fear his power, I do not know. As for Maudra Argot, she sent her piece of the crown, though she did not attend in person. After the blessing ceremony, Ethri returned to Cera-Na to bear the news, but I stayed here."

"You shouldn't have," Tavra said. "It's dangerous. There is a storm coming. It may not be in the sky, but it is black as Skeksis cloaks and rains sharp as their teeth and claws."

Tae's cheeks colored, but she crossed her arms and didn't back down.

"I know that. But the last time I faced a storm near Ha'rar, I could do nothing to stop it. You had to save me. This time, I will do everything I can to do the saving."

Naia and Kylan glanced at each other and Amri remembered he was the only one who had seen Tavra's memories and heard from Onica about her Far-Dream of the storm. Naia and Kylan had no idea what Tavra and Tae were talking about.

"There's no point arguing about it now," Onica said, breaking the strange quiet. "Tae is here and she's brought my ship. Instead of telling her she was wrong to do so, we might as well accept it."

Naia pounded the table with a fist. "Right. The storm is coming either way. We'd be better off prepared."

Amri spoke his thoughts aloud, though he didn't know if any of them had the authority to guess at the answers. "What do you think Maudra Fara will do, now that she's challenged Seladon? Stone-in-the-Wood lies closest of all the clans to the Castle of the Crystal. They are Rian's people—surely they believe and stand behind him by now. Do you think they'll . . ."

"The Stonewood are loyal and Maudra Fara is a fierce *maudra* for her people," Kylan said. "I learned that much when she forced us to leave instead of offering us sanctuary. If she's decided to stand with Rian, and knows that the Skeksis will come for her people first . . ."

"She may go to war with them," Tae finished. "She said as much when she challenged Seladon. And Naia, your mother, Maudra Laesid. What do you think she'll do?"

"Fight," Naia replied without hesitation. "She didn't lose her leg running away from battles . . . But this is wrong! Now isn't the time that any of them should be fighting among themselves. We need to unite, not break apart!"

"This is as I feared," Tavra said quietly. She walked down Amri's arm and to the table, where they could all hear her. "The Skeksis are using Seladon. That is the real reason they killed my mother. They found out she was planning to resist them, and knew Seladon would be easier to manipulate."

"And because they knew you were gone," Amri finished. He thought again of what Naia had said on Tappa's back. That Tavra should be All-Maudra. He hated the thought, not because it wasn't right but because it felt so impossible. He didn't want to think about all the ways it would have changed the past, and how it could have changed the future, if it were only meant to be.

"Do you know where Seladon is now?" Onica asked Tae.

"That's the thing. After she took on the living crown, no one has seen her. There are rumors among the Vapra that she has left Ha'rar and that only the Ritual Master and the General remain. I was trying to follow them into the citadel tonight when I found you. Hoping to find out whether Seladon has been killed like the All-Maudra, or taken captive by the Skeksis. The fact is, so long as she does not rise against them, the Vapra remain docile, if uncertain."

"Like the Stonewood, the Vapra are loyal," Tavra murmured. "And now I see it is to a fault. If their leader does not raise her voice against the Skeksis, neither will they. But if that leader is not given a voice . . ."

An uncomfortable, cold silence fell on the room. It almost felt like death. What was the point of going on, if this was the Ha'rar they had finally arrived in? After all they'd overcome, just to arrive to find the All-Maudra murdered. The Vapra fire unlit, their throne overtaken by a daughter who had bent to the Skeksis. Amri slumped and put his head in his hands.

"This can't be. There has to be something we can do," he whispered.

Tae slammed her fist on the table.

"This isn't fair, Tavra! It should be you leading the Vapra— your voice that should be heard. It should be you standing against the Skeksis for the Vapra, not Seladon! Everyone has always known it should be you!"

Tavra's reply was more morose than ever. "Even if I wasn't this way, I have no right to the throne. Seladon is the oldest."

"You could challenge her," Tae insisted, all fire and wind. "And you would win."

"Clearly I would not, as I lacked the fortitude to withstand the Skeksis when I discovered their truth, leading to this predicament."

"And yet you fight on, like a true leader—"

"Because there is nothing else I can do!"

Tavra glinted, reflecting the firelight from the candles in the cabin. It was the only sign of emotion from her crystal body . . . that, and the spike of pain that barbed her voice.

"Of course I wish I could displace Seladon. Lead my people. But I can't! The Vapra cannot see me. Ha'rar cannot hear my voice. I cannot wield a sword against the ones that killed my mother. I cannot even hold the one I love. So let it go, Tae. Let *me* go and find another hero to put your faith in."

Tavra slipped through the cracks in the table planks, a moment later twinkling as she disappeared into the bedchamber. Anything to escape the conversation, Amri imagined. He felt a hard rock in his chest when he thought about how she must feel, trapped in a body that wasn't her own, unable to do what she otherwise might.

Onica was the one to break the solemn quiet.

"We came here hoping to light the fire of resistance in Ha'rar," she said. "We were nearly too late in Cera-Na, and in the Wellspring of the Dousan. The All-Maudra told us in a dream that she had lit the Vapra fire, but we don't believe she has. There was no sign of it when we lit the fire on the *Omerya*, or in the Dousan Wellspring caves. We need to find a way to unite the Vapra. But I don't know how we will be able to reach them all with the Skeksis in the city."

Tae sighed, running her hands through her hair and tugging briefly on her ears.

"The Skeksis requested the Vapra gather on the steps of the citadel tomorrow night. Some believe Seladon will make an appearance there and explain what the future holds for Ha'rar. Others believe the General will announce she's dead as well. Perhaps if the Vapra are gathered in one place, we might be able to reach them then . . ."

"But the General and the Ritual Master will be watching," Kylan finished with a pensive sigh. "If we speak to the Vapra then, and even if we're able to light the fire, the Skeksis will know. Our secret rebellion becomes a declaration of war, and I don't know if it's one we'll be able to win in the open."

Amri thought of the Mariner, watching the Sifa hearth fire light with rainbow flames from the deck of the *Omerya*.

"If they don't already," he murmured.

Tae reached out to hold Onica's hand in hers. "Onica, will you look into the fire for us?" she asked. "Ask Thra what we should do, and see if Thra answers?"

"Hmm. I will try."

Onica rose and went to the clay hearth, as she had the first day they'd met her. Amri cleared the table, leaving only the clay bowl. When the burning herbs were ready, they joined hands. Amri set his thoughts aside, trying to be present as Onica closed her eyes, deeply inhaling the dark scent of the smoke. He listened to Onica's steady breaths in the otherwise quiet little cabin. Amri tried to match the Far-Dreamer's breathing. His eyelids drooped as the smoke filled his lungs, clearing his mind. The ship rocked on the waves, but he felt one with the motion, as if he were the one floating on the current.

Nothing came out of the darkness. After a while, Onica shook her head. At first she looked like she might reach out again, initiate the meditation once more, but in the end she leaned over the bowl, grinding the herbs and putting out their smoldering.

"Nothing?" Tae asked, as if she'd hung all her hope on it.

"Thra is not answering," Onica replied solemnly. "It does not always, and we must find peace within that. It has been a long day, for all of us. There's nothing we can do for the Vapra tonight, and we cannot help them if we do not help ourselves."

She stood, wrapped her shawl around her shoulders, and left them, slipping behind the curtain that separated the cabin from her sleeping quarters. Amri chewed on his lip as the rest of them sat at the table in silence.

"Is she all right?" Kylan asked.

Tae stared after Onica, as if she could will the Far-Dreamer back to the table and the smoke. But nothing stirred, and so Tae gave it up, shaking her head. "I don't know. I guess she's right, though. We should rest while we can."

Amri started to protest, but he wasn't sure what to say. Onica was the Far-Dreamer and had seen nothing, and that seemed to be that. He exchanged a glance with Naia as they found quilts to bundle up in for the night. She reached out and squeezed his hand.

"It will be all right," she said, but her usual warmth and confidence were tempered. They all knew what they were up against. It didn't feel right to go to sleep, safe in Onica's cabin, while the Skeksis slowly plucked the fires from the hearths of the Vapra. Soon there would only be one light to look to, and it would not be the Waystar but the darkened heart of the Castle of the Crystal.

Amri stared at the herbs swaying overhead. One by one he heard his friends drift off to sleep, Naia snoring gently nearby, as he remained awake in thought. What the Vapra needed was something to remind them that there was hope. Something to remind them that they were not alone. It was what all the Gelfling needed, but now that the Skeksis walked in the citadel halls and held dominion over all of Ha'rar, it was the Vapra that needed it the most.

No, not something. Someone. But Tavra had no body and no voice. No way to reach her people in her current state. So small and silent, forgotten as soon as she disappeared from sight.

A creak and a CLUNK echoed off the planks of the small ship's hull. At first Amri thought it was just the boat bobbing against the wharf, but then it came again, followed by a splash.

"Naia. Did you hear that?"

His friend didn't stir at his whisper. He reached out and touched her shoulder gently, but she only snored and rolled the other way.

CLUNK.

He bolted up and then it was gone, the cabin still and silent. Only the fire moved, white coals undulating with red heat. Naia and the others slept, undisturbed.

"Tavra?" he whispered, but not even the princess answered.

Chills raced up Amri's back as a drumming, like a thousand thick fingers, drilled along the hull right behind his head. He stood, wrapping his blanket around his shoulders as if it would protect him from whatever was out in the water, padded across the cabin, and peeked out onto the deck.

A water spirit that lures childlings into the sea . . .

The night was frozen, the light of the Waystar refracting against the sky so it appeared three times as bright. Like a star, beaming down from the mountain cliffs that surrounded the city, as if calling out to the Vapra below. Calling silently, with its voiceless song.

Amri walked out, staring up at it. It had guided ships into the wharf, had brought travelers north as they came to meet with the All-Maudra. To see the beautiful Ha'rar, a place whose name was known as far and wide as the Gelfling race had traveled. A place now as vulnerable as Domrak. As silenced as a Silverling in the body of a spider.

He jumped at a splash off the side of the boat. The waves lapped against the hull, disturbed by whatever was in the water. Amri followed the sounds with his ears. It was something big, bigger than a Gelfling, clunking against the boat as it circled. Amri tightened his grip on his blanket and neared the edge, looking over.

The waters were black and impenetrable. He saw his reflection, lit by the Waystar, and wondered if this was what the darkness was like to daylighters. Mysterious and frightening. Filled with everything and anything, terrible and infinite.

Amri gasped out as a shape broke the waves. A long back with an even longer tail, silvery and dark. It collided with the hull and the entire ship rocked with an echoing *CLUNK*, and Amri grabbed hold of the rail to keep from losing his balance. He raced after the shape as it submerged again.

"Naia! Tavra! There's something out here!"

He neared the other end of the ship and saw the creature again. He grabbed a coil of rope, cursing as he tried to remember a knot—any knot. Why weren't his friends coming? Why hadn't they heard all the clunking?

At last, he got a slipknot out of the rope. Hands shaking, he waited. The waves came again, the water shimmering, and he threw the rope. It landed in the water just as the creature breached, snagging it. Amri's hands burned on the rope as it caught the thing, dragging the line as it dived with an incredible strength and speed.

"Naia!" he shouted. She didn't answer. She didn't come.

A loop of the rope came racing up behind him. Before he knew what was happening, it caught him around the ankle. He lost his footing as the line shot over the side of the rail, tangling around his legs. Then he was falling over the rail, crashing into the frigid ocean water below.

CHAPTER 22

Amri knew better than to scream underwater, but he couldn't help it. The shock of the cold water snapped at him like the jaws of a monster, charging into every limb. Bubbles poured from his lungs. When they popped on the surface, Amri wondered if his friends would hear his cry for help.

"Oh. Hello, there."

He clenched his last breath in his teeth. He looked around, trying to find the owner of the voice, but the water was murky as ink.

A blurry shape rushed below him, sweeping against his leg. The rope that was tangled there fell away, as if all its knots had been dissolved by magic. Amri spun in the current as the creature, huge and inconceivable, disappeared back into the depths of the water.

His lungs should be burning by now, he thought, pressing his hand against his throat. He remembered what it had been like in the Wellspring, his vision getting steadily foggy, saved only because he had been there with Naia. This time, floating in the ocean that felt like space, he felt none of those things. He didn't even feel the cold anymore.

"Am I dead?" he asked.

The water filled his mouth, but he didn't drown. He turned when he saw movement, but the creature that circled him, long and streamlined, was always just out of sight. It swooped through the thick water, giving scant glimpses of its long tail and powerful limbs that propelled it through the water as easily as a bird in flight.

"Not at all," it said, as if the waters themselves had spoken.

"Um . . . am I going to die?"

"That is a strange question."

Amri squinted as the thing passed again, close enough that he felt the currents of the water it displaced. He reached out, touching flowing cloth and soft hair. The creature's voice was familiar, though he couldn't place it. Salty like the sea, strong and everlasting.

"Are you a Mystic?" he asked.

"Hmm . . . I am pretty mystical."

The phrase was familiar. Amri had said it to Kylan and Naia about urLii, so long ago when they'd all visited the Tomb of Relics together. The first time he'd brought them to somewhere familiar to him. A place in the caves that was in his domain, far away from their world. Where he'd been home and they'd been strangers— and all he'd wanted to do was leave.

His lungs were still unstarved for air. He treaded the water, wondering how long it would take him to reach the surface, and what he would find when he got there. If he really was dead, would that be the end? Was this strange, glittering water the only thing keeping him from passing on?

"I'm gonna go," he said.

"Wait."

The creature came closer, a multi-limbed monster hovering before him. Its face was almost close enough for him to see, its countenance still uncomfortably familiar. It lifted one limb, reached it close enough to Amri that he could see the texture of its skin, dark and satiny.

"You *are* a Mystic," he gasped. Tavra's song of the water spirit echoed in his mind, bringing with it the vision of the lanterns guiding the way up the coast. "You're the one who lights the lanterns? The water spirit?"

It came closer, swirling the waters, enshrouded in a black-and-silver streaming mantle that folded and unfurled with the water. Amri's heart hammered when he saw its face, for a moment seeing the shrewd eyes of skekSa the Mariner.

"Are you skekSa's opposite?" Amri gasped.

"Opposition is a falsehood. Like day and night—convenient words, but only part of the truth. For there exists such a thing as dawn, and also dusk. All phases in the turning of the spheres. I am merely a swimmer of the seas."

"So you are a Mystic! Are you here to tell me how to help the Vapra?" Amri asked. In the past, the Mystics had come to their aid when they had needed it most. He hoped as much as he could hope that this was one of those times as well.

"You already know how to help the Vapra," the swimmer said, echoing his intonation so it was like hearing his own voice bubbling back at him.

"So you're not going to help."

"A compass is nothing without a ship."

"Then point me in the right direction!"

"I already have."

Amri tried not to show his frustration, as if it might scare the Mystic off. urLii had been like this, too, though back then if Amri had known he was a Mystic, he might have tried harder to learn from the absentminded old creature that frequented the Tomb of Relics. Amri swallowed his pride and spoke slowly and calmly.

Think, Amri!

"The lanterns and the Waystar led us here. But Ha'rar is a daylighter place, and the Vapra are daylighters themselves. I don't know anything about the city, or the snow, or the mountains. Just like I don't know anything about the sea or the desert. How can I possibly know how to help the Vapra? You should be speaking to Tavra instead of me!"

"I am speaking to whom I should be speaking. To the Shadowling that brought a song from deep caves to an oasis lake. Tell me, what is the difference between the waves of the sea and the waves of the sand?"

The Silver Sea. The Crystal Sea. Amri thought of Onica's ship and Periss's sand skiff. The way the Crystal Skimmers had leaped through the desert dunes like the hooyim of the ocean. Before he replied, the swimming Mystic continued:

"What is the difference between crystals of stone and crystals of water?"

"Crystals of water?" Amri asked. Then he remembered. "You mean ice?"

"Deatea. Fire. Deratea. Air. Kidakida. Water. Arugaru. Earth. Four words with one center sound. Four elements with one central heart. Water becomes steam. Is that not air? And then it burns. Is that not fire? Dawn becomes day becomes dusk becomes evening becomes night. Becomes dawn once again. Where does one end and the other begin? Is there such a thing?"

Amri's mind spun. Maybe he was drowning, after all. A swirl of bubbles rose, clouding the water between them. Amri shuddered, thinking of skekSa's behemoth ship. The bubbles came with more force, obscuring the Mystic's face. His time was ending and he still didn't have answers.

"But I'm a Grottan," he called desperately. "I don't know anything about waves except that I'm scared of the ocean. I don't know anything about the daylighter world except that I'm clumsy at walking in it!"

You're not clumsy at walking. You're clumsy wearing shoes.

Amri reached out, but he couldn't find her. Not anymore. More and more air came from below, the breath of Thra perhaps, and he surrendered to it. Rising higher and higher until . . .

"Amri!"

Amri's eyes flew open. Naia leaned over him, shaking him by the shoulders. When she saw he was awake, she leaned back.

It was still night. He was lying on the deck of Onica's ship, wrapped tightly in the blanket he'd brought out. His hair and clothes were not wet, though he was damp with melted snow. He blushed as Naia touched his shoulders, his cheeks, his neck, as if making sure all his parts were still intact. When he noticed what she was doing, her cheeks turned pink, too. She punched him gently in the shoulder.

"What were you doing out here?" she hissed. "It's so cold!"

"I thought I heard . . ."

Naia pulled him to his feet. A thin layer of snow had fallen, coating the deck. The waves that sloshed against the ship were silent, even. There was no swimming creature lurking below.

They went inside. The others were still asleep, and Amri sat at the table, while Naia put water on the fire.

"I had the strangest dream," he said. It tasted like a lie. It couldn't have been a dream, could it? He stared at the bundle of herbs in the center of the table, cold and dormant in the clay bowl. He shook his head. "Must have been a dream."

Naia brought him a cup of hot water and sat beside him. "What about?"

He told her, trying to speak quietly enough that they wouldn't wake the others. The cabin was small, though, and by the time he reached the end, Tae and Kylan were up. Even Onica came to listen, standing in the doorway, hands folded.

Amri finished and waited for them to agree that he had imagined it. That his mind had been opened by the fernsage smoke and brought him a vision that was a collection of his hopes and fears.

"The longer I'm awake, the more like a dream it seems," he said.

"Even if it was a dream, that doesn't mean it's not important," Onica replied. "Do you have any idea what it means?"

Amri blushed. "You're the Far-Dreamer. Aren't you supposed to be the one that knows . . ." Even as he spoke, he thought of what the Mystic had said. Dawn to day to dusk. Being a Far-Dreamer didn't mean it was her responsibility to know everything there was to know about dreams. Perhaps he had been putting too much stock in titles.

You already know how to help the Vapra.

He stood, pushed the cabin door open again, and went out into the night. It was the daylighter world out there, with the ocean to his back and the mountains of Ha'rar straight ahead.

But what were the mountains, if not miles and miles of stone and rock?

"Amri, where are you going?" Tae called after him. "It's dark out there, and dangerous! The Skeksis—"

"—can't see well in the dark," he said over his shoulder.

He didn't wait for the others, scampering over the side of the ship onto the icy wharf. They didn't need to come along. Even so, he heard Naia coming after him as he retraced his steps back to the stair that would take them up the cliffs back into the city.

"You forgot your sword," she said, handing it to him.

"Thanks."

He slung it at his hip, even though he didn't need it. Not this time. He marched up the stairs, and she fell in line behind him. She didn't ask what he was doing or where he was going. Didn't protest or try to tell him to stop. Her silence was determined, comforting. Once again, when he would otherwise have been alone, Naia was beside him.

They reached the street above. Though the hike from the wharf to the city was a long one, the Waystar grove on the bluffs above seemed no closer than before. A night wind blew, putting out some of the fires in the lanterns that hung under the Vapra eaves. It was so cold, not even snow fell, and that was good. The colder it was, the harder the ice.

Amri leaned down and pulled the straps off his sandals. Naia stood by and watched, hand on the hilt of her dagger. Ready to protect him from anything, even as he did something she didn't totally understand. He tried not to worry what Naia would think of him, acting like a Shadowling in the middle of the Gelfling capital. He couldn't worry about it. He had to be who he was.

He tossed the sandals aside, letting his back curve to the shape he had tried so hard to straighten. Barefoot, he crouched on the frozen stone pathways, and for the first time, his fingers and toes tasted the street of Ha'rar.

The vibrations reached him immediately, strong and clear through the dense rock and crystal ice that laced the stones of the city. He could feel the Vapra footsteps in their homes, pacing and fretting. Wondering what had happened to the All-Maudra and her daughter who had so quickly assumed the living crown and disappeared. He could hear the grumbling of the Skeksis in the citadel, whose ice and stone walls reverberated with their ugly voices and heavy feet. He could taste the ocean crashing against the cliffs, the endless waves that rolled in from the north. The gentle bobbing of Onica's ship against the wharf.

He could hear the trembling as clearly as he could hear the

Grottan in Domrak—maybe even more so. From the street to the Vapra homes to the citadel, the ocean and the cold blue mountains. It was all connected, intertwined somehow. As if some perfect, pure mineral laced the entire city in a web of crystal, originating from a source high in the mountains that looked down on Ha'rar.

Amri closed his eyes and pressed his ear against the street, listening. The song was different. It wasn't mineral like in the underground rivers of the Dousan Wellspring. Wasn't rock like the deep Caves of Grot. This was fluid, like the sea or the lakes or rivers. Clear and pristine. Diamond-hard, carrying the thousand sounds of the city from one end to the other.

It was crystal, but not of stone.

He opened his eyes and looked up, following the song of the crystal, this time with his eyes. Traced it all the way up the cliffs to the glowing white light that shone down from above. It was so simple, now that he knew. Now that he'd listened.

Naia peered at him curiously as he pulled his sandals back on so he could get back to Onica's ship without freezing the soles of his feet. The night faded as the dawn came slowly over the jagged horizon.

"We have to get Tavra and Kylan to the trees of the Waystar grove," he said. "I know how to send a message to the Vapra of Ha'rar."

CHAPTER 23

They planned to leave that evening, when they could move under the cover of the night. Until then, Amri found a corner of the cabin and crawled under a pile of pillows, blocking out the daylight. He dreamed of the stone tree in the belly of Grot. He stood before it as it died, limbs like roots, or roots like limbs. Knowing that if he could be breathed in by the ancient thing, flow into its veins and up its trunk, when he emerged on the other side, he would be a pink blossom on the slender boughs of the Sanctuary Tree.

He heard whispers. A thousand voices, all as one. The shadows moved with infinite limbs. When he woke, it took everything he had not to slap away the spider tapping the back of his hand.

"Is it time?" he asked.

"Yes. Are you ready?"

He nodded, staying under the pile of cushions in the dark for a moment longer. He imagined what it would have been like, if Tavra had been in her Gelfling body at this moment, huddled under a pile of Sifa quilts with him, talking to him from a finger's width away. It was an amusing scenario, but for once he kept his mouth shut about it.

"What about you?" he asked instead.

"I came here to ask you a favor."

"What's that?"

"In case anything should happen to me tonight. Someday, when the fires are lit. When it's safe. Would you find my sister Brea and tell her what happened? I want her to know that I didn't abandon her."

"No," he said. "I'll make sure you get to tell her yourself."

He sat up, emerging from his pile like an unamoth from a cocoon. Kylan looked up from where he sat at the table, holding his magic *firca* in his palms. Preparing for what he would do when they reached the Waystar, no doubt. Amri could only hope it would work.

"Good evening! Here, this one's got an opening for a sword," Naia said, twirling the cloak over his shoulders. It was silver and white, which felt wrong to him. All the cloaks he'd ever worn in Grot were black, to blend in with the caves. But it made sense. They were about to be climbing up the ice- and snow-laden mountains. Silver would blend in much better.

"Do I look like a Silverling?" he asked, pulling his hair out from inside the cloak collar.

Naia's ears turned pink. She looked away and mumbled, "Not a bit."

The cabin door creaked and Tae came in, the moonlight falling across her shoulders. She had changed out her Sifa sailing gear for a Vapra cloak, her wings peeking out from the slits in the back. A light dusting of snow clung to her red-gold hair.

"It's time," she said. "The Vapra are making their way to

the citadel. The General and the Ritual Master have not shown themselves. Neither has Seladon. There may be other Skeksis in Ha'rar as well, but I can't be sure. Even with the Waystar, it's getting very dark."

Amri let the cold air knock the sleep from his mind and body. He needed to be alert, awake. He could feel his eyes opening, blooming like night flowers in the dark.

"I'm ready," he said. "Naia? Kylan?"

Kylan stood, tucking his *firca* in his jerkin front. "As ever."

Naia was always ready. She clasped Onica's hand.

"We're counting on you in case of trouble," she said.

"The sails will be unfurled, the lantern lit," Onica said. "I will head for the bay below where the Waystar trees grow. Should anything happen, fly down to me and we will escape to fight another day. I believe in you."

With no more than that, the five of them left Onica and her ship in the harbor and hurried along the wharf. Amri cast a look back onto the Silver Sea, hoping to catch a glimpse of the swimmer in the water, but if she really was out there, she did not show herself.

As Tae had said, the Vapra of Ha'rar were already gathering near the steps that led up to the citadel. Huddled in their silver cloaks, whispering quietly among themselves. Amri heard the consistent sound of fear, and apprehension. He heard Seladon's name, and Tavra's. The sibilant sounds of the Skeksis Lords' names. skekUng, skekZok. skekSil, the Chamberlain. skekSo, the Emperor.

"Keep looking up," he said, though none of the Vapra heard him. He and his friends retreated in the other direction, away from the gathering crowd. The only thing that crossed their paths were the flurries of snow blown by the wind, from the far end of the mountains and across the city.

Tavra told Amri the way to the place where Ha'rar met the mountain, and he led Naia, Kylan, and Tae through the streets and up the narrow winding stairway of ice and stone. Against the cliff, they were protected from the wind, but Amri could see the trees on the mountain higher up swaying. It was going to get colder.

They passed a few dwellings built right into the mountain, but before long the stairway eroded to a simple steep footpath. Then, after only a short moment more, the footpath dissolved and they trudged through knee-deep snow in the forest.

As soon as they left the dim lanterns of the street, the others slowed their pace. Even Naia's steps were less confident as she picked her way over icy rocks and slippery, snow-coated slopes. Amri helped his friends along, cutting their path through the night, using Tavra's voice from his shoulder like a compass to guide their direction.

"I can't see a thing. Is this what it's been like for you, traveling in the day?" Naia asked as they reached a rocky ledge too high to step over. He made short work of it and crouched on the top, grabbing Naia's hand and pulling her up and over. She didn't wait for him to say yes before she added, "I didn't realize."

"It's all right," he said. "Not everywhere in Thra is caves and rocks." *Though night and ice is close enough*, he thought. Or at least he hoped it would be.

They paused to look down into Ha'rar. It was like looking into a picture, all painted in blue and black and white. The citadel, on the far end with its back to the sea, shone with the reflections of the stars and the moons.

"My directions are useless past this point," Tavra said. "The winds change the snow and ice too frequently. Follow the light, but be cautious. There are crags hidden by the ice, and snow-shelves that would send us falling to our deaths."

Tae brought up the rear. She seemed the least affected by the cold, perhaps from frequent visits to Ha'rar. She gave him a confident nod and added, "Our path is up to you now, Amri."

Something he'd longed to hear, but now that he had, it felt heavy on his shoulders. It was up to him to guide them—and protect them from danger. He knelt and touched the freezing stones. Under the deep snow, the mountain path still existed. He could feel its sturdiness.

"This way," he said, and the others followed without hesitation.

They climbed the mountain as the moons climbed the sky. The wind was so much stronger on the bluffs, casting sheets of snow off the trees. Amri's eyelashes started to freeze with crystals, the wind so cold, not even his breath clouded in front of him. The Waystar's light was powerful, shining from somewhere up ahead. They paused as they looked through the trees and rocks. The light seemed to come from everywhere, so bright that it obscured their path more than illuminated it.

He touched the stones and stopped when he heard a different kind of voice in the earth. He frowned. "There's something strange up ahead . . . A building of some sort. Does someone live up here?" he asked.

"Not that I'm aware of," Tavra said. "But these cliffs are ancient. Not many travel this far. If someone came up here and built something, I doubt anyone would know. Or care."

"It would be a nice way to live if you wanted to be alone," Naia remarked.

"And if you didn't mind freezing," Kylan added, teeth chattering.

Amri led the way. The dark of the night dissolved under the nearing radiance of the Waystar's light, shining on a stone structure surrounded by trees. It was nothing special from the outside, just a tall mound of stones and ice with a simple wood door.

They knocked, but no one answered. No firelight flickered inside. It had all the appearance of abandonment, but the door opened easily when Naia gave it a strong tug. Inside was a single round room, barren except for a stone table and a fire well. A wood staircase wound up the wall in a spiral, toward a chamber at the very top of the tower. It looked like what the inside of a spiraling seashell must look like, if it were big enough to build a home inside.

"What is this place?" Amri asked aloud.

"This hearth has been lit recently," Kylan said. He held his hand out over the coals as Tae brought a bundle of kindling from a pile of sticks and timber. "Within days."

"I don't know who's to thank, but I'm grateful for a place to warm up before we head out to the Waystar grove," Naia said.

"It shouldn't be much farther," Tavra agreed. "But we can't stay too long. We must reach the Vapra while they are gathered before the citadel. Before the Skeksis cow them with whatever lies they are about to deliver."

Amri nodded. "Warm up and then we'll go."

While Kylan started the fire, Amri touched the parchments that were strewn across the stone worktable. The soft, cold paper was thick and fibrous, covered in ink-drawn maps and charts. He recognized the coastline of the Silver Sea, from Kylan's book, meticulous and fine-detailed, every landform and eddy and bay lovingly titled and detailed. Cera-Na and her fingerlike headlands, even the sand river they'd taken into the desert. The Caves of Grot, the Claw Mountains. The long tail of the Black River, the lifeline of the Skarith Basin.

There were other charts, too, but they were not of the land. Amri recognized stars and the Sisters, the patterns of the wind drawn across the sky where it intersected with the path of the Brothers. The pictures of the seasons and the ninets, how the phases of the moons changed course as Thra moved through time and space.

"They're written in ink, not dream-etching," he said, touching the black letters. Naia joined him, looking over his shoulder. She brightened, pointing.

"Look, this is Sog. See how the water crosses through the

wetlands to the south and joins the sea? Great Smerth is here." She pointed to a spot in the depth of the swamp. Amri paged through the other maps, arranging them on the big stone slab so the Black River lined up. The single line that drew them all together, until they had a map of the Skarith Land.

"Our world," he said, feeling a chill. He touched the Dark Wood, the ink that drew the shape of the Castle of the Crystal. It was hard to believe how much of it they'd seen in only the past few days. And to arrive in Ha'rar, after how long they'd spent trying to reach it.

"You know what you're going to say?" he asked Tavra.

"Yes," the Silverling spider replied. "I don't know if it will be enough, but it is all I have. I can only hope that my words can move the Vapra to believe that there is hope . . . even without my mother and Seladon to guide them."

"They still have you," Naia assured her. "Even if your voice is small. If Amri's right, and if Kylan can do what he did with the Sanctuary Tree, then . . ."

They turned as Tae backed away from one of the small holes in the stones that served as a window, ears twisting forward.

"Someone's coming!" she whispered.

Heavy footsteps crunched through the snow, just outside the door. There was nowhere to run; whoever was coming would soon find them, and Amri could only hope the owner of the domed building was a hospitable type. Perhaps the swimming Mystic who had given Amri the wisdom to find his way up here.

The door slammed open. A monstrous black creature stood

there, mountain wind tearing at her heavy coat. She doffed her plumed hat and shook the snow and ice from its feathers before fitting it back upon her brow.

"*You,*" skekSa the Mariner said in her deep, velvet voice. "What are you doing here? Who told you of this place—where is its keeper?"

Her menacing eyes fell upon Amri and his friends, then the star charts and sea maps. Amri found his hand on the hilt of Tavra's sword. skekSa reached back and slammed the door, throwing the latch so there was no escape. She leveled the room with her gaze, hot breath steaming from her nostrils.

"Tell me, and I will let you live," she growled. "Where is urSan the Swimmer?"

CHAPTER 24

"We don't know what you're talking about," Naia said. skekSa swept closer, filling the room. She tilted her head at Amri, counting the number of Gelfling before her, then leaned over the worktable and smoothed her claws along the paper and ink, touched the tomes and scrolls. Her gaze lingered on the maps they'd been looking at, then came back to the Gelfling before her.

"Maybe I believe you."

"Why are you in Ha'rar?" Amri asked. "Weren't you supposed to stay with the Sifa in Cera-Na?"

"Why would I? They abandoned me. Without their navigators and charts, I cannot escape this infernal mainland. Then Emperor skekSo called me to Ha'rar when things got, how shall we put it? Complicated. With All-Maudra Mayrin. And I remembered that there *is* someone with the charts I need, who keeps them in her tower near the Vapra Waystar grove."

What is a compass without a ship? Amri remembered what the swimming Mystic, urSan, had said. As he watched skekSa tear through the scrolls and maps on the worktable, he realized the inverse was also true.

"What is a ship without a compass?" he murmured.

"What did you just say?"

skekSa glared at him, as if he'd said some secret word that had revealed a hidden weakness. She stepped away from the worktable and loomed over him, feathers on her neck rising so she looked twice her already intimidating size.

"Nothing," he lied.

"*Hm.* You know, I met with my friend Lord skekZok earlier this night," she purred, tongue sharp with a barely softened threat, "about the Stonewood traitor. Apparently, Lord Chamberlain skekSil ran afoul of a group of Gelfling south of Ha'rar. One in particular—a Vapra, to his memory, but I think he may be mistaken—threw Sifa fire dust in his eye. You wouldn't know who that might have been, *my little apothecary?*"

Amri tried not to shrink back. "He was asking for it."

"Oh, you can burn out both his weepy eyes for all I care. The part that fascinated me, my dears, was the Chamberlain's description of the Drenchen of the group. A rough-and-tumble little thing with healing *vliyaya*, who'd broken into the Castle of the Crystal and lived to escape. Ritual Master skekZok is very keen in this aspect, you see. And since we are friends, he and I, then you can imagine I am keen as well."

Naia stood tall, drawing her dagger. Amri pulled Tavra's sword from his hip. skekSa barely noticed, circling the room until her back was to the door again, standing between them and the exit.

"Of course, I didn't fully understand his interest in you when we met in Cera-Na," skekSa continued. "But now that I do, and now that he's offered me a reward for your capture, how fortunate it is that you are here before me, trapped in this tiny room."

"I'm not going with you," Naia said. "And I'm not going to the castle. And I'll die before I let you drain me like you drained Mira and Tavra!"

skekSa held out her hands. It was meant to be pacifying, but all Amri saw were her claws.

"Hush, my dear. skekZok doesn't plan to set you before the blasted reflector. We merely need you and your twin brother for . . . information. Your bodies may have the answers to a question many of us have been asking."

Kylan spoke up, standing firm beside Naia. "Aughra said you're wrong. She said it's not going to help you understand how to drain your other halves."

skekSa scoffed.

"Is that what they think? Unfortunate. Now listen. I've no more time for games, so here is my proposal. I will let the three of you"—she pointed at Amri, Kylan, and Tae—"escape. But you must leave this mountain immediately, and you must never get in my way again. And in exchange for your lives, I get to keep you, my Drenchen dear. To myself."

The pit in Amri's stomach, left from when he'd swallowed his fear and gone aboard skekSa's ship, felt like a buried seed struggling to come to life. He'd tried to leave it in darkness to die, but skekSa's words were like light to it, bringing it to sprout. He'd been right. The whole time.

Naia pointed her dagger at skekSa. Before Amri could stop

her, she said, "I'll take that deal, but I won't go with you without a fight."

"Naia, no—"

Kylan's protest was cut off by skekSa's grin. She knocked aside her coat, baring the glinting gold handle of a long blade slung at her waist, putting a hand on the grip and sliding it loose with a deadly, metallic scrape.

"I accept your challenge," she said.

"Naia, you can't. Don't do this!"

Amri grabbed Naia's arm, but Tae pushed him away toward the door.

"I'll stay with her," the Sifa said, brandishing her dagger. "Get out of here with Kylan. We came up here to do something, and we're going to do it. I need you to make sure of it. All right?"

She looked at him, confident and determined. Amri tried to remember that she was Maudra Ethri's first-wing, daring and courageous as any Sifa could be. Without Tavra, Tae was their best chance. He nodded, backing away. Kylan didn't move, hand drifting like he was going to stay and fight. Naia glared at them with defiant spring-blue eyes.

"Go!" she said.

Amri grabbed Kylan and ran. Past skekSa as she stepped aside, shoving open the door and squeezing out onto the blustery cold mountain slope.

"We can't just leave them in there with skekSa!" Kylan yelled, grabbing Amri by the collar.

"skekSa won't kill Naia!" Amri shouted. "They want her alive.

Remember? They kept Gurjin alive. So if they do the same for Naia, we still have time to think of something!"

Kylan wouldn't give up. "Maybe not Naia, but what about Tae—"

"We have to trust her!"

The song teller shut his mouth and glared, eyes red from the cold and anger. Amri tried not to care, turned away and fixed his sights on the cold light of the Waystar. A moment later, he heard Kylan following. He hated it, leaving Naia and Tae behind. Trudging through the cold snow as if his heart weren't aching with worry.

He felt a gentle prick on his cheek.

"We will succeed," Tavra said softly. Ardently. "We have to. Then we will return to Naia and Tae and make sure we all leave this place alive."

They left Naia, Tae, and skekSa behind in the stone hovel, heading up a steep incline toward the Waystar. The slope was almost vertical in places, and Amri helped Kylan up and up, closer and closer to the glowing above. When they finally climbed over a ledge of icy rock, Amri gasped.

A grove of trees grew in a circle on a pointed bluff that stretched out over Ha'rar. They glowed blue and white with such radiance, it was as if six stars had fallen to earth and bloomed. They had reached the grove of star trees the Vapra called the Waystar.

"Quickly," Tavra said, shaking them from their awe. "Look, below. The Vapra gather and the Skeksis will soon come."

Below, the citadel was alight with little flames. Even Amri's eyes found it difficult to see through the dark, against the Waystar's light. But he could imagine the Vapra gathering on the front steps of the citadel. Huddling in the cold, feeling alone. Hoping that soon, All-Maudra Seladon would appear to them and tell them what their futures held. They hoped for reassurance, for strength in the face of uncertainty. And that was what they were about to get.

"All right," Amri said, looking between the trees. "Let's do this."

He held out a hand and touched the faceted bark of the nearest tree. Its light came from its core, neither hot nor cold to the touch. He closed his eyes and listened to the tree's song. Listened to how its roots burrowed down through the mountain, followed the water and ice that spread like veins through all of the city below.

But this tree's reach was not complete. Its roots were still young. Amri moved to the next, and the next. Touching and listening, feeling the vibrations of life. Seeing in his mind's eye how far the roots ran, which tree would bring Tavra's message the farthest and widest.

Then he found it. Not the tallest tree of the copse, but the sturdiest, with a wide base and gnarled roots. Its glow was not even the brightest, its layers of bark somewhat dimming its inner glow. Amri smiled when he touched the tree's skin with both hands. He could hear everything through its body—the whole mountain, every buried water source and frozen river vein. Every street of Ha'rar, every trickle of water that ran below every Vapra home.

"This one," Amri said. "This is the one."

Kylan stood beside him, touching the tree's bark. "Are you sure?"

Amri had never been so sure of anything. All the anxiousness and worry about whether he would be able to find the right tree, deliver the message—light the Vapra fire—washed away as he looked upon the ancient tree.

"It has grown here since long before the Vapra arrived," he said. "Before Ha'rar. This tree knows the entire mountain, the entire valley. Runs under the citadel and through every street of Ha'rar. If it agrees to carry Tavra's message, every Gelfling in the snowy land will see her dream. Hear her voice, and know they are not alone . . . Are you ready?"

Kylan gulped, eyes wide, staring at the tree. He took his *firca* from his jerkin and glanced to Tavra. "I'm ready. Tavra?"

Tavra darted down Amri's arm, hesitating on his hand before stepping onto the bark itself. The light from inside the tree glowed when she touched it, filling her crystal body with its radiance.

"Ready," she said. "Amri, if this works and we light the flames of resistance within the hearts of the Vapra, I and the rest of my clan will be indebted to you and the Grottan."

A wave of calm washed over Amri as they stood in the Waystar's light.

"Light and dark are not in opposition," he said. "The Vapra. The Grottan . . ." He nodded to Kylan. "The Spriton—all of the clans. We may be seven, all distinct and special. But we are all a part of the clan called Gelfling. It is time to gather as one."

Tavra twinkled. "Indeed," she said.

"Now go on!" Amri cried. "Do the thing! We don't have much time left."

Kylan nodded and raised his *firca* to his lips. He played the first tone, a harmony that Amri recalled from when the song teller had played before the Sanctuary Tree. As he did, the brightness of the ring of trees intensified, light rippling along the boughs of the trees and into their transparent leaves.

"And now Tavra . . ." Amri breathed. He closed his eyes and pressed his forehead against the tree's rough bark. Tried to dreamfast with it, the way Naia could. It wasn't a gift possible for him, but he tried anyway. *Please. Carry Tavra's song to the Gelfling below. Let them know the truth, before they are blinded by the Skeksis' lies.*

A light flashed in Amri's mind, like a spark lit in the place where dreams were born. He saw the three of them standing before the copse of trees. *Three* of them—Tavra was with them, resplendent in her Vapra gowns, a silver circlet on her brow. As Kylan played the *firca*, its song resonating into the tree's core, Tavra spoke. As she did, her words were etched upon the tree, her voice stitched along its crystal heart.

"Hear me, Vapra," Tavra began. Her voice was in Amri's mind. In Kylan's song. She paused and looked at Amri in the strange dreamfast, her lavender eyes glittering like twilight. Amri couldn't help but feel pride, a part of him in her words when she began again:

"Hear me, Gelfling of Ha'rar. I can only hope you hear me and recognize my voice. I do not have much time, so I can only tell you part of all I have to say. And it is that the Skeksis have lied to all of us. The dream on the pink petals is true. The Skeksis have begun draining us, deep in the Castle of the Crystal. My mother the All-Maudra knew this and planned to rise against them. And in punishment, the Ritual Master and the General murdered her."

Amri felt a tremble in the dream, as if the earth itself was shivering. The whispers that shuddered through the tree's veins and the ice and rock were from the Vapra. From anyone who was listening, who heard Tavra's voice.

"I do not know what the future holds for the Gelfling, but I know this: No matter what the Skeksis say to you, no matter how dark the night may seem—there are friends in that darkness, waiting for you. Readying the torches we will bring against the Skeksis, when it is time for their reckoning. We will survive. We will endure. Wait for our signal. Let it guide you and we will be victorious, so long as we are together."

It felt like the beginning of an electric storm crawling across the earth and skin. Amri felt the warming of kindling and a thin string of smoke. He felt footsteps, the earth shaking. Distant voices as Tavra finished:

"I know this and I wait for you, though it may be in the darkness. For in the shadows, we will light the fires of resistance."

"Amri—Kylan—!"

CRASH!

Amri fell out of the dream as one of the Waystar trees cracked in half. It toppled, throwing clouds of snow and shards of ice into the air, refracting the light and splintering into rainbows. The snow and ice settled, and Amri climbed to his feet, drawing Tavra's sword from his hip.

skekSa stood in the wake of the destroyed Waystar tree, giving her deadly sword one flick and sending the remains of the ice from its blade. Black blood dripped from across her beak, her eyes furious and vengeful. She let out an angry roar as she knocked the broken tree out of her way.

"I told you to leave," she rumbled.

Naia appeared beside Amri. Across the copse, he saw Tae alight near Kylan. He wasn't happy skekSa had come up the cliff after them, but at least she seemed to be slowed down by her weight in the snow.

"We tried to stop her, but she's so strong," Naia said. She had a cut on her cheek, an ugly bruise growing on her forehead. Yet fierce as ever, her brother's dagger in her hand. "Did Tavra's message . . . ?"

"The dream went out. It's up to the Vapra now—are you all right? What happened?"

"She said—" Naia flinched and shook her head. "It doesn't matter. She's a liar like the rest of them."

"Now what have you done?" skekSa growled. "Stupid little Gelfling. I gave you a way out. And this is how you repay me? This is how you abuse my benevolence?"

"Benevolent? Is that what you think you are?" Tae shouted. She pushed Kylan behind her, baring her dagger that had already tasted skekSa's flesh. "The Sifa trusted you. Have trusted you

for trine upon trine. Was it all a lie?"

skekSa composed herself, just a fraction, standing straighter and sniffing.

"Little Tae," she said, though a snarl sharpened the edge of her beak. She grabbed another of the Waystar trees and cracked its limbs in her claws, careless with her impossible strength. Its glow died like an ember pulled from the fire. "I would have taken Ethri and the Sifa across the Silver Sea. Far away from the Emperor and the castle and all of these stupid politics. But Ethri decided not to go. It was you who defied me. Declared your true allegiance. I am not an ally of the Sifa. I am your *master*."

Tae drew herself back, wings flinching as skekSa swept forward. Amri tried not to back away as she loomed over them, standing in the center of the circle of trees.

"Now, as your lord, I will tell you the same thing the General and the Ritual Master are telling the Vapra below. At this very minute. The rebellion is dead and a lie, burnt to cold ash along with the All-Maudra. The Vapra, and the rest of the Gelfling, have only one fate: To bow to the Skeksis, and to gaze upon us with immortal fear. To cower in utter subservience."

Her voice fell low and sinister as her breath clouded around them like a fog.

"There will be no more fires," she said. "And there will be no resistance."

Amri kept his back straight and pointed over the cliff.

"Then what's that?" he asked.

skekSa's piercing eyes glinted as she followed his gaze. Together,

Skeksis and Gelfling watched. Peering through the dark, as one by one, the gold flames of the Vapra torches turned blue.

Then purple and red and pink. Like the flames they'd lit aboard the *Omerya* and the one that had resurrected the Wellspring. From above on the bluff, Amri could only see the fires, lighting one after the other like stars awakening at dusk.

"They heard you," Amri whispered, but Tavra was not on his shoulder. He realized he didn't know where she was and hoped she was with Kylan and Tae.

The Waystar trees pulsed, then flashed, engulfed in the mystical, unburning fire like a miniature sun. The city below was lit as if it were daytime, rippling in unending colors. The light fell upon the icy streets, refracting into rainbows until the citadel itself ignited with the light of the fire in the sky. It was too bright. Amri covered his eyes, though he desperately wanted to watch.

When he was able to look again, he fell silent with the rest of them.

Blazing on every faceted, icy wall of the Vapra citadel were dream-etchings, burned across the citadel like ink on parchment. Like the etchings on the deck of the *Omerya* and the cloisters near the Wellspring . . .

Like on a wall, Amri realized. A wall engulfed in the flame.

He stared in wonder at the etchings as they rippled across the broad surface of the citadel, unraveling for all to see. The depictions of the *Omerya*, the Sifa, Maudra Ethri. The shade-filled leaves of the Wellspring Tree, protecting the Dousan from the darkening storm.

And now the next verse of the song, which they had told that very night atop the frozen bluffs: Shining like a star, radiant with light, was the image of a Vapra soldier-princess, the crest of six trees emblazoned on her living crown.

CHAPTER 25

SkekSa stared, wide-eyed, rage saturating her dark eyes and making her look more Skeksis than ever. Amri tried not to let it frighten him. Not now that they'd had their victory lighting the Vapra flame. All that was left was to escape the Mariner's clutches. Survive, like Tavra had said.

Naia stood beside him, turning her sights from the citadel to the Skeksis. Across the ring of trees, Tae did the same, protecting Kylan as he put away his *firca*.

skekSa gnashed her fangs and gestured with her sword. It was longer than Amri was tall, heavy and sharp and wickedly hooked, made for killing.

"I'll give you one more chance. Come with me, Naia, and I will let the others go. If you resist, I will kill them and take you with me anyway. If it comes to that, their blood will be on your hands."

"I'll die before I go with you," Naia said.

skekSa's purr turned into a vicious growl in her throat, deep and primal.

"Have it your way."

She charged at Tae, swinging her sword. Even if its edge were not sharp, the sheer power and weight of it would crush a Gelfling if it struck. Tae leaped, wings taking her up so her toes touched the gleaming metal of the blade. She ran along the sword, leaping again and slashing with her dagger.

"We have to help her!" Amri said, raising Tavra's sword. It was hard to imagine bringing it against the Skeksis, especially when he still had no real skill with it. But what else could he do?

"Take care of Kylan," Naia said. "Remember thirty parries? We'll try to hold her back. Onica was supposed to bring her ship around to the bay!"

She grabbed his shoulder and squeezed. Then she ran ahead, dagger shining in the Waystar light, loosing a mighty battle cry that caused even skekSa to pause. Amri watched for only a moment as Naia and Tae converged on the Skeksis Mariner, blades inescapable as a storm at sea or in sand.

He found Kylan near the old Waystar tree that had carried their message, Tavra on his shoulder. On the other side of the tree was the edge of the cliff, and after that, a long, hard fall into the sea.

"We can't let her destroy the trees," Kylan said. "Not after they helped us send Tavra's message—"

"We have to save ourselves first!" Tavra said.

"But how?" Amri cried, glancing over the cliff, but no Sifa lantern broke the black darkness of the ocean that stretched below the cliff. If they could escape at all, it would be down the mountainside. And to do that, they had to get past skekSa—

"Amri, look out!"

Amri turned at Naia's warning. Unnaturally fast, skekSa rushed at him, sword dropping from the sky like lightning. He raised his sword in time to block the blade, but she twisted hers to the side. The hook caught and wrenched his sword from his hand, sending it flying. Unarmed, he backed away, trying to keep from shaking as he put himself between the Skeksis and Kylan.

Naia and Tae caught up. Before skekSa could cut Amri and Kylan down, Naia was on skekSa's back, Tae slashing with her dagger as she came around the front. skekSa stumbled back, unable to grab Naia and avoid Tae's flurry of attacks at the same time.

Skeksis blood stained the snow and skekSa roared, finally leaping back and away from the reach of Tae's vicious blade. Distance gained, skekSa reached over her shoulder and tore Naia from her cowl, throwing her aside. Her entire body steamed with rage as she lumbered again toward the Gelfling huddled at the foot of the ancient Waystar tree.

"She's coming for us," Amri said. "She still doesn't want to kill Naia, but she'll certainly kill us if she has the chance!"

Tae panted from where she crouched, in front of Amri, Kylan, and Tavra. Wings splayed, dagger poised to defend them with every ounce of silver metal. She glanced back, her eyes darting from Amri to Kylan and finally landing on Tavra.

"Whatever happens," she said, "protect them. Light the fires. I believe in you."

Before they could ask what she meant, Tae tossed back her cloak, baring her wings, brilliant and blue. As skekSa approached, she leaped into the air. The wind froze across the scales of Tae's wings, glittering like the stained glass that laced the citadel.

She folded her wings, dropping from the sky with astonishing speed. skekSa lifted her sword against the Sifa, but she was too slow.

Tae's dagger bit. skekSa's sword flipped into the air, and Amri caught his heart in his teeth when he saw that the Skeksis's severed hand still clutched the hilt as it flew.

skekSa screamed. She grasped the stump where her hand had been.

"*How dare you!*" she cried, over and over. "*HOW DARE YOU!*"

Tae landed before skekSa, up to her knees in snow, showered in the frozen spittle spraying from skekSa's beak. She drew her dagger back, as if she might take another of the Skeksis's hands. Her eyes were up, but Amri saw movement below.

"Tae, look out—"

One of skekSa's smaller arms slipped out from the Skeksis's coat. Something flashed, and a *BOOM* rang through the mountain air. A cloud of smoke exploded from skekSa's hip, blasting Tae off her feet. She crashed into one of the Waystar trees, leaving a red mark on its glowing white bark where she struck. Then she fell into the snow and did not rise.

The smoke cleared. skekSa coughed and reached into the depths of her coat again, drawing out a leathery, egg-shaped device and holding it in her tiny palm. Her breath rasped in anger and pain, her blood still falling on the white snow. She stumbled to one knee.

"I can't believe this," she panted. "Can't believe it one bit."

"Onica," Kylan said in the tense silence that followed. The song teller's eyes were wide with fear from what they had witnessed. From where he stood, he could see over the cliff. His voice cracked as he whispered, "I can see her lantern light . . ."

"Go to Tae," Amri said. They had to assume she was alive, that she had survived the blast. He didn't know what they'd do if she hadn't.

"But what if she's—" Kylan didn't finish.

"We'll have to figure out something! I'll find Naia . . . Hurry!"

Kylan nodded and ran to where Tae had landed as Amri went the other direction. He found Naia in a mound of snow, groaning. He stooped and pulled her up. If they could just make it to the cliff before skekSa came after them again—

"Are you all right?" he asked. "Are you hurt? Onica's reached the bay."

"I'm hurt, but I'll be fine," Naia said. She slipped off Amri's shoulder to bear her own weight. He was worried she would try to fight again, try to take on the Skeksis even though he had no idea how. To his relief, she shoved him toward the cliff and said, "We'll have to fly down. It's our best chance!"

They trudged through the snow as quickly as they could. Amri could see Kylan kneeling beside Tae up ahead. It didn't look good.

"Oh no," Naia breathed. "Tae—"

"You're not getting away."

skekSa's voice brought them to a halt. skekSa had seen them, seen the direction in which they were headed. In spite of her grisly wound, skekSa took hold of one of the Waystar tree limbs, using it to pull herself to her feet. In her little hand, she still held the egg-like contraption that had blasted Tae. Without breaking stride, she hurled it at them with deadly aim.

"Naia!" Amri lunged, snatching a fallen branch from the snow and flinging it as he knocked Naia aside.

His aim was good. The egg exploded in the air, the blast knocking him into a spin in the freezing snow. He lost time, felt cold on his cheek. Then Naia's arms around him as she tried to lift him. He tried to get his feet under him, but he could barely breath, let alone move.

She let him down, and he saw her step over him, brandishing her dagger as skekSa reached them. Amri groaned and tried to get up. Tried to master his limbs that refused to obey, even as skekSa stepped up, casting her shadow upon them. She had found her sword, held it in the hand that was intact, carelessly bleeding from the other as if it meant nothing.

"I don't want to do this," she said slowly, her blade tasting the snow at her feet. Her voice turned hard at the end, wicked as her sword. "I told you we had a deal—you ungrateful fool."

She struck. Her blade rippled white with the Waystar's light—

Then *blue*, through iridescent Sifa wings.

Sparks flew from metal clashing, and skekSa cursed, then screamed as the tip of a Vapra sword sliced her claws, flipping her deadly sword out of her grasp and this time sending it over the cliff and plummeting to the sea below.

"NO!"

Amri tried to move again. The world still swung below him; his ears still rang. His eyes were still hazy, trying desperately to focus.

But even so, he could see who stood between them and skekSa: a Sifa with hair gold as the sun, holding Tavra's sword. Shining on her neck was a crystal spider, silver and blue as the moon.

The ringing dulled enough that Amri could hear Tavra's words, stern and commanding in Tae's voice.

"Get out of here, to the cliff," she said. "Run! Fly!"

"Out of my way!"

skekSa lunged for Naia, but was blocked by the ruthless blade in Tae's hand. Not even skekSa's three remaining hands could catch her as she leaped to the air, flitting and diving and spinning like a flurry of snow in the wind.

Naia hoisted Amri's arm over her shoulder, and he willed his feet to move. Willed himself to look away, to trust that Tavra had the skills and that Tae's body had the strength to fight skekSa. By the time Naia got him to the cliff, Amri could control his feet again. Kylan was waiting where Tae had fallen. Amri shoved Naia at him when the air shook with skekSa's frustrated roar.

"Tavra and Tae can't hold her off forever!" he told Naia. "Take Kylan and go!"

Naia nodded. She grabbed Kylan and leaped just as skekSa and Tae erupted from the grove. The Mariner thrashed at the Sifa with a tree branch, trying to strike her down like an annoying bug.

But Tae was too quick. She swept back on the wind, well ahead of skekSa and alighting beside Amri.

"Quickly," Tae said. "Hold on!"

But he knew it wasn't Tae. Not really. It was Tavra who spoke to him as she slipped her arm around his waist. Tavra, using the power of the crystal-singer to move Tae's body. The way she'd moved Amri's, back in the Crystal Sea. Amri had seen what had happened to Tae when she'd been struck by skekSa's explosive device. She'd been unconscious—unmoving. It was only Tavra that was keeping her in motion right now.

skekSa lunged for them, snatching, but she was too late. Amri held on as Tavra spread Tae's wings and leaped off the cliff, flying toward the lantern on Onica's ship.

The fall was like leaping into space. Though Amri didn't remember the ocean being warm, he could feel the temperature rise as they dropped, melting the frost from Tavra's wings. No—they were Tae's wings, weren't they? Amri's mind spun. He didn't know anymore.

Morning was coming, sunlight creeping across the horizon in the distance and slowly melting the cold of night from the capped waves of the Silver Sea. Above them, skekSa's curses turned into screams. They'd escaped.

"You saved us," he said.

"I'm trying." He glanced into Tae's face, and he saw Tavra looking back at him. It was eerie, and heartbreaking. "The others are up ahead. Reach out and grab them. I don't think Naia will be able to make the landing."

Naia's black wings were half-spread, slowing her descent but not flight-worthy enough to break their fall. Tavra understood the currents here, bringing them close enough that Amri could take hold of Naia's hand. When he had her, the five of them rode the snowy current the rest of the way down.

As soon as their feet touched the deck of Onica's ship, Tae collapsed. Amri grabbed her by the waist and lowered her as Naia scrambled to her side, spreading her hands and bathing her in blue light. Onica leaped from the mast where she'd been waiting, eyes filled with tears.

"What happened? Is she all right?" she asked. "Tae!"

Naia's expression was grim but not hopeless. She stopped healing Tae long enough to say, "She's hurt badly, but I think I can save her. Let's get her inside, where it's warm. Quickly!"

In the cabin, surrounded by candles and the scent of herbs, Amri sat by Naia's side as she focused. The power of the Drenchen girl's *vliyaya* was strong, almost tangible in the air like a scent of water and life. Washing away the bruises and cuts, mending the broken bones and cracked wing Tae had sustained in her vicious battle with skekSa.

In the end, the glowing eased and Naia put her hand on Tae's forehead.

"I've healed her body," she said, brow creased with pain. "But she was deeply injured by that explosion. Even though I've mended her cuts and broken bones, her mind still sleeps. I cannot even sense her dreams. I don't know when she will wake . . . if ever."

It was hard to imagine. The Sifa merely looked as if she were sleeping.

"I didn't mean to . . . ," Tavra began. She rested on Tae's cheek, glistening like a tiny moon in a cloud of sun-gold hair. Amri sighed and shook his head. The moon had eclipsed the sun during a storm in Ha'rar, after all.

"You didn't do anything wrong," he said. "You brought her body back here so Naia could heal her. You saved us all, and you couldn't have without her. That's what she would have wanted. When she wakes up, I'm sure that's what she'll say."

The air reverberated with the sound of a metallic whistle. Amri pressed his hands over his ears as it rang through the chill air. He knew that sound. And with a dread knot in his gut, he knew what would come next.

Amri ran out onto the deck, followed by the others. The ship trembled as the sea shook. He grabbed hold of the rigging on the ship as waves rolled out from the ocean and crashed across the back of an enormous black shell. A deafening moan trembled through the water and echoed against the steep cliff. Terror shot through Amri's body as a behemoth mouth rose from the depths, water gushing from its enormous hooked-beaked maw.

It gaped, spreading its jaws. The ocean churned, sucked into the black abyss of the creature's throat. Onica's ship was caught in a vortex of inescapable currents, and Amri watched the slowly brightening sky disappear as the monster ship closed its jaws, swallowing them into a sea of darkness.

CHAPTER 26

Amri woke with his cheek against a hard, wet surface and a bitter taste in his mouth and filling his nose. He sat up in the dim light. The room was small and without windows, doors, or corners, like a bubble made of ligaments and muscles that had gone stiff with disuse. Of course there was a dungeon in the belly of skekSa's monster ship.

"Take it easy."

Over the pounding in his head, he hadn't even realized he wasn't alone. Tae sat beside him, her calm hand resting on his shoulder as he groaned. From the cautious, stern look in her eye, he knew that it wasn't really Tae. Not yet. The spider hiding in her hair glimmered.

"Tavra," he said.

"It seems I must protect Tae's body a bit longer," she replied.

He sat up. Kylan sat beside him, Onica kneeling at Tavra's side. They looked relieved to see he was awake, but none of them were in a position to be happy about anything. They were in a cell, albeit a strange one. Captives, despite the fight they'd put up and the casualties they'd taken. Amri tried not to dwell on it.

"What happened? How long was I out?"

"We don't know," Kylan said. "But I don't think very long."

Amri bolted upright, realizing one of them was missing.

"Where's Naia?"

"Escaped," Tavra replied. "Which is what we must do, as soon as we are able."

She was right. Amri stood. Fighting the throbbing in his head, he pressed his hands against the sticky, pulsating walls to no avail. Arteries of slow-moving blood branched and tangled between the bulging contours of the wall. When Amri pushed his ear against the wall, all he could hear was that pulse, moving slow as the earth, and a deep, pained rushing sound that was so intermittent, he almost didn't realize it was the behemoth ship's breath.

"I wonder if skekSa ever truly meant to help the Sifa," Kylan said as he inspected the closed valve in the wall. Amri joined him, but it felt pointless. It was the doorway, but they had no means of opening it without skekSa and her awful whistle. As much as things might have changed—as much as Tavra wanted to talk about escaping—they were trapped.

"Skeksis alliances shift like the tide," Onica murmured. "Perhaps she did. But now we've lit three of seven fires. The Gelfling alliance rises. This changes things for the Skeksis, too."

Amri jumped when a dreadful, familiar voice purred through the membrane:

"Not for long."

Amri and Kylan jumped as the wall opened like a mouth. Lord skekSa stood in the corridor beyond. Her severed arm was wrapped in blackening gauze, countenance hardened and threatening. Amri backed away, wondering if she had come to kill them, after all they'd done.

Tavra and Onica rose at his shoulders, Kylan remaining at his side. He wasn't alone. He remembered Naia's bravery in the face of the Skeksis, and dug in his heels. He wouldn't be afraid, not even when facing a creature so fearful.

"Where are you taking us?"

skekSa sniffed, as if the question had a disgusting odor.

"Somewhere nicer than this dungeon. But don't be fooled. I'm still very cross with you."

She stepped aside, flourishing with her stump. Reminding them what they'd done to her and that she was not about to forget it. Her gesture was toward a tunnel that led into the cavernous labyrinth of her ship, where they were at her mercy.

"Come along, then," she snarled. "Little heroes."

Despite her tone, Amri smiled.

Heroes.

Though they were surrounded by darkness, the word lit the image of torches in his mind's eye. Naia was out there, somewhere, bearing her light. She would not give up on them. Neither would Tavra and Onica and Kylan, at his back. They would protect him as he would protect them—with his life. Not as song tellers or Far-Dreamers or soldiers. Not as daylighters, Spriton or Vapra or Grottan, but as Gelfling.

Having no other choice, Amri and his friends followed skekSa down the snaking passageway. But Amri held his head high. He would not be defeated. Until the day that he could no longer, he would resist. The flames within his heart blazed, and not even the shadows of the Skeksis could drown its light.

GLOSSARY

Arathim: A race of ancient arthropods, including crystal-singers and silk-spitters. Their color and shape varies widely from family to family, with number of legs ranging from three to twelve.

armalig: This slow-thinking but fast-moving creature is motivated by food and so easily tamed. Often used by the Skeksis for pulling their carriages.

bell-bird: An ancient, extinct bird whose bones and beaks are said to resonate with Thra's song.

bola: A Y-shaped length of knotted rope with stones tied to each of the three ends. Used as a weapon, the bola can be swung or thrown, enabling the wielder to ensnare prey.

Crystal Skimmer: These large, flippered creatures are very social and travel in pods. They are native to the Crystal Sea. Easily trained by Gelfling, these majestic beasts are used by the Dousan clan to cross large expanses of the desert.

daeydoim: Six-legged desert-dwelling creatures with large dorsal scales and broad hooves. Frequently domesticated by desert nomads.

firca: A Y-shaped Gelfling wind instrument, played with both hands. It was Gyr the Song Teller's legendary instrument of choice.

fizzgig: A small furry carnivore native to the Dark Wood. Sometimes kept as a pet.

Grot: A cavern deep in the eastern mountains, the home of the mysterious Grottan Gelfling clan.

hooyim: One of the many colorful leaping fish species that migrate in large schools along the northern Sifan coasts. Often called the jewels of the sea.

Landstrider: Long-legged hooved beasts common to the Spriton plains.

maudra: Literally "mother." The matriarch and wise woman of a Gelfling clan.

maudren: Literally "those of the mother." The family of a Gelfling *maudra*.

merkeep: A delicious tuber. It is a traditional food of the Stonewood Gelfling.

muski: Flying quilled eels endemic to the Swamp of Sog. Babies are very small, but adults never stop growing. The oldest known muski was said to be as wide as the Black River.

ninet: One of nine orbital seasons caused by the configuration of the three suns. Arcs in which Thra is farthest from the suns are winter ninets; arcs in which Thra is nearest are summer ninets. Each ninet lasts approximately one hundred trine.

swoothu: Flying beetlefur creatures with strange sleeping patterns. Many act as couriers for the Gelfling clans in exchange for food and shelter.

ta: A hot beverage made by mixing boiling water and spices.

Three Brothers: Thra's three suns: the Great Sun, the Rose Sun, and the Dying Sun.

Three Sisters: Thra's three moons: the Blue Moon, the Pearl Moon, and the Hidden Moon.

trine: The orbital period of Thra moving around the Great Sun, roughly equivalent to an Earth year.

unamoth: A large-winged pearly white insect that sheds its skin once every unum.

unum: The time for Thra's largest moon to circle Thra once, roughly equivalent to an Earth month.

vliya: Literally "blue fire." Gelfling life essence.

vliyaya: Literally "flame of the blue fire." Gelfling mystic arts.

xeric: One of twelve Dousan nomadic groups, each led by a designated sandmaster.

zandir: A flower native to the wetlands near Cera-Na. Its pollen can cause the lowering of inhibitions and talkativeness, so it is often used in truth-telling potions.

APPENDIX A

THE GELFLING CLANS

VAPRA
Sigil animal: Unamoth

Maudra: Mayrin, the All-Maudra

The Vapra clan was an industrious race with white hair, fair skin, and gossamer-winged women. Considered the oldest of the Gelfling clans, the Vapra resided in cliffside villages along the northern coasts, making their capital in Ha'rar. Chosen by the Skeksis, the Vapra's *maudra*, Mayrin, doubled as All-Maudra, matriarch leader of all the Gelfling clans. Vapra were skilled at camouflage; their *vliyaya* focused on light-changing magic, allowing them to become nearly invisible.

STONEWOOD
Sigil animal: Fizzgig

Maudra: Fara, the Rock Singer

This clan was a proud and ancient people who dwelled on the fertile lands near and within the Dark Wood. They made their main home in Stone-in-the-Wood, the historical home of Jarra-Jen. Many Stonewood Gelfling were valuable guards at the Castle of the Crystal. They were farmers and cobblers and makers of tools. They were inventive, but pastoral; like their sigil animal, they were peaceful but fierce when threatened.

SPRITON

Sigil animal: Landstrider

Maudra: Mera, the Dream Stitcher

Age-old rivals of the Stonewood clan, the Spriton were a warrior race inhabiting the rolling fields south of the Dark Wood. With such bountiful land to raise crops and family, this clan's territory spread to cover the valley in several villages. Counted among the most fierce fighters of the Gelfling race, the Spriton were often called upon to serve as soldiers for the Skeksis Lords and guards at the Castle of the Crystal.

SIFA

Sigil animal: Hooyim

Maudra: Gem-Eyed Ethri

Found in coastal villages along the Silver Sea, the Sifa were skilled fishermen and sailors, but very superstitious. Explorers by nature, the Sifa were competent in battle—but they truly excelled at survival. Sifan *vliyaya* focused Gelfling luck magic into inanimate objects; Sifan charms enchanted with different spells were highly desired by travelers, craftsmen, and warriors of all clans.

DOUSAN

Sigil animal: Daeydoim

Maudra: Seethi, the Skin Painter

This clan made their settlements on sandships—amazing constructs of bone and crystal that navigated the Crystal Sea like ocean vessels. Resilient even within the arid climate of the desert, the Dousan thrived. Their culture was shrouded and unsettlingly quiet, their language made of whispers and gestures, their life stories told in the intricate magic tattoos painting their bodies.

DRENCHEN

Sigil animal: Muski

Maudra: Laesid, the Blue Stone Healer

The Drenchen clan was a race of amphibious Gelfling who lived in the overgrown Swamp of Sog, deep in the southernmost reaches of the Skarith region. Sturdier and taller than the rest of their race, the Drenchen were powerful in combat, but generally preferred to keep to themselves. Though one of the smallest Gelfling clans, the Drenchen had the largest sense of clan pride; they were loyal to one another, but remained as distant from other clans as possible.

GROTTAN

Sigil animal: Hollerbat

Maudra: Argot, the Shadow Bender

A mysterious, secretive breed who dwelled in perpetual darkness in the Caves of Grot. Generations in the shadows left them with an extreme sensitivity to light—and solid black eyes that could see in the dark and large ears to make out even the faintest of echoes. The Grottan clan was said to number less than three dozen Gelfling, and their life span was said to be unheard of, lasting three to four times as long as other Gelfling.

APPENDIX B

LOCATIONS OF THRA

Black River: The main waterway within the Skarith Basin. It flows from high in the Grottan Mountains north to Ha'rar, where it empties into the Silver Sea.

Castle of the Crystal: Also known as the Skeksis' castle, this obsidian tower is where the Skeksis Lords live, and where they protect—and control—the Crystal Heart of Thra.

Cera-Na: A bay on the western coast of the mainland where the Sifa gather.

Crystal Sea: A desert of crystalline sand just southeast of the Claw Mountains. Frequented by electric storms and sandstorms.

Dark Wood: The large forest that fills most of the Skarith Basin. Also called the Endless Wood, it seems to go on forever.

Domrak: The home of the Grottan clan, a network of caves deep in the Grottan Mountains.

Grottan Mountains: A ridge of rocky mountains on the west border of the Skarith Basin.

Grottan Sanctuary: A deep mountain valley overgrown with giant stone mushrooms. An ancient nesting ground for bell-birds, this is where the Grottan Gelfling often go to meditate.

Ha'rar: The northern, snowy home of the Vapra clan. Made the capital by the Skeksis when they ordained the Vapra All-Maudra.

Kira-Staba, the Waystar grove: A grove of glowing trees growing on the bluffs that overlook Ha'rar and the Silver Sea.

Nenadi-Staba, the Low Tree: A low-lying, gnarled-root tree growing in the wood near Sami Thicket.

Olyeka-Staba, the Cradle Tree: A towering tree in the Dark Wood, said to be the tree from which the entire forest originates.

Omerya-Staba, the Coral Tree: A floating coral tree made of thousands of marine colonies, converted into a living, sailable ship by the Sifa clan.

Oszah-Staba, the Wellspring Tree: A tree growing in the Dousan Wellspring. Its enormous leaves prevent storms from damaging the oasis.

Sami Thicket: A village hidden in a forest within the Spriton Plains, and home of the Spriton clan.

Sifan Coast: A long series of rocky shorelines along the north and western sides of the Claw Mountains. Inhabited by the Sifa clan.

Silver Sea: The frosty, fog-enshrouded sea north of the Skarith land.

Skarith Basin: The land that lies between the Claw Mountains to the west and the Grottan Mountains to the east. The region within includes the Crystal Sea, the Dark Wood, and the Spriton Plains.

Smerth-Staba, Great Smerth the Glenfoot Tree: An ancient tree growing in the heart of the Swamp of Sog.

Spriton Plains: A vast series of rolling plains and meadows south of the Dark Wood. Home to the Spriton clan.

Stone-in-the-Wood: Home of the Stonewood Gelfling, this village nestled deep in the Dark Wood is large and fortified with stones and rocks. Some say it was the first Gelfling village.

Swamp of Sog: A lush, dense jungle in the southernmost part of the Skarith Basin.

Tomb of Relics: A cloistered hall in the Grottan Mountains where ancient artifacts are kept safe by the Grottan Gelfling.

Vliste-Staba, the Sanctuary Tree: A pink-petaled tree growing on the mountains near the Grottan Sanctuary. Its roots are made of glittering stone and penetrate deep into the mountains.